LISTENING FOR GHOSTS

ALSO BY DAVID RABE

PLAYS

The Basic Training of Pavlo Hummel
Sticks and Bones
The Orphan
Streamers
In the Boom Boom Room
Goose and Tomtom
Hurlyburly
Those the River Keeps)
A Question of Mercy
The Dog Problem)
The Black Monk
An Early History of Fire
Good for Otto
Visiting Edna
Cosmologies

FICTION

Recital of the Dog
A Primitive Heart
Dinosaurs on the Roof
Mr. Wellington (illustrated by Robert Andrew Parker)
Girl by the Road at Night

SCREENPLAYS

Casualties of War
I'm Dancing as Fast as I Can

LISTENING FOR GHOSTS

A NOVELLA AND FOUR STORIES

BY

DAVID RABE

DELPHINIUM BOOKS

For Marsha Jane Rabe, my sister. She's been with me almost from the start.

CONTENTS_

THINGS WE WORRIED ABOUT
WHEN I WAS TEN

High on the list was trying not to have the older boys decide to de-pants you and then run your pants up the flagpole, leaving you in your underwear, and maybe bloodied if you'd struggled—not that it helped, because they were bigger and stronger—and your pants flapping way up against the sky over the schoolyard. They mostly did this to Freddy Bird—nobody knew why, but it happened a lot. It was best to get away from him when they started to get into that mood—their let's-de-pants-somebody mood. Oh, there's Freddy Bird. You could see them thinking it. You had to slip sideways, not in an obvious way but as if you were drifting for no real reason, or maybe the wind was shoving you and you weren't really paying attention, and most important, you did not want to meet eyes with them, not one of them. Because they could change their mind in a flash if they noticed you, as they would if you met their eyes, and then they'd think, Oh, look, there's Danny Matz, let's de-pants him, and before you knew it, you'd be trying to get your pants down from high up on the flagpole while everybody laughed, especially Freddy Bird.

Meeting eyes was, generally speaking, worrisome. It could lead anywhere. I'd been on the Kidnickers' porch with the big boys when they were tormenting Devin Sleverding—pushing him and, you know, spitting on him and not letting him off the porch when he tried to go. Fencing him in. And I felt kind of sorry for Devin, but I didn't let it show, and I made sure that I stayed on the big boys' side of the invisible line that separated them from Devin, who was crying and snorting and looking like a trapped pig, which he was, in a sense, and waving his hands around in that girly way he had, his wrists all fluttery and floppy, which he should have just stopped doing, because that was how he'd got into trouble with the big boys to begin with. (That was another thing we worried about, a sort of worry inside a worry: Along with not wanting to meet anybody's eyes, we had to make sure that we never started waving our hands around like girls, the way Devin Sleverding did.)

So the older boys had formed a circle around him, and if he tried to break out, they'd push him back into the middle of the ring, and if he just stood there, hoping they'd get tired or bored and go play baseball or something, well, then one of them would jump at him and shove him so hard that he staggered over into the boys on the other side of the circle, who would shove him back in the direction he'd come from. That was what was happening when our eyes met. I was trying to be part of the circle and to look like I belonged with the big boys and thought he deserved it, waving his hands like a girl. Just stop it, I thought. His snot-covered, puffy red face looked shocked and terribly disappointed, as if seeing me act that way was the last straw, as if he'd expected something more from me. And I don't know where Devin got the stick—this hunk of wood covered in slivers that had probably been left on the Kidnickers' porch after somebody built something—but he had it and he hit me over the head. I saw stars, staticky, racing stars no bigger than mouse turds. Blood squirted out of my head, and I fell to my knees, and while everybody was distracted, Devin made his break. I was crying and crawling, and one of the big boys said, "You better go home." "Okay," I said, and left a blood trail spattering the sidewalk where I walked and alongside the apartment building where I lived and on just about every one of the steps I climbed to our door, which entered into the kitchen, where my mom, when she saw me, screamed. I had to have stitches.

Another thing I worried about was how to make sure that I never had to box Sharon Weber again. It was my dad's idea. We'd gone down to Red and Ginger Weber's apartment, which was on the ground floor of our two-story, four-apartment building. I was supposed to box Ron Weber, who was a year older than me, but he wasn't home, so Red offered his daughter, Sharon, as a substitute, and my dad said sure. Nobody checked with me, and I didn't know what to say anyway—so there I was, facing off against Sharon, who was a year younger than me, but about as tall. She hit me square in the nose, a surprise blow, and I just stood there.

"C'mon, Dan," my dad said. "Show her what you got." I wanted to. But I was frozen. I didn't know what I could do—where to hit her. She was a girl. I couldn't hit her in the face, because she was pretty and, being a girl, needed to be pretty, and I couldn't hit her in the stomach, because that was where her baby machinery was, and I didn't want to damage that; I couldn't hit her above her stomach, either, because her chest wasn't a boy's chest—she had breasts, and they were important, too, to babies and in other ways that I didn't understand but had heard about. So I stood there, getting pounded, ducking as best I could, but not too much, because I didn't want to appear cowardly, afraid of a girl, and covering up, not too effectively, for the same reason, while Sharon whaled away on me.

"Dan, c'mon now," my dad said. "What are you doing? Give her a good one."

I couldn't see my dad, because my eyes were all watery and blurry—not with tears, just water.

I guess it had dawned on Sharon that nothing was coming back at her, so she was windmilling me and side-arming, prancing around and really winding up. My dad said, "Goddamnit, Dan! Give her a smack, for god's sake." Red was gloating and chattering to Sharon, as if she needed coaching to finish me off. "Use your left. Set him up." My dad was red-faced, his mouth and eyes squeezed into this painful grimace, the way they'd been when I spilled boiling soup in his lap. He could barely look at me, like it really hurt to look at me.

He grabbed me then, jerked me out the door. Once we were outside, he left me standing at the bottom of the stairs while he stomped up to our apartment. I ran after him and got to our part of the long second-floor porch we shared with the Stoner family just in time to see him bang the door shut. I heard him inside saying, "Goddamnit to hell. What is wrong with that kid?"

"What happened?" my mom asked.

"I'm sick of it, you know."

"Sick of what?"

"What do you think?"

"I don't know."

"Never mind," he said. "Goddamnit to hell."

"Sick of what? At least tell me that."

"Why bother?"

"Because I'm asking. That ought to be enough."

"Him and you, okay?"

"Me?" she said. "Me?"

I heard another door slam. When I opened the apartment door to peek in, I saw that the door to the bathroom, which was alongside the kitchen, was closed.

My mother was wearing a housedress that I'd seen a million times. It buttoned down the front and never had the bottom button buttoned. She had an apron on and a pot holder around the handle of a pot in her hand. Everything smelled of fish. She looked at me standing in the doorway with the Webers' boxing gloves on. "What happened?" she asked.

"I was supposed to box Ron Weber, because Dad thought I could beat him, even though he's older, but he wasn't home, so Sharon—"

"Wait, wait. Stop, stop. What more do I have to put up with?" She grabbed my arm and pulled me into the kitchen.

"What happened? What happened? What happened?" she said too many times. "Carl," she shouted at the bathroom door. "What happened?"

"I'm on the crapper," he said.

"Oh, my god." She walked like a sad, dizzy person to the table, where she sat down real slow, the way a person does when sliding into freezing or scalding-hot water. She put her chin in her hands, but her head was too heavy and it sank to the table-top, where she closed her eyes. I stood for a moment, looking down at my hands in the boxing gloves, wondering how I was going to get out of them. What if I had to pee? How could I get my zipper down and my weenie out? I went into the living room, which was only a few steps away, because the apartment was really small. I sat on the couch. I wished I could go up into the attic. It wasn't very big and had a low, slanted roof, but it felt far away from everything, with all these random objects lying there, as if history had left them behind. One of them was Dobbins, my rocking horse, who had big white scary eyes full of warnings and mysteries to solve, if he could ever get through to me. But the only way up to the attic was through the bathroom, which was off limits at the moment because my dad was in there on the crapper. I worked on the laces of the gloves with my teeth, trying to tug them loose enough that I could clamp the gloves between my knees and pull my hands out, and I made some progress, but not enough. So I gave up. I sat for a while and then I lay down on the couch.

*　　*　　*

Another thing we worried about was that, if it rained and it was night—not late, because then we had to be in bed, but dark already, and wet, the way a good heavy rain left things—and our parents wouldn't let us go out, or wouldn't let us have a flashlight because we'd run the batteries down, then other kids would get all the night crawlers that came up and slithered in the wet grass. We worried that they would all be snatched up by the kids whose parents weren't home, or who had their own flashlights. It was strange to me that night crawlers came up at all, because when they were under the dirt, they were hidden and safe. Maybe, though, if they stayed down there after a heavy rain, they would drown. I didn't know and couldn't ask them. The main thing was that they weren't regular worms but night crawlers, big and fat, with shiny, see-through skin, and we could catch them and put them in a can with coffee grounds and then use them as bait or sell them to men who were going fishing but hadn't had time to go out and catch some themselves.

When our parents did let us go, we raced out our doors and, in my case, down the stairs, then walked around sneakily, searching the grass with a flashlight, the beam moving slowly, like the searchlight in a prison movie when prisoners are trying to escape. When the light struck a night crawler, we had to be quick, because they were very fast and they tried to squirm back into the holes they'd come out of, or were partway out of, and we had to pinch them against the ground with our fingers and then pull them out slowly, being careful not to break them in half. Because they somehow resisted—they hung on to their holes without any hands. We could feel the fear in them as they tried to fight back, so tiny compared with us, though we were only kids, and when we got them out, the way they twisted and writhed about seemed like silent screaming. It was odd, though, how much they loved the dirt. We all knew that there were awful things down there. Germs. Maggots. You could even suffocate if dirt fell on you in a mudslide. We almost felt as if we were saving the night crawlers, dragging them out and feeding them to fish. It was impossible to figure it all out.

Another thing we worried about was having to move. What if we had to move? It happened every now and then to people we knew. Their families moved and they had to go with them. A big truck showed up, and men in uniforms took all the things out of the house and put them into the truck. It had happened to the Ballingers, for example. "We're moving," Ronnie said. "Gotta move," his younger brother, Max, said. And the next thing we knew, the trucks were there and the men in and out and then the Ballingers were gone. Every one of them. The house was empty. We could sneak into their yard and peek in the windows and see the big, scary emptiness, so empty it hurt. And then other people, complete strangers, showed up and went in and started living there, and it was as if the Ballingers had never been there.

Or Jesus. We all worried about Jesus. I know I did. What did he think of me? Did he, in fact, think of me? At Mass, I took the Host into my mouth, and the priest said that it was Jesus, and the nuns also said that it was Jesus, in this little slip of bread, this wafer that melted on my tongue. You weren't supposed to chew it or swallow it whole, so you waited for it to melt and spread out holiness. Hands folded, head bowed, eyes closed until you had to see where you were going to get back to your pew, and there was Mary Catherine Michener entering her pew right in front of you, her eyes downcast, a handkerchief on top of her head because she'd forgotten her hat, and her breasts—which had come out of nowhere, it seemed, and stuck out as if they were taking her somewhere— were big, as if to balance the curve of her rear end, which was sticking out in the opposite direction. Did Jesus know? He had to, didn't he, melting as he was in my mouth, trying to fill me with piety and goodness while I had this weird feeling about Mary Catherine Michener, who was only a year or two older than me and whom I'd known when she didn't have pointy breasts and a rounded butt, but now she did, and seeing them, I thought about them, and the next thought was of confession. Or of being an occasion of sin. I did not want to be an occasion of sin for the girls in my class, who could go to Hell if they saw me with my shirt off, according to Sister Mary Irma. And so confession again. Father Paul listening on the other side of the wicker window, or Father Thomas, sighing and sad and bored.

Being made an "example of" by Sister Mary Luke, the principal, was another nerve-racking thing that could happen. You could be an example of almost anything, but whatever it was, you would be a kind of stand-in for everybody who'd committed some serious offense, and so the punishment would be bad enough to make everybody stop doing it, whatever it was.

Or getting sat on by Sister Conrad. That shouldn't have been a worry, but it was. And though it may sound outlandish, we'd all seen it happen to Jackie Rand. But then, almost everything happened to Jackie Rand. Which might have offered a degree of insurance against its ever happening to us, since so much that happened to Jackie didn't happen to anyone else, and yet the fact that it had happened to anyone, even Jackie, and we'd all seen it, was worrisome. Sister Conrad, for no reason we could understand, had been facing the big pulldown map and trying to drill into our heads the geographic placement of France, Germany, and the British Isles. This gave Jackie the chance he needed to poke Basil Mellencamp in the back with his pencil, making him squirm and whisper, "Stop it, Jackie." But Jackie didn't stop, and he was having so much fun that he didn't notice Sister Conrad turning to look at him.

"Jackie!" she barked. Startled and maybe even scared, he rocked back in his desk as far as he could to get away from Basil, and aimed his most innocent expression at Sister Conrad. "Stand up," she told him, "and tell us what you think you are doing."

He looked us over, as if wondering if she'd represented our interest correctly, then he turned his attention to his desk, lifting the lid to peek inside.

"Did you hear me? I told you to stand up, Jackie Rand."

He nodded to acknowledge that he'd heard her, and shrugging in his special way, which we all knew represented his particular form of stubborn confusion, he scratched his head.

Sister Conrad shot toward him. She was round and short, not unlike Jackie, though he was less round and at least a foot shorter. All of us pivoted to watch, ducking if we were too close to the black-and-white storm that Sister Conrad had become, rosary beads rattling, silver cross flashing and clanking. She grabbed Jackie by the arm and he yelped, pulling free. She snatched at his ear, but he sprang into the aisle on the opposite side of his desk, knocking into Judy Carberger, who cowered one row over. Sister Conrad lunged, and Basil, who was between them, hunched like a soldier fearing death in a movie where bombs fell everywhere. "You're going to the principal's office!" she shrieked.

We all knew what that meant—it was one step worse than being made an example of. Stinging rulers waited to smack upturned palms, or if we failed to hold steady and flipped our palms over in search of relief, the punishment found our knuckles with a different, even worse kind of pain.

Sister Conrad and Jackie both bolted for the door. Somehow—though we all marveled at the impossibility of it—Sister Conrad got there first. Jackie had been slowed by the terrible burden of defying authority, which could make anyone sluggish.

"I want to go home," he said. "I want to go home."

The irony of this wish, given what we knew of Jackie's home, shocked us as much as everything else that was going on.

Jackie leaned toward the door as if the moment were normal, and he hoped for permission, but needed to go. Sister Conrad stayed put, blocking the way. He reached around her for the doorknob and she shoved him. I may have been the only person to see a weird hopelessness fill his eyes at that point. I was his friend, perhaps his only friend, so it was fitting that I saw it. And then he lunged at her and grabbed her. We gasped to see them going sideways and smashing against the blackboard. Erasers, chalk sticks, and chalk dust exploded. Almost every boy in the room had battled Jackie at one point or another, so we knew what Sister Conrad was up against. We gaped, watching her hug him crazily. Her glasses flew off. Jackie shouted about going home as he fell over backward. She came with him, crashing down on top of him. They wrestled, and she squirmed into a sitting position right on his stomach, where she bounced several times. The white cardboard thing around her head had sprung loose, the edge sticking out, the whole black hood so crooked that it half covered her face. Jackie screamed and wailed under her, as she bounced and shouted for help and Basil ran to get Sister Mary Luke.

Getting into a fight with Jackie Rand was another thing we worried about. Though it was less of a worry for me than for most. Jackie and I lived catercornered from each other across Jefferson Avenue, which was a narrow street, not fancy like a real avenue. Jackie lived in a house, while I was in an apartment.

He was rough and angry and mean, it was true—a bully. But not to me. I knew how to handle him. I would talk soothingly to him, as if he were a stray dog. I could even pull him off his victims. His body had a sweaty, gooey sensation of unhappy fat. Under him, a boy would beg for mercy, but Jackie, alone in his rage, would be far from the regular world. When I pulled him off, he would continue to flail, at war with ghosts, until, through his hate-filled little eyes, something soft peered out, and if it was me that he saw, he might sputter some burning explanation and then run home.

As a group, we condemned him, called him names: "Bully! Pig eyes! Fatso!" The beaten boy would screech, "Pick on somebody your own size, you fat slob!" Others would add, "Lard-ass! Fatty-Fatty Two-by-Four!"

The fact that Jackie's mother had died when he was four explained his pouty lips and the hurt in his eyes, I thought. Jackie's father seemed to view him as a kind of commodity he'd purchased one night while drunk. The man would whack him at the drop of a hat. This was even before Jackie's father had failed at business and had to sell the corner grocery store, and before he remarried, hoping for happiness but, according to everybody, making everything worse. Jackie's stepmom, May, came with her own set of jabs and prods that Jackie had to learn to dodge, along with his father's anger.

All of us were slapped around. Our dads were laborers who worked with their hands. Some built machines; others tore machines apart. Some dug up the earth; others repaired automobiles or hammered houses into shape. Many slaughtered cows and pigs at the meatpacking company. Living as they did, they relied on their hands, and they used them. Our overworked mothers were also sharp-tempered and as quick with a slap as they were with their fits of coddling. And after our parents and the nuns were done, we spent a lot of time beating one another up.

Still, Jackie's dad was uncommon. He seemed to mistake Jackie for someone he had a grudge against in a bar. But then, as our parents told us, Jackie was "hard to handle." He would "try the patience of a saint," and his dad was "quick-triggered" and hardly happy in his second marriage.

As Jackie and I walked around the block or sat in a foxhole we'd dug on the hill and covered with sumac, these were among the mysteries that we tried to solve.

"Too bad your dad lost his store," I told him.

"He loved my real mom," Jackie said, looking up at the light falling through the leaves.

"May is nice."

"I know she is. She's real nice."

"He loves you, Jackie."

"Sure."

"He just doesn't know how to show it. You gotta try not to make him mad."

"I make everybody mad."

"But he's quick-tempered."

"I'd try the patience of a saint."

More than once, I went home from time spent with Jackie to stare in wonder and gratitude at my living mother and my dad, half asleep in his big chair, listening to a baseball game. Sometimes in church I would pray for Jackie, so that he could have as good a life as I did.

In daylight, we did our best, but then there was the time spent in bed at night. It was there that I began to suspect that, while there was much that I knew I worried about, there was more that I worried about without actually knowing what it was that worried me—or even that I was worrying—as I slept. The things with Mr. Stink and Georgie Baxter weren't exactly in this category, but they were close.

Mr. Stink was a kind of hobo, who built a shack on the hill behind our apartment building, and he had that name because he stank. We kids were told to stay away from him and we did. He interested me, though, and I looked at him when I could, and sometimes I saw him looking at us. We all saw him walking on the gravel road between the hill and our houses, lugging bags of junk, on the way to his shack.

Then one night I was in our apartment, doing my homework, while Dad was listening to baseball, and my mom was rocking my baby sister in her lap and trying to talk my dad into listening to something else, when this clanking started. It went *clank-clank-clank* and stopped. Then *clank-clank-clank* again. "What the hell now?" my dad griped. It went on and on, and Dad couldn't figure out what it was, and Mom couldn't, either. It started at about nine and went on till ten or later, and Dad was on his way to complain to the landlord, whose house was next door, when he decided instead to talk to Agnes Rath, who lived in the apartment under us. It turned out that Agnes was scared sick. When Dad knocked, she turned on her porch light and peeked out between her curtains, and seeing that it was him, she opened her door and told him that Mr. Stink had been peeping in her window. She'd seen him and, not knowing what to do, had turned off all her lights and crawled into the kitchen. Lying on the floor, she'd banged on the pipes under her sink as a signal. So that was the clanking. Agnes Rath's signal. Well, a few nights later, a group of men ran through our yard and my dad ran with them, and then, not too long after that, fire leaped up on the hill around the spot where Mr. Stink had his shack, and nobody ever saw him again.

Then Georgie Baxter got married and moved into an apartment on the ground floor of the building next door to

Jackie. Georgie and his new wife, who everybody said was "a real looker," couldn't afford a long honeymoon. They got married on a Saturday, but because Georgie had to work on Monday, they came back to their apartment Sunday night, and what awaited them was a shivaree. People came from all directions, men, women, and kids, everybody carrying metal buckets or pots and beating on them with spoons to make a huge loud racket. Jackie and I were doing it like everybody else, beating away on pots with big spoons, though we had no idea why, all of us together creating this clamor as we closed in on the apartment building with Georgie and his new bride inside. I stood with my pot and my spoon, beating away, whooping and feeling scared by the crazy noise we were making and the wild look in all the grown-ups' eyes, as if they were stealing or breaking something. I wished more than anything that I knew why we were doing what we were doing.

About a week later, Jackie came and told me to hurry. At his house, he took me upstairs. It was Saturday, and he put his finger to his lips as he pulled me to the window and we looked down at Georgie and his new wife, in their bed without any clothes on, rolling and wrestling, and she looked like pudding or butter. After a while, Jackie fell on the floor kind of moaning, like he had the time we went to the Orpheum Theatre to see the movie *Dracula*. Perched way up high in the balcony, we'd watched the ghost ship land in the mists with everyone dead, and when Dracula swirled his cape and lay back in his coffin, Jackie got so scared he hid on the floor. I looked down at him now, and then back at the window, and the pudding woman saw me. She glanced up, and though I ducked as fast as I could, she caught me looking in her window. If she told, what would happen? Would I get run out of town like Mr. Stink? If she told Georgie, or started banging on water pipes to alert people, would they come swarming and pounding on pots to surround me? My fate was in the hands of Georgie Baxter's wife. What could be worse? Because she knew that I knew that under her clothes she was all pudding and bubbles. It was a horrible worry, but I didn't tell anyone, not even Jackie. That worry was mine alone, and it was maybe the worst worry, the worry to end all worries.

But then Jackie wandered into his kitchen one Saturday to find his stepmother, May, stuffing hunks of beef into the meat grinder. Her head swayed to music from the radio on the shelf above her, and her eyes were busy with something distant. Jackie had gone into the kitchen because he was thirsty, so he stood on a chair to get a glass from the cupboard above the sink. He filled the glass to the brim from the faucet and drank every drop. The chair made a little squeal as he slid it back under the kitchen table. That was when Stepmom May screamed. Seeing the black hole of her mouth strung with saliva, Jackie was certain he had committed some unspeakable crime. She raised a bloody mess toward him, her eyes icy and dead, and he knew that she was about to hurl a half-ground hunk of beef at him. When instead she attacked the radio, yanking out the plug and circling her arm with the cord, he thought that she had gone insane. It was only when she wailed "My thumb!" that he understood. A hand crank powered the meat grinder, moving a gear that worked the teeth inside its cast-iron belly. With her right hand turning the crank, she'd used her left to stuff the meat into the mouthlike opening on top of the apparatus. Her thumb had gone in too deep, and she'd failed to notice, or noticed only when she'd ground her thumb up with the beef. She ran out the door, the radio tied to her arm, rattling along behind her, and left him standing alone, blood dotting the worn-out ducks in the uneven linoleum, and the trickle of hope that had survived the loss of his real mom draining away.

When Jackie told me what had happened, as he did within minutes, it was as if I'd been there to see it, and I felt his deep, deep worry. It played on us like the spooky music in *Dracula*. It was strange and haunting and beyond anything we could explain, with our poor grasp of nouns and verbs. And yet we knew that Jackie needed to try. A downstairs door banged, and Jackie ran from where we stood on my porch, around the corner of the banister, taking the steps two at a time until he landed in the yard.

Finding Agnes Rath, who nervously peered over her grocery bag at Jackie, he made his report: "stepmom may cut her thumb off in the meat grinder!"

Suppertime was near, so people were coming and going. Suddenly, Jackie heard Red Weber approaching, followed by his wife. Racing up to one and then the other, Jackie backtracked in the direction of their door so he could announce his dreadful news before they trampled him in their haste to get home: "stepmom may cut her thumb off in the meat grinder!"

Henry Stoner, who lived beside us on the second floor, came around the corner, lunch bucket under his arm, and Jackie retreated up the stairs, never missing a step; he took corners, eluded rails. "stuck it in and turned the crank!" he shrieked. "stuck it in and turned the crank!" Mrs. Stoner was home already, her shift at the plant having ended earlier than her husband's. She came out onto the porch and, in a gush of neighborly concern, prodded Jackie for more details.

"How is she?" Mrs. Stoner asked.

"just ground it up!"

"Did you see it?"

But he could not budge from his point. The thing against which he had crashed clutched at him, like the tentacles of that monster squid we had all seen in *Wake of the Red Witch*. Now Jackie was being dragged down through inky confusion to some deep, lightless doom. If he was ever to discover the cause of the terror endangering him and me and everyone he knew, as he believed, and I did, too, the search for an answer had to begin with what he'd seen. "just stuck it in! and turned the crank, Mrs. Stoner! just ground it up!"

"Can we do something for you, Jackie?"

Though he had time to look at her, he had time for nothing more. Mr. Hogan, who lived on the gravel road behind our house and who used our backyard as a shortcut home every night, was crossing. Jackie hurtled down the stairs and jumped in front of Mr. Hogan, who was fleshy and soft and smelled of furniture polish. Startled, Mr. Hogan took a step back. Before him stood a deranged-looking Jackie Rand. "just stuck it in and ground it up!" he yelled.

"What?"

"stepmom may cut her thumb off in the meat grinder! stepmom may cut her thumb off in the meat grinder!"

"What?"

"blood!" he shrieked. "stuck it in and ground it off! blood! blood!"

Over the next hour, the four families in our building worked their way toward supper. Last-minute shopping was needed, and errands were run. Butter was borrowed from the second floor by the first floor, an onion traded for a potato. The odor of Spam mixed with beef, sauerkraut, wieners, and hash, while boiling potatoes sent out their steamy scent to mingle with that of corn and string beans, peas, coffee, baked potatoes, and pie. All to the accompaniment of Jackie's "blood!" and "stepmom may!"

My mother, looking down over the banister, said to my dad, "He looks so sad."

"Not to me."

"You don't think he looks sad?"

"Looks crazy, if you ask me. Nuttier than a pet coon, not that he doesn't always."

"Don't say that. Why would you say such a thing?"

My father went inside, leaving my mother alone. I felt invisible, perfectly forgotten, standing in the corner of the porch watching my mother witness Jackie's second encounter with Red Weber, who had returned from somewhere. "stepmom may! stuck it in, Mr. Weber! cut it off! blood! turned the crank! stuck it in!"

Annoyed now, he brushed Jackie aside and snapped, "You told me! Now go home. Go home!"

Without a second's hesitation, my mother called down to invite Jackie up for dinner.

"Stepmom may," he said as he came in our door. "turned the crank!" he addressed my dad. "blood!" he delivered as he took a seat. And glowering at my baby sister in her high chair sucking milk from a bottle, he said, "stepmom may cut her thumb off in the meat grinder!"

"Am I supposed to have my goddamn supper with this fool and his tune?" my dad asked.

"Can't we talk about something else?" my mother said to Jackie.

Outside, a door slammed. Jackie could not rest. He bobbed in what might have been a bow. "Thanks for inviting me to dinner. It was real good." He was gone, not having taken a bite, the screen door croaking on its hinges.

"Goddamnit to hell," my dad said. "What does a person have to do to have his supper in peace around this nut factory!"

From afar, there was the rise and fall of Jackie's voice as he chased whomever he found: "stepmom may! cut her thumb off! stuck it in and turned the crank!"

It was then that I understood. If Jackie understood, then or ever, I can't say. But the answer seemed simple and obvious once I saw it. If Stepmom May could do that to herself, what might she do to him? If she could lose track of the whereabouts of her own thumb, what chance did he have? What was he, after all, but a little boy, a small, mobile piece of meat? Certainly her connection to him was weaker than her connection to her own hand. Would he find himself tomorrow mistaken in her absentmindedness for a chicken, unclothed and basted in the oven? Must he be alert every second for her next blunder? Would he end up jammed into the Mixmaster, among the raisins and nuts?

What might any of our mothers do to any of us, we had to ask, given the strangeness of their love and their stranger neglect, those moments of distraction when they lost track of everything, even themselves, as they stared into worries that were all their own and bigger than anything we could hope to fathom?

I'm not sure how the word spread, but it did. We all heard it and knew to gather in the Haggertys' empty lot. It was a narrow strip that ran down from the gravel road that separated the hill from the houses where we lived. Nobody knew what the Haggertys planned to do with the lot. It wasn't wild, but it wasn't neat and cared for, either, and we all went there as soon as we could get out after supper. We came from different directions and then we were there, nodding and knowing, but without knowing what we knew. For a while, we talked about Korea and the Chinese horde and the dangers that had our fathers leaning in close to their radios and cursing. We got restless and somebody wanted to play pump-pump-pullaway, but other people scoffed. We tried red rover, and then statue, where you got whirled around by somebody, and when the boy who'd spun you yelled "Freeze!" as you stumbled around, you had to stop and stay that way without moving an inch, and then think of some kind of meaning for how you'd ended up. We did that for a bit, but we all knew where we were headed. Finally, somebody—it might have been me—said, "Let's play the blackout game."

The light had dimmed and the moon was now high, high enough that it was almost above us in the sky, with lots of stars, so we were ghostly and perfect. Our mood had that something in it that made everyone feel as though this was what we had all been waiting for.

To play the blackout game, you'd stand with someone behind you, his arms around your chest, and you'd take deep breaths over and over, and the other boy would squeeze your chest until you passed out in a downpour of spangling lights. The person behind you would then lay you down gently on your back in the grass, where you wandered around without yourself, until you woke up from a sleep whose content you'd never know. We took turns. Jerry went, then Tommy and Butch. I went, and then Jackie was there, and he wanted to go. Freddy Bird got behind Jackie, and Jackie huffed and huffed and sailed away, blacking out. Freddy Bird let go and stepped clear. Jackie toppled over backward. His butt landed and then his body slammed back, like a reverse jackknife, and, finally, his head hit with a loud crack. A hurt look came over him, and a big sigh came out of his mouth: "Oh-h-h-h." More of a gasp, really, and he lay very still. Motionless. Pale, I thought. We all stared. He didn't move. Freddy Bird was no longer pleased with how clever he was.

We waited for Jackie to wake up and he didn't. It seemed longer than usual.

"We didn't kill him, did we?"

"You don't die from that."

"It's because he's out twice. Once from the breathing stuff and once from banging his head."

We waited. Jackie didn't move. I went closer.

Staring down, I had the crazy thought that Jackie Rand was like Jesus. Not that he *was* Jesus but that he was kind of our Jesus, getting the worst of everything for everybody, getting the worst that anybody could dish out, so that we could feel okay about our lives. No matter how bad or unfair we might feel things were, they were worse for Jackie.

"Should we maybe tell somebody?"

A tiny tear appeared in the corner of each of Jackie's eyes. He was the saddest person on earth, lying there, I thought. The tears dribbled down his cheeks, and then his eyes blinked and opened and he saw where he was. His big pouty lips quivered. He reached to rub the back of his head, and he started to cry really hard, and we knew that he was alive.

THE LONGER GRIEF

ONE

He was reading about Wyoming. At the same time, a huge buttress of masonry coupled with a slab of reinforced concrete floated past. Occasionally, he looked up. Meanwhile, strings of cottonwood took up their tentative place in his mind. He saw them in some flickering of existence that muffled the real word. Snow feathered a birch tree. Mounds of snow dappled a hillside and collapsed into the level expanse of a meadow. The so-called real world, he thought. He was reading about a woman who had lost her dog. She prowled through picturesque vistas on her search. She investigated the down-sweep of rugged gullies. He could see her widespread steps, fighting for balance against the demands of gravity. Outside, the mangled environs of New York City shot past. His wife had been dead almost ten weeks now. Marie had died at the age of forty-one. Cancer.

From the hollow of Grand Central Station, he headed north through a deteriorating urban landscape. He turned a page and saw the symmetry of white space and type altered by a pencil slash in the margin, a faint underscoring. A tiny asterisk hung alongside, having been placed there by Marie, a kind of paw print of her sensibility. He could feel her puzzlement, her interest, and the sensitive, eager action of her mind. English had been her second language, Dutch being her first, and though she had been fluent, she felt hemmed in at times and developed the habit of marking words whose meanings were not quite clear to her or that in other instances charmed her. The western landscape where the dog had run off was not one she'd ever seen, but the mountains, the big sky of rumors intrigued her, and she and Thomas had promised they would go there someday. So in a sense the light tracing beneath a word was like her saying, Thomas, look here. In the narrative, the woman climbed a game trail. He accompanied her, floating along, as he knew Marie must have done when the book was in her hands. Now I sniff and smell only dirt. He could see her there, on her hands and knees. Nose to the dirt. He felt close to her and to Marie, too, the three of them invested in the search, hoping for the best. Many of her books bore her imprint, and so did many of his. But this one had been among the last she'd engaged before her brain surrendered to the battering of chemo and illness. He'd come into the bedroom, hurrying for an appointment. She'd been in the chair by the window, a book closed in her lap. He wished he could say with certainty that it had been the Wyoming book, but he couldn't.

"I can't make sense of it," she said, fingers tapping the cover.

She could have meant anything, given the busy absurdity of their days. "What?"

"The book. The words. The first of a sentence goes away before I'm partway to the end." She smiled, as if that was the best thing to do.

Outside, rusty girders and miserable brick hurtled from view as the hollow of a tunnel rose up to enclose the sinking train. Overhead the lights flickered. It was Friday, and late afternoon, and though he sat alone, there were throngs of commuters. As he glanced around, he knew the woman wasn't going to find the dog. He could feel her failure in the austerity of the prose. If he were to speak of his wife to any of his fellow passengers, not a single one of them in this crowd of hundreds dispersed throughout twenty or more cars would know of her or care to know. Certainly none of the teenagers in garish T-shirts, open jackets, and untied, high-tech running shoes. Not any one of the salesmen, or advertising executives, or corporate types in day-old suits bowed over their iPhones, or computers, or clustered together talking of golf, or the shifting Dow.

When the train surfaced, he looked to the window beside him. The setting sun made the glass into a glare, blotting out all sensation. Seconds passed before the crumbling brick reappeared, the rows and racks of curtained windows linked by the black stitches of fire escapes, their ladders, railings, and landings. Laundry hung on a few balconies. An occasional potted plant, or displaced tree, offered token greenery. On some, empty lawn chairs waited. On others, bicycles leaned. A scream of graffiti flamed into view, a rush of red, yellow, and purple letters in an assertion of individuality flying toward him. A kind of tombstone, he thought.

Turning back to the book, he plucked up several words his wife had hoped to acquire for refined understanding and later use. Suspiration. Cantankerous.

A loud bark of hilarity lifted his eyes to a tailored haze of blues and grays off to his right, where a covey of business executives filled a set of wide seats facing each other. A broad-shouldered young man, some sort of bright, vain upstart, stiffened his neck and dipped his chin in a half-hearted effort to prevent smugness from corrupting his satisfaction at having pleased his entire clique. The cherry-bright lips of the woman beside him, the only female among them, parted in glee, her hands stroking the wool of her skirt straining over her thighs as if to calm them. The gray-haired man, whose back was to Thomas, seemed the likely target of the joke, as he shifted uncomfortably. It was impossible to try to look into the softness of tissue and receptivity that opened darkly into the woman's mouth, her tongue brushing the edge of her teeth, without feeling the pointlessly veiled sexual suggestion she would certainly deny with mugging expressions that reinforced it.

The steady rain of cards, letters, emails, and phone calls offering condolences, love, memories, and what kindness they could had tapered off in recent weeks. Still, he stepped off the rattling elevator each night carrying a handful of mail withdrawn from the box in the vestibule. Once in the door to their apartment, he stared at the answering machine on the bookshelf that he had bolted to the wall with Marie balancing it from below while he secured the supports, her shoulder pressed against his thigh, her breath sounding with clock-like steadiness, and whenever he glanced down into her gleaming eyes, she would shrug happily. He and Marie had moved into the apartment three years earlier, but they had been allowed only fourteen innocent months before her illness was diagnosed. Though he did not exactly welcome the cards, the letters, and even the emails, he did not view them with the same distaste prompted by the voices on the answering machine. He might feel as he opened an envelope and read that he stood on a strange planet, having been flung far from the world the sender occupied, but the written word provided a semblance of comfort. He felt it brought a gentle, considered quality—at least that—tactile sensations, the whisper of the paper as he scanned the messages, the scratch of passing pens, implicit fingertips on a keyboard pausing and advancing, leaving words behind. He knew that whatever view the writer held of him, they were wrong, their belief that they could help him misguided, because they did not know the extent of his exile and disruption—that he was stopped, his life stopped, his estrangement from the norms they pursued unconditional. Still, he did not despise them for the delusion that they might affect him, as he did those who used the telephone. It was irrational and he knew it, but he felt inclined to anarchy. The phone calls felt abrupt, intrusive, easy, squeezed in. He could hear them thinking, Oh, right, I better call Thomas. I almost forgot. At times he played them angrily, allowing each caller mere seconds before erasing them. There'd been evenings when the signal light twitched with what he felt must be an infinite number, and increasingly, in the weeks following Marie's funeral, the voices awaiting him belonged to women, some of them women he had not heard from in years, their sympathy ringing fake, no matter how sincere they tried to sound. Often, they ended with an invitation, presented as an afterthought, to join them for dinner, a movie, a party, a walk in the park, or a cup of coffee. He loathed them most, despising their ignorant desire to get on with things.

He loathed the people across the aisle almost as much, the disgust of his thoughts enveloping their pointless health and good humor. They were so naïve and self-satisfied, thriving in spite of their fundamentally clueless nature. They were still laughing. The woman reached now, one hand clasping the young male's knee, while her other, in a reflex of nervous grooming, patted her auburn hair. Her mouth formed a smile, as if panting, her big white teeth everywhere. He couldn't believe it, now that he really looked at them. What had they been talking about before? A movie, and then some interdepartmental prank. Was it possible that they were as oblivious as they seemed? Each of their lives teetered on a house made not of cards but of razor blades. Was he the only one aware of the uncertainty underpinning even the most rudimentary routines? An undertow of disorder surged beneath the rattling train, poised to burst through the next instant to scorch their faces, rip the skin from their smiles. He wanted to wake them to what he knew. Had none of them ever lost anyone they loved?

He observed them with an even more single-minded intensity. The older man wore a worsted wool herringbone suit somewhat more sober than the attire of his companions. It was unlikely that the expensively trimmed gray fringing his ears came only from worries about the market, his equities, his promotions, his golf and tennis scores. And the others, for all their uncomplicated aplomb, must have lost a parent or sibling. Were they fools who had yielded to the relief offered in platitudes—cowards who took shelter in the slop of some self-help book or talk show on "grieving and closure." He hated the phrase, knowing he'd never have "closure," nor did he want it. Closure of what? The hole in his life?

His station stop had been called. He was on his feet, having slipped his bookmark into the last pages he'd read. As he reached to gather his bags, the trembling that shot through the floor bloomed into a full-fledged jolt that flung him against an empty seat across from the group he'd been watching. They hooted at one another, turning surprise at the violence shaking the entire car into a whoop of exhilaration. The backs of his calves hit something, and he caught hold of a metal hoop in the backrest of a random seat to keep from falling. But when he grew steady, he was almost leaning over them. They thought that their banter made them safe, that they were free to be prodigal with their lives. The force of his focus awoke the older man first, and then the young woman looked up, flirty even with him. He felt biblical and wild with his book clutched in his hand, like some Old Testament prophet recently back from desert with his vision of wisdom and wrath. I'm losing it, he thought.

"Yes?" said the younger man, following the gaze of the woman.

Thomas wanted to tell them that he and his wife had been trying to get pregnant when she came down with cancer. After months of debate, the innocent blaze of her desire to have their child had won him over. It had parted the barrier of his foggy reluctance, and they'd abandoned all forms of birth control. In the last month before the diagnosis, she had received a job promotion, advancing to junior partner. She had just completed a year of radical periodontal work, her gums slit open, the bacteria scraped off so the bones in her mouth would be healthy for the long life she planned. Four times the periodontist had gone in with his gleaming light and flashing instruments. Years before, wanting to quit smoking, she'd succeeded only in cutting back, but all the doctors agreed, the oncologist being the most emphatic, that she bore no blame for her illness. They should know that, too. They should know it all.

"Lighten up, buddy," said the thick-chested young man. The subtle rearrangement he gave his shoulders hinted that he was ready to stand, if necessary, to enforce his warning.

"Did you hear the name of this station stop?" said Thomas.

The young man said, "Chappaqua," and raised his eyebrows in a request for appreciation from the woman, who tittered her enjoyment.

"Thanks," Thomas responded. They weren't worth it.

"No problem."

As he departed, they scoffed behind him, and the reflex ease with which they judged him alien to their lives startled him. He was about their age, he thought, most of them striking him as early to mid-thirties while he was only in his early forties. Of course, his clothing might seem unconventional to their eyes: a long silk scarf elaborated by fringe, dark blue linen trousers imported from Italy, a lightweight out-of-fashion raincoat purchased a decade ago by someone at Barneys and by him at a thrift shop recently.

The train shivered to a halt, a squeal leaping up from beneath the metal floor. As he exited the car, stepping across the gap, the track below flashed in a lateral gleam. He hastened along under the artifice of lights hung at regular intervals against the dusk inching closer.

The first set of stairs appeared shorter than he remembered. He thought how his sister, Kathy, would be waiting in the parking lot, or her husband, Robert—someone would be there to pick him up in one of their Volvos. A construction of large but ambiguous purpose steered him into a covered crossover, which brought him to a lengthier stairway. He wasn't certain why he'd made the journey, whether he had been attracted to the idea of a visit or had merely needed to escape the city. Staying in the apartment had become risky. Everyday objects such as cups and pillows, an ashtray, a book, her dresser, her closet, her clothing, even a doorway—all were charged with unusual powers. A cup that she had touched at some ordinary moment could freeze him. Like the blow of an assailant, this or that incident or object demanded his attention with the power of a sanctified relic transforming the present in a physical rush of effects that wiped out reality. For an instant he wouldn't know where he was. Then pain would identify whatever he looked at and wherever he stood. The object, a bowl, or blouse, or whatever, while making Marie feel concrete and nearby, would have failed to yield contact with her, producing instead some new aching state in which she was evoked while remaining lost, and the emptiness became both the measure and the assertion of what was no more. Early that afternoon, one such encounter with a postcard toppling from a bookshelf brushed accidentally had left him sobbing on the fire escape. Looking down onto the dingy streets, he saw a white van the exact shape of the blue van that had borne her body off through the uneasy traffic on the day she died. Retreating to the apartment, he began to think of going to visit his sister.

It had not been in the least unusual for him and Marie to head north for a weekend prior to the discovery of her illness, but after her diagnosis, they spent even more time in the third-floor guest room of the old farmhouse in which Kathy and her family lived. Marie hungered for the hours spent in its gracious old confines, viewing the three-flight climb to their room as a pilgrimage to a healing site, the children, her niece and nephew, Molly and Kenny, yammering and playing or fighting somewhere in the house, or out in the yard, the towering trees wavering outside the window, the forest flowering in spring and thickening in summer. She had seemed to think it possible that she might flee her disease, or at least diminish her awareness of it, and now he was fleeing the fact that she had not escaped the tenacious embrace that had finally taken her.

Nearing the base of the stairs where the transparent plastic extended for a few more yards before opening onto the yellowish arc-lighted parking lot, he saw the Volvo station wagon pull into view and stop. In the back seat two shapes wavered. It was the children, he realized. They were wrestling, and the instantaneous rage that their frivolity set loose unsettled him. Tempted to hasten to the car in a fury, demanding that they stop and ordering them to behave, he saw that coming here might have been a mistake. He hoped that the plastic tunnel enclosing him had made it impossible for anyone in the car to see him. He wanted to retreat and find a place to hide until another train could return him to New York. But then he saw that one of the Volvo's windows was down and someone was waving. He stood unmoving, constrained by ambivalence bordering on incapacity. Still he forced a gesture of greeting and started for the car. Perhaps he shouldn't see anyone, he thought.

TWO

His uncertainty in that moment was a version of the mood plaguing him regularly these days, one that had nearly sabo-

taged the lunch he'd planned with his father. It had been scheduled for a Monday on the seventh of the impossible weeks
dragging him on day after day following Marie's funeral. His
reasons for initiating the luncheon had been many, or at least
the feeling that had compelled him to begin the series of calls
that sorted a selection of days, times, and locations until they
found an acceptable arrangement had suggested a complex
purpose. Admittedly, he had lacked specifics, other than his
need to ask for money. But his melancholy and longing for fa-
milial connection had felt equally real and even more pressing.
It was generally thought that his father had money, though the
actual amount and nature of his wealth were unknown. It was
one among many opaque matters so deeply hidden that he and
his sister allowed that one day they might find that the money didn't actually exist. In the past, Thomas had been content
with this state of affairs, almost privileged in his ignorance,
as if not knowing, and more importantly, not caring proved
something special about him. Much of his life had been gov-
erned by the impulse to establish himself as independent and
different from his father, largely immune to whatever expectations the man had for his son. He and Marie had pooled
their incomes. Given her established position at the law firm,
her contribution had been the steadier and larger of the two.
Thomas freelanced carpentry and worked as an assistant to a
sculptor. He'd been disciplined lately, accepting carpentry jobs
that consumed him for short periods and paid well. To date,
his moods and occasional unreliability had not worn out the
sculptor's tolerance. But even in the best circumstances he
could foresee, paying for the co-op apartment, maintenance
and mortgage would quickly overwhelm him without Marie's
help. Because his childhood had been spent in the midst of ac-
coutrements that signaled prosperity, his belief in that hidden
wealth allowed him to consider approaching his father in the

way he was. His parents had owned, and his father continued to own, the brownstone he'd grown up in. They'd spent summers in a large, rambling beach house on Long Island Sound. There had been a housekeeper and a cook at the brownstone. The living quarters consisted of four floors with an elevator to ride or a stairway to climb or descend. If he'd wanted to avoid whoever might be on the elevator, or the stairs, he would make the opposite choice. This option, along with the numerous floors, had provided a flexibility of alternatives and space that left him feeling free at one hour and lonely in another.

Having walked for a bit into the busy glare of the New York day before waving down a cab, he now impulsively asked the driver to pull over a few blocks short of his destination. The vulnerability and need that had carried him to this point evaporated. Resentment at having to manage the upcoming encounter with his father by manufacturing the necessary gadgetry of personality to talk and smile had struck, turning into a refusal to proceed that felt insurmountable. Aware that he'd requested the lunch, he no longer wanted anything to do with the obligation he'd created. He decided to skip it but continued to walk.

After marching another block, he settled for hoping that while covering the remaining distance, he would at least find a way to know what he wanted. Once that was clear, he could reconstitute his character, if he were proceeding, or simply turn away and make excuses later. Fine, he thought, negotiating the flow of pedestrians approaching and passing, or carrying him on in their protective muddle across streets packed with honking but grudgingly cooperative traffic.

The brevity of the interlude before the Players Club rose up in front of him felt unjust. He veered across the street, starting a loop around Gramercy Park. If Marie were alive, he could call her and consult, or at least express his confusion. Anger surged, tears threatened, because she wasn't available for that or anything. He shook his head as if to rattle its interior free of the congestion clotting it. His family was such a mess, really, constantly entangled in moves and countermoves that left them all stymied and segregated by restrictions and punitive moods legislating who could do what with whom without risking offense. There had to be offense. Always. Tainting even Marie's death.

Though the history of their most recent fiasco was lengthy, and though the last chapter could be thought to have come out of nowhere, he knew that Agnes, Marie's sister, had originated the idea that led to it. And he knew, also, that it had gone awry, as most things did. He blamed himself for not seeing how banal the proposition was, really, utterly false in its assumptions and expectations. But his emotions had been a quagmire then, engulfing and sloppily yearning for miracles to pit against the misery of loss. Not that he was a paragon of clarity now. But he had not only gone along with Agnes, he'd championed her proposal.

His mother was dead nine years now—cancer, too—and his father, Benjamin, had rather quickly found a girlfriend, Melanie Haynes. There were those who believed Melanie and Ben, as she called him, had been involved before Thomas's mother died, even before she was ill. But no one knew for sure. Thomas had tried not to care as the years marched on, even when Melanie moved in with Ben after barely a year, and he didn't want to start caring now, somehow mixing those feelings in with his loss of Marie. The connection he sensed between these two women felt capable of urging him to act in ways he didn't understand, couldn't diagnose, and wanted to ignore.

When first proposed by Agnes in the minutes following the memorial for Marie, the idea had felt beautiful and loving. Everyone had been in attendance—Benjamin, Melanie, Thomas, Agnes, along with Kathy, her husband and children. He should have seen the impossibility of goodwill and good intentions having any effect, given the difficulties on display from the start. He now felt almost certain that Melanie had instigated the way his father usurped Thomas's control of the seating arrangements. Whatever the case, Benjamin and Melanie acted together. In a show of force that only Thomas could have contravened, they claimed the front row. They designated the seats beside them for Thomas, Agnes, and Marie's uncle, while Kathy and her family were pushed into the shadowy rear of the little hall. Thomas had sickened when he saw what was going on, but he had been too debilitated to do anything about it. The idea that he needed to straighten out family discord when he was the bereaved husband enraged and exasperated him, and then the near violence of these emotions disheartened him further. He wanted to honor and mourn Marie. The purpose of this gathering was to celebrate her life and share in her loss. But there they were, his family members, in two warring camps.

Having taken their place of prominence in the moments before the memorial began, his father and Melanie sought him out with beckoning looks intended to draw him to join them. Agnes and the uncle were already in place. At one point he'd heard Kathy's young son, Kenny, whispering about how he wanted to go up and sit with Grandpa. Kathy's sharp explanation that he couldn't was too loud. Kenny's sigh, along with the hurt in his young eyes, stirred Thomas, if not to action, at least to thoughts of action. By then he was wedged between his father and Melanie, listening to Marie's friends and coworkers memorializing her generosity, kindness, intelligence, and her overall love of life. For as long as possible, he resisted the impulse to glance back at Kathy. When he yielded, finally, it was as much to make sure she was still there as to read her mood. Her caring, almost pitying smile presumed a shared perspective on the proceedings, which had the opposite effect, reminding him instead that none of this strife would exist if Kathy had not picked a fight with Melanie over a tamale pie recipe two years ago. They had all been getting along fine. If not exactly enjoying one another, the veneer of amiability they had all agreed to maintain was holding, until that evening at the dinner table in the beach house.

Benjamin and Melanie were hosting, everyone gabbing away—Kathy and her husband, Robert, along with Thomas and Marie, who had yet to learn the dark news awaiting her. Melanie had prepared an elaborate meal and the compliments were flying, the wine flowing. Everything garnered praise, but the subject of "the incredible tamale pie" commanded repeated attention, with Benjamin instigating and Melanie blushing. After maybe the fifth iteration, Kathy wondered aloud if she might be able to see the recipe. Melanie hooted, a sound of shock that surprised them all. The full scope of her displeasure was dimly concealed in the seconds it took her to mount her playful refusal. "Not going to happen, Kathy. No. No."

"I see," said Kathy. "A state secret, is it?"

"One you'll never know."

"I meant it as a compliment."

"Of course. But I don't share my recipes."

Kathy raised her palms in mock apology, scrunching her face and hunching her shoulders as if she were shrinking in shame.

A week later, Thomas visited the beach house again, this time alone. Marie was out of town on business. Kathy had begged off—too much going on with the kids. After lunch, Thomas had taken a long walk on the beach. The waves had surged into a cove below him, the weather unusually rough.

He threw stones as far as he could, watching the wind bend their trajectory.

Upon his return he found a note left by Ben and Melanie, who'd gone shopping. When the phone rang, he hesitated to answer, but then did. It was Kathy calling from Chappaqua. "Thank goodness it's you," she told him. "I hope you're surviving. Are they around?" He explained that they were out for groceries, and she asked, "Okay now. Tell the truth. How are you doing there with that bitch?" He said he was doing fine. "She's such a bitch, her and her stupid recipes. How do you stand it? Poor Daddy. Hopefully, he'll wake up to the cretin she is. How can we help him? We have to help him." Once more he tried to mollify her, but she surged back with, "Oh, she is, too, a bitch. You know it. So snotty with every breath. Just admit it. Next time I'm there, I'm going to steal her stupid recipes. I'll burglarize her. I don't know how. But somehow. And then I'll make her goddamn tamale pie and feed it to her."

He'd heard the car pulling up outside, Ben and Melanie returning. "Gotta go. They're back."

"Who called?" his father asked as they entered, setting down bags on the table.

"Nobody," Thomas said, not wanting to mention Kathy.

"But it's blinking," said Melanie.

Oh, god, Thomas thought, watching his father scoot over to push the Play button and return to the groceries, expecting to listen while continuing the task at hand. But nothing continued. Ben, holding a package of chicken breasts, froze. At the same instant, Melanie, who was mid-pirouette from the counter to the refrigerator with cauliflower in one hand and a head of lettuce in the other, stumbled and nearly fell. Thomas stood, stricken with dread, as the machine broadcast his entire exchange with Kathy.

Melanie sputtered. She flailed her arms as if to ward off an absent enemy and ran from the room. Then she reappeared, almost immediately, circling back to deliver a woeful expression of abuse, humiliation, helplessness—whatever being struck dumb could convey. "I don't blame you, Thomas," she said. "I don't. You are blameless." With that, she departed, finally, at least for that evening.

Benjamin called after her, "Don't you worry, Melanie. I'll take care of this. I'll see to it." He turned on his son. He stomped and shook his head. He erupted in staccato bursts that covered disappointment, betrayal, and regret for having tried to make things work. Now he had to contend with poor Melanie weeping, and all because his daughter was a troublemaker, incorrigible and provocative, as she had always been. Like Melanie circling in and out of the room, Benjamin circled subjects and themes, returning to regret, adding bewilderment and hurt, even replaying the message, before rediscovering disappointment as the quintessential characteristic of this event and perhaps of his whole life. He'd tried to make things work, but they never did and never would. And then, shifting his focus slowly, he told Thomas to leave the room, because he wanted to be alone when he called Kathy.

Thomas backed away, watching his father approach the phone. But then, pausing before dialing, he held Thomas with the saddest look. As if wanting to give Melanie's remarks his full approval and sympathy, he said, "I know you did your best. I could hear you trying. But Kathy—well, Kathy, as we both know, is unrelenting when her mind is made up. When she smells blood. She's a banshee. Or worse. She wants trouble. I've never known what to do about her." His nod was a reissue of his dismissal, as his concentration went to the phone. Thomas slipped away, relieved to quit the oncoming disaster.

He waited several hours before calling Kathy from a bar where he'd gone for a drink. He hoped the interval gave her enough time to recover from the worst of her reaction to whatever their father might have said to her. However, she sounded heartbroken. Sobbing for one patch of conversation, she veered seconds later into outrage. Some of the same concepts her father had used made their appearance: betrayal, disappointment, and disbelief. How could their father side with that transparent, superficial bitch? She asked again and again, howling, almost begging for an answer. Thomas tried to console her with assurances that it would all blow over after a little time had passed. But she didn't want it to blow over. The hell with him. He'd cursed her, she said, told her he was done with her, never wanted to speak to her again. Brought up ancient history, ancient troubles. The hell with him.

"Okay," Thomas told her. "But you know he didn't mean all that."

"What I know is that he did mean it. That's what I know."

"Not the worst of it."

"That most of all. The worst most of all. He said it over and over. It's what he really wants anyway. You know that's what he's always wanted."

"No," he said as a suspicion with enough certainty to arrest him crept to the forefront of his crowded mind. It urged him to realize that Kathy had provoked the fight, intentionally, whether he knew it or not, or she knew it or not. First the tamale pie and then that call. If her recklessness with him on the phone, trying to draw agreement from him about Melanie— thank god he'd refrained—had failed to prompt the desired conflict, she would have found another way. That was what he needed to know. Because she wanted to force her father to choose between her and Melanie, hoping he would side with her, all the while knowing the impossibility of that hope.

From then on, when Thomas and Marie spent time with Kathy, their father was nowhere to be seen, nor was Melanie, of course. The reverse was true when he and Marie visited his father and Melanie. The consequence of that phone call meant that Thomas had not seen his father and sister anywhere near one another, let alone in the same room, until the memorial when he sat between Melanie and his father, while Kathy and her family hovered in the back rows. It was the sadness of that petty, pointless division that moved Agnes to act. She felt that her sweet sister would have found the situation intolerable. It had to be rectified, she'd whispered to Thomas, as the service ended. With the brevity of life, the finality of death and loss, the vulnerability they all shared so emphatically before them in Marie's death, they did not dare waste this moment. They had to transform it, she told him, use it to create reconciliation between Kathy and her father, between Kathy and Melanie. It was what Marie would want. Stumbling about in the aftermath of the service, the possibility of Marie working in their lives to bring healing gave Thomas a sense of her ongoing goodness affecting the world that compelled him to agree.

As the guests spilled out into the shimmering afternoon, Agnes, who felt Kathy should take the initiative, made her proposal. At first Kathy refused, but after a moment she admitted that she often wished the hostility would end. Rather quickly then, she converted. They were all to have dinner that night as their final gesture of farewell to Marie. Benjamin and Melanie had made the arrangements, inviting everyone, so it was possible to imagine that they had some inclination in the direction of rapprochement. It was even possible to think that the process was underway.

In the moments that found everyone stalled near the coat-check booth, waiting for their table to be prepared, Kathy asked her father if he would go outside for a private moment. He agreed, readily, suggesting further goodwill. She smiled at Thomas, and he watched through the front window as they

stood in the artificial spill of light from within. She would tell
him later how carefully she'd explained that she was sorry for
what she'd said on the phone that day, and how she hoped that
in Marie's name it could all be forgotten. She said she could
feel her voice quivering as she went on, hoping they all could
find a fresh start. When she began to feel frightened, she tried
to close quickly with her earnest belief that they both must
know that this was what Marie, who was kind and loving to
everyone, would want for them.

Thomas saw his father flinch as if she'd spit at him. He re-
coiled further, shook his head, seemed through the distorting
window to grow pale. The restaurant door opened with the ar-
rival of other patrons and Thomas thought he heard the words,
"How dare you? I can't believe it." In Kathy's re-creation, done
for him later, their father scolded her, pinched words fighting
to escape his pinched mouth. "'I can't believe the gall. What in
god's name is wrong with you?'" And more: "'There's no point.
You don't like Melanie and she doesn't like you. One thing
doesn't have much to do with the other. I'd say there's no point.
We've tried and it doesn't work. No, no, I think that would just
be a big waste of time.'" After glancing out and staring into the
traffic, which puzzled Kathy, making her think he was about
to wave down a cab, he turned back. "'So how is everything
else?'" he asked before walking back inside.

Kathy followed him, her eyes glistening, her body quivering. She shook her head sadly, and Thomas began to wait for
his father's wrath. Everyone else was oblivious, chattering excitedly. Benjamin, having taken Melanie by the hand, pursued
the maître d'. "We need our table. We're hungry. Everyone in
my party is hungry," he said without looking at anyone. "Let's
go. Let's eat." With Melanie in hand, he led them off after the
expansively apologetic maître d'.

It was with that thought that Thomas stopped pacing. He

stood on the opposite side of the park from the Players Club, his hands locked in fists around the metal of the fence. He had circled the block at least once, maybe more. He looked past shrubs and flowers, another strip of fencing, across the narrow side street to the door of his destination.

In the end he surrendered, feeling almost hypnotized. Approaching the dining area warily, he surveyed the room, the tables, and then his father, who sat bowed over *Time* magazine with a pot of coffee. As Thomas sat, Benjamin continued to read a moment more. Then he leaned back to consider his son from an enhanced distance, which Thomas saw did nothing to diminish the dismal impression he made. "You've about used up our allotted time."

"Sorry."

"You do know what time we agreed on?"

"Yes."

"And you decided to ignore it."

"No."

"Is this about money? I'm wondering why you insisted we do this and then you're here like this, barely available, barely present. Not really doing it. My guess is it's about money."

"No."

"I suspect it is."

"I just wanted to see you."

"How do I look?"

"What were you reading?"

"A magazine. This magazine. The news."

"I can see that."

"Then why ask?"

"I guess I was thinking more specifically."

"I've already forgotten. I'd like a reason, though, any reason why we're sitting at this table. Do your best."

"Did you eat yet?"

"Huge quantities of bread. Rolls. Breadsticks." He waved at the waiter, and gestured that Thomas needed a coffee cup. "I do have something to talk to you about, even if you've lost track of why you brought us here."

"I didn't say that."

"If I take the moment, you may have a chance to rediscover your purpose. I don't know what Kathy told you about our conversation outside that restaurant the night of the memorial, but it was sickening. I have to tell you, I was incensed. I've been wanting to tell you, because you should know. What she tried to do disgusts me. What has she told you?"

"Not much."

"You know what she was trying to do."

"Not exactly."

"Well, let me tell you. She was trying to take advantage of poor Marie's death—to use our grief to wipe away some of her misdeeds. So she could be forgiven. In Marie's name. She actually said that. Trying to get back in my good graces and pretend to make friends with Melanie whom she does not like—not at all. It was such a self-serving lie. It says something about her—and nothing good—that she could come up with that. To get herself out of trouble. Well, I didn't fall for it. But it reminded me how devious she can be. If she could come up with that type of conniving idea, what couldn't she come up with? My god. I was incensed. And I let her know what I thought, too. She won't be trying that again. Or on the other hand, she probably will. Because that's the kind of person she is." The expression with which he introduced a pause suggested he took under consideration certain amplifications that might strengthen his argument, and while this silence could have also seemed an invitation for Thomas to respond if he cared to, it wasn't. "I'm hungry," Benjamin said, ending one thing and moving them on to the next. He scanned for a waiter and beckoned to the one he found.

They ordered in a rush, as if indifferent to all but the speed that would get them fed and out of each other's company. Benjamin picked up the magazine with a gesture that appeared to prepare them for the fact that he was going to read, but then he shifted toward Thomas, taking him in slyly, a film of vagueness settling over his gaze. "So how much do you want?"

"What?"

"The money you want. How much?"

THREE

As he climbed the steps toward the guest room in his sister's home, reaching the second floor and looking up the stairwell toward the lightless third floor, Thomas faltered. He felt that the room awaiting him was not the one he sought. Dinner had been ready when Robert, who had picked him up at the station with both kids carrying on in the back seat, delivered them all up the curving driveway to the house. The children stormed the front door, turning their entrance into a race, as if it mattered who was first to the food.

Kathy hugged Thomas while ordering the kids to wash their hands. Robert, with Thomas's luggage in hand, headed straight to the guest room, glancing at his watch more than once. Thomas, for no reason he could name, trailed along. By the time they returned, Kathy and the kids were at the table. "Don't let it get cold," she said. The phone rang almost immediately with the first of several business calls that Robert had to take. He apologized and told everyone to please go on without him. But as the calls continued, the incessant stopping and starting gave the dinner a hectic mood. Kathy added her regrets after the third interruption. Eating rapidly and noisily at first, the kids gradually slowed, and Kathy took the moment to look intently at Thomas and tell him how glad she was—how glad they all were—that he'd chosen to visit. Then she instructed the children to say "good night" to Uncle Tommy, which they did, politely, one after the other, before being herded upstairs for their baths and bedtime.

Thomas sighed. The truth was that the hubbub had helped by insulating him from any obligation to socialize. The irritability that had possessed him on the train felt like a phantom poised to return. He nibbled a little of the chicken still on his plate and then wandered around. With ice, tonic water, and gin, he mixed a drink. In the library, he sat down in one of the large leather chairs and stared out the window at the patio. He remembered it in summer with benches and lawn chairs and the big yard beyond.

Kathy appeared in the doorway, bearing a glass of wine and another installment of regret. She was exhausted and had a headache, and Molly still needed a story read. She might not be back down. Was he confident that he knew where to look for anything and everything he might need? And tomorrow morning, she wanted him to know, she and Molly were going horseback riding with Greta, who ran the stable. He was invited along if he wanted. No need to decide now. He smiled, gestured with his drink, and she smiled back, raising her wineglass.

On the stairs, where hesitation held him, he glanced down the way that he'd come, and then up the remaining interval. In that eerily intimate space that awaited him with its piles of pillows and quilts, Marie had suffered an endless and exquisitely inventive series of torments. She had loved traveling to the house and to the countryside, hoping to enjoy the natural surroundings, the wind, the night sky, and the children, imagining a possible respite, a few days of distraction, but the nausea had pursued her, the nightmares, the coughing, the dread of suffocating in her sleep, of drowning in her own sputum, her body shrinking around her in the measurement of some dreadful withdrawal of life itself, as if life were an addiction whose enchantments had seduced her and now she must give them up.

The book waited where he had placed it on the night table earlier. In it the woman remained where he'd left her, too, looking for her dog through the pages of Wyoming with the underlined words that he'd forgotten to look up. In a curious leap of association, the scribbles on the catacomb walls scattered throughout Rome came to him. Thin, willful scratches, he remembered seeing with Marie at his side; they were not unlike those she'd left behind.

He picked up the book, hoping it would serve to fortify him against the feelings of displacement and alienation that he'd tasted on the stairs. He and Marie had lain together in this room, savoring every good moment, struggling past those that were bad, weeping together, or separately, sleeping or trying to, one of them lying awake while the other dozed, whispering together, plotting for hope, imagining recovery, remembering health. So much had happened here, but nothing remained. The dainty impractical bedside table, the lamp with sailboats on its shade, the grapes spreading in snatches of purple upon the wallpaper, the very pillows on which she had sweat and burrowed into him, as if he could oppose the demon closing its inhuman arms around her, as if he could intervene with his pathetic flesh and rout the dragon from her dreams—all bore no evidence of those precious, irreplaceable hours.

The window across from the foot of the bed was high above the ground below, the night sky imminent. The landscape sloped upward, pushing the peaked outline of a neighboring house into view. He fell upon the pillows, fluffy and colorful on the neatly made bed. Tomorrow he would go riding with his sister and niece and the woman who ran the stable. In the meantime he would lie there remembering Marie's ashes in their canister decorated with flowers amid books and photographs on a bookshelf in the apartment. He needed to decide what to do with them. And he needed to find out where his mother was buried. He didn't know, which was odd, and he wanted to know, which was normal. He remembered her funeral service, but only one thing from the rest of the day. They had all come down the steps of the church, and his father had announced, "Let's go for ice cream." Not a bad idea, except it wasn't going to be ice cream before the cemetery, as some thought, and others hoped. He wasn't going to the cemetery, and so no one went. They all stood around awkwardly posed to protect their good clothes from the dripping ice cream they licked from cones. Benjamin liked to end things. If you knew him, you knew that about him. Friends and family might struggle to grasp his affinity for terminations, but he never doubted their worth. Still, there had to be a way for Thomas to find out where his mother was buried. Not that he would put Marie's ashes there. Both had died of cancer. Was there something to be understood about him or them from this coincidence? Was a coincidence actually something?

He heard murmuring and tried to quiet his thoughts to minimize their interference. Was he hearing voices, barely sensible and ghostly? And was that music? One of the kids? But it was too late, wasn't it? He slipped from bed into the hall and went as far as the top of the stairs, where his altered vantage brought certainty that it was his sister and her husband he heard, though he couldn't tell where they were. They seemed to be moving. But their direction was unclear, until they became a degree more distinct, and he worried they were climbing the back stairs, perhaps even heading up to see him.

"Well, a lot of it is transference," Robert was saying. "Not all. But some. The devastation."

He retreated a foot or two, still wanting to hear.

"So you think he's just indulging."

"No. No, not at all."

"It's what you said. You just said that."

"No, I didn't."

Momentarily their volume held steady, as if they had paused not far away.

"Couldn't it be that he loved Marie that much? Just that much."

"But it's so extreme."

"Yes, it is."

The next seconds added nothing more, not even footsteps. Her tone was provocative, and Thomas ventured onto the stairway, where sound might reach him with less difficulty. He tried to focus his hearing, filling the silence with a depiction of their postures dictated by discord, maybe even one of them walking away.

"I'm not saying he didn't love her," Robert answered. "Of course he loved her. Of course he did. But there has to be transference in it, too. Where else do all those feelings come from?"

"Is that a real question?"

"I think so."

"Be sure. You might want to reconsider."

"What's wrong with it?"

"Maybe even withdrawing it."

"Why? Tell me why."

"It's icy. A bit icy."

"I don't see that. I'm asking. I don't know where else passions come from."

"The heart. They come from inside us. From our feelings. From us."

"Which comes from where?"

"I'm going to bed."

"Me, too."

"If you must."

"I do. I'm sleepy."

"Because you are far afield with all this."

"All this what?"

They lowered their voices as they moved in the direction of the children's rooms, their speech melting together, their individualities blurring into a hum, though by hastening down a short way, he believed he made out Kathy's last fading sentence or two.

"Well, for some people the death of a spouse is the worst possible thing. The very worst. I know you don't believe that could be the case, but for some people it is. For some people it's devastating."

Thomas stood for a second, and then he went back to bed, intending to sleep. That was what you did in bed at night alone. They'd been talking about him, disagreeing about his behavior. Transference, according to Robert. Kathy had defended him. He should sleep, but he didn't really want to sleep. He had little interest in whether he did or didn't. By the end, Kathy had escalated from provocation to accusation. He wondered if Robert had responded when they were out of earshot, or if he might be responding now, or had he simply accepted her judgment.

Thoughts of Marie called, busy thoughts pointlessly directing him to revisit all the books he'd read on alternative therapies, as if rescue were somehow still possible. *Your Cancer Is Not as Smart as You. Hidden Cures. The McMillan Cure. The Gerson Cure.* Marie had a friend whose sister was a nun and they'd prayed with her and with other nuns, too. When they sat with a Tibetan Lama, he guessed Marie's birthday correctly, startling them. The next minutes filled with faith in his extra-sensory powers. They peered into his smile. What would come of it? They went to an Ashram and chanted, *Om, Om, Om,* and left soaring in an ecstatic state. All the time doing chemo. Going to the Chemo Room in the oncology wing. Seeing Dr. Markowitz and the doctors whose consultations he advised. Sitting elbow to elbow in recliners with other patients and their companions sipping coffee, reading magazines. Or going to the Chemo Bay, where there were more patients. Never stopping. Oh, the needles. How Marie hated the needles. She had always hated needles. With nuns praying and priests saying Masses and *Om* on their lips, they joked that they had become spiritual vandals, whose indiscriminate eclecticism put them in danger of confusing the otherworldly patrons they implored. He researched juice cures. Turmeric. Frankincense. He read about hyperbaric oxygen therapy and wondered: Could they? Should they? Where?

But then they ended up in that lead room in New Jersey. Where else would you go for a lead room but—

The voices intruded again, infiltrating the seams of his thoughts, urging him to wonder if he dreamed. He glanced at the door to make certain he'd closed it. The conversation, if that's what it was, had grown louder. Alarmed beyond what reason could soften, he scampered into the hall, then inched down to the second floor. What had he heard? With the kitchen more or less below him, he understood the intrusion had not come from there. But still he heard his sister and Robert. He imagined them having continued their disagreement, having then gone down for a drink of some kind, wine or beer, and now they were returning. Detecting an edge in them now, he hoped they weren't fighting.

The hall he looked into advanced through shadows to the central stairwell, where it went past the children's rooms, little Kenny's first and then Molly's, before ending at the master bedroom, where whatever was happening persisted at what felt to him like reckless volume. He hastened in that direction, less concerned with stealth than he had been. He didn't want them fighting. People who loved each other should not fight. He and Marie had quarreled infrequently, but he regretted every instance. No matter how few, there had been too many. If his sister and her husband were arguing, he would knock on the door and tell them to stop. Or pretend he needed something. His presence would be enough. What could he pretend to need?

Proximity translated the ruckus beyond their door into the protest of a bed frame and mattress under fluttering sheets. He heard laughter. Helpless giggles burst through Kathy's effort to stifle them, convincing him that Robert tickled her, as she had tickled Thomas when he was small. A child's voice called, "Mom, is that you? Mom?" It was Molly. He was outside her room. The bedroom grew hushed. He turned and fled, the effect of Kathy's giggles, now quieted at the sound of Molly's voice, letting gratitude moisten his eyes.

Back in bed he thought: Time to rest. Call it a day. Time to sleep. Instead, he followed Marie around with vials and plastic organizers of drugs and vitamins and tumblers of carrot juice. When she had the strength to feel playful, she had teased him that he'd become "a stalker," begging him to leave her alone. He thought about the vials, envisioned the organizers, and the bright orange carrot juice. He heard the hum of the juicer. He heard her teasing voice. He gained twenty pounds cooking fattening foods, trying to feed her, trying to make sure she gained weight. They meditated. And they visualized, too, battling blood and dread by breathing together, finding sweetness there, like children in a fantastical tale of adventure with warriors, demons, and grave trials. It would work if they had souls. Only if they had souls. Only if they had spirits. They marshaled allies to help them push past doubt, the first of the dragons. They found a scientific study where two groups of college students had been given specific images to focus on. One group imaged neutrophils while the second group imaged T cells. At the conclusion of the study, in a result labeled "peculiar and highly suggestive," the appropriate cells in each group increased, while other cells remained unchanged.

Encouraged by the possibility that science supported their hopes, they launched warrior maneuvers, ethereal forays of invention dispatching fabricated white knights on white horses with swords, lances, and flapping banners to do battle. While the disease, like some inimical brute, signaled its whereabouts falsely, hiding its advance, firing from cell to cell its lethal message. He was drifting now, sliding toward sleep, which was probably all right. It was time. Time to sleep. But what time was it? He had no idea. And what was time? And where was Marie? Was she in time or out of time? Wait, he thought. Wait, wait, wait. Not now. Not yet.

He wasn't in the right room, he realized. He needed to leave it, so he did. He descended, carrying his books. The room he was looking for was somewhere else. Higher, it seemed, as if there were another floor above the third, and if he could climb to it, he would find everything he sought. But he was going down. After a while he would ascend. By going down first, he would rise up later to discover every missing thing preserved with the care it deserved. He knew the room, could see it in a detailed conception, a set of lines and measurements, a mechanical drawing from which the fully dimensioned reality would emerge, a room in which the past waited, and where he would not be alone with this sadness and his books, one in which the dog would no longer be lost, and the other which would help him decipher Marie's special words.

He sat up. He waved his arms as if to drive sleep away. He hated sleep. He switched on the bedside lamp and the light alarmed him, as if it were noise. The instant he spotted the bundle of his trousers on the floor, he turned the lamp off and reached out, groping through the afterimage left by the glare.

Clothed in the trousers and a T-shirt, but barefoot, he went downstairs, stepping softly straight to the liquor cabinet. He collected tonic and ice from the refrigerator.

Snow with pearls of dust at their core, he read. Wyoming was a wide, craggy, uncorrupted emptiness. The room where he sat was littered with the children's cups and trinkets, a set of diminutive sneakers, a plastic gun with a part of the handle missing. They broke everything. For them an essential aspect of play seemed to be destruction.

The floor lamp behind him was the only light in the downstairs, and at the periphery of its reach he saw a fragmented cookie surrounded by crumbs and bits of frosting. "Cantankerous" was underlined. He wondered if she had ever found out the meaning. He would look it up, even though he felt he knew.

The glass he held now contained only gin. The first drink, almost from the first sip, delivered mellow, flowing sensations that had lobbied for more, and straight this time, and he'd filled a medium-size water glass. Maisy had taken note of him when he was in the kitchen, eyeing him with interest, and now she ambled in, her ears up, gaze steady. He'd significantly depleted the gin bottle. There might be concern when Kathy noticed, but there would be allowances, too. He'd restock it before going back to New York. He took a sip, and then a gulp. "Sweet" was the way everyone had described Marie. "Lovable." "God made a terrible mistake taking her," his sister once said.

He could slip now from the Wyoming landscape, where the woman, astride a horse, rode into a shelf of canyon, calling the dog's name. With a shift of his eyes, he could leave her behind in the words becoming specks. The details of the room flooded him. The debris of the children came over the rim of the glass poised at his lips: a foam football on the coffee table, its colorful edges nibbled white by Maisy, who sighed and flopped down on the floor. Was this what it was like, life and death? Just a step. Just a shift. And you went from one to the other. From the book to the room, from the room all the way back to Wyoming. Two parallel worlds. Except death would be one from which you could not step back.

He awoke in a cool dark. His skin was sheeted in icy moisture. He was in his underwear, and he was out of doors. Starless sky hung behind the sweeping furls of a willow tree whose waves were too close. He sat up, disorientation giving way to facts. He was out on the roof. It was a kind of plateau with a shingled floor. In a tumble of thoughts, scrambling to construct order, he tried to remember. His head hurt. He had the dictionary. Had he lugged it with him, along with the book on Wyoming and a scrap of paper? His head hurt. Had he heaved the window up, the sill and frame parting with a ripping sound to create a hole to let him slither out, headfirst? The rooftop had seemed a kind of prelude, an antechamber, a way of approaching something he needed to know. Now he was cold, his physical discomforts pushing aside those unpleasantries he might think of as emotions. He had come out here to look at the sky directly. Or maybe he'd wanted to look up Marie's words under the sky? But had he done it all in a blackout, as it seemed, from which he had now emerged? He had not drunk enough to black out. A couple of drinks. No more. A big one, for sure. But nothing he couldn't handle. His predicament was the result of something else, something unusual, even unnatural, a deathlike captivation darker than ordinary sleep, and dangerous. Because he had moved about in it. He could have fallen to his death in his sister's yard.

He crept back into the room and onto the bed. He opened the dictionary and removed the page of notebook paper. In a kind of arbitrarily punctuated run-on sentence devised originally to accommodate the words he wanted to look up for Marie, he saw that other words had intruded, words from elsewhere with mysterious roots and implications. *Suspiration*, he read. *Cantankerous. Myself. Docility. Today.* Tomorrow. *Exigent. Time. Grief. Sadness. Life. Death. Love. Her. She. Yesterday.* Their spacing grew haphazard as they staggered to a weary end: angerignatsssss.

On the day of her cremation, he had traveled to the funeral parlor alone in the early morning hours. His request for a private viewing was allowed under the gaze of the manager, whose piety was a shallow performance of caring that Thomas experienced as he might have an insult. Still he met it, and matched it with whispering solemnity and cloying gratitude. He entered the big room with the casket at the end. She lay in satiny padding like a jewel in a case about to be taken away, the dire transformation of her vitality complete in the mannequin she had become. His glance found the man still behind him, a dark suit with glinting glasses where eyes might be expected. He posed in the dimly lit archway, a paragon of stillness, his gaze fixed on the floor in a show of deference, which he must have practiced on hundreds of other mourners year after year.

It wasn't exactly envy Thomas felt, but he did wonder what the man, who appeared in his late fifties, might understand after decades of immersion in the varieties of grief. Did he even recognize his opportunity? All the people that came through his doors struck down by loss, or coping stoically, or blind to it, or utterly indifferent. And then there was the clergy, the ministers, priests, and rabbis with their varied consolations. What did it all add up to? Thesis against thesis, the discrepancies, and occasional commonalities. Did they add up? Or were they no more than posture and confusion, their limits and conflicts best ignored in order that some comfort be possible?

He blinked, looking into the daylight blasting the window. He lay in his sister's guest room. He sat up. He got up. He dressed and went out the door and down the stairs. People like to do the things that they have done before. They like to get out of bed and go down the stairs and see the room they expect to find waiting where they expect it to be, the table where they expect it and the refrigerator where they expect it, and they like to find the people they expect standing or sitting where they are expected. Upon opening the kitchen door at the bottom of the stairs, Thomas was glad to find the kitchen beyond it, and then amazed at the sight of his sister seated at the table, sipping orange juice from a glass while the pen sticking from her fingers wiggled across a piece of paper, paused, and repeated. "Hi," she said, smiling up at him. "Hi."

"Hi."

"You slept in. I guess you needed it."

"I guess I did."

"No guess to it. It's noon."

"It can't be. Noon? No, no."

"Yes, Mister Lazy. So I've moved our horse riding adventures to tomorrow."

"How is that possible?"

"I just called her and switched. You've met Greta, haven't you? She's very accommodating."

"Yes. Sure. I've met her. Briefly at some point. But what I meant was—how is it possible I slept that late?"

"I don't know, but it is."

"Good for me," he said. His amazement, which increased as he became aware of it, registered in the cheery ping of his voice, the bright playful energy of their exchange. It satisfied him to imagine that he amused her, or at least pleased her, though last night, alone in his bed, he could never have anticipated either this desire or its delightful gratification. It was as if his sister had transformed him by saying, "Hi," when he entered, her greeting manifesting some alternative Thomas, who might or might not be who he actually was. The chain of impulses flying about and dragging him with it all night was gone now. He could barely remember them, though he knew they pertained to Marie.

Kathy set her empty glass in the sink, still gazing at the piece of paper on which she'd written a list. "I've got to run to the mall. Do you want to come along? Keep me company."

"I don't know," said the part of him that didn't know. It spoke with a voice calling from the gloom he'd escaped. It didn't want to be forgotten. "Maybe," said the alternative version the kitchen had prompted. He was considering the mall, and not merely the local mall where she was going and where he'd shopped occasionally, but any mall, trying to remember the last mall he'd been in. What were malls like, what happened in them, what had happened to him in the last one, and how had he felt about what happened?

"Or you could stay here if you want. Just hang out. Molly is making a poster for school and Kenny is at soccer practice. You could flop and continue doing nothing. Or you could hang out with Molly. Or even help her out if you felt like it."

"What kind of poster?"

"I want you to do what you want. It's for school. She's hard at it."

"You don't know what kind of poster?"

"Last time I checked, she hadn't quite made up her mind.

The subject is assigned—but there's latitude in her approach. It's for English. You sound interested. I won't be gone long." She squirmed into a stylish denim jacket. "She's in her room. But if you want to work with her, and if you feel like it, you guys could bring all her supplies down to the dining room table and spread out."

"Yeah. Okay. It sounds kind of fun."

"It's entirely up to you."

He was chattering and cheerful, watching her zip up and go. He located tomato juice in the refrigerator and coffee in a half-full carafe still hot on the counter. He sat at the table sipping alternatively from the glass and the cup, wondering why he didn't feel worse after his behavior last night. It seemed he had been out on the roof, which didn't seem possible. The memory was persistent, though inconclusive. Not to mention preposterous. He thought he remembered getting back in the window, but not getting out. But how would he ever know? On what basis, by what standard, could he determine if the fragmented actions he recalled had been enacted or dreamed? Did sleepwalking explain it?

Molly sat with her chin in her hand supported by her elbow on the small table, markers and pens lying about, her concentration absorbed by the poster board spread out before her. "Hi, Molly," he said.

There was a delay before she looked at him, blinking as if to clear away something in the air between them. "Hi, Uncle Tommy."

"Can I come in?"

She nodded, "Sure," and he took a position behind her. Peering past her shoulder, he saw the black wavy dashes and subtly elongated Vs rising wing-like from a turmoil of colors that were parted by two bands that snaked and narrowed in a suggestion of perspective and horizon. "It's very good," he said.

"Do you think so? I don't know."

"I do. I'm impressed. I'm very impressed by your choice. It shows something special about you, I think, that you like Van Gogh."

She tensed and, without turning her head, peeked at him, as if she hoped to keep hidden her alarm by limiting her physical availability. "What do you mean?"

Puzzled by her concern that he sensed without clear evidence, or any idea what caused it, he went on carefully. "He's a painter. Or he was a painter, I should say. A wonderful artist. He's dead now."

"Like Marie."

"Well, yes."

"Are you thinking about her? And because they're both dead, that's why you thought of him. I heard Mommy say to Daddy that she thinks you think about her a lot. Maybe always."

What was happening to him? Who was he now? He dragged a red hassock from across the room so he could scrunch down close to her. "Well, actually, I do think about her a lot, but I mentioned Van Gogh because your poster—at least what you have of it—reminded me of one of his paintings. One of my very favorite ones. What is your poster about?"

"Earth. The earth." She studied her work and, finding it worrisome, emitted the tiniest sigh of unmistakable concern. "Will people think I'm copying him? Because that would be cheating. I don't want people saying I cheated."

"Oh, no. I don't think they will."

"I don't want people saying I'm a copycat. I saw it in a book. Are you saying that?"

"Not at all. Absolutely not."

"But you knew right away what I was drawing. Where I got my idea. So everybody will know."

"I think it's okay. There's something called an homage."

"Mom has all these art books, and I saw it, and the poster is supposed to be about the earth. That's the assignment. I didn't want to do just a globe. I know three other kids who are doing globes. But this seems better to me."

"I think it is better. Much better than a globe. And it's fine if you copy as long as you admit it. All you have to do is say you did what you did because you admire him—because Van Gogh inspired you. That's what I said before. Homage. That's what an homage is."

"What?"

"What you're doing."

"Really?"

"Yes. Exactly."

"This is an homage?" With a breath she grew erect, patting the poster board edges with the sides of her palms to square the image and consider it anew. In the next instant, she sought him directly, her brow furrowed. "You're not teasing, are you?"

"No. Absolutely not."

She swept up a pen and bent to the task, her arcing hand creating brown sickle shapes, which she followed up with similar gestures, leaving yellow and green that overlapped and filled in.

"What are the words going to be? Have you thought about the words? If it's a poster, it needs words, doesn't it?"

"I don't want too many words."

"You're right there. But a few. Do you think you should use his name? Van Gogh's name?"

"Do you?"

"It could be a good idea. Then people would know it was an homage."

She sat back and searched the ceiling in what seemed a childish pose of thought. "Do you mean like call the poster, *The Earth by Van Gogh*?"

"Yes. Or *Van Gogh's Earth*. Like that."

He watched her work for a while. She layered in some odd colors, blue and pink, and added what he thought were too many crows. "Do you believe in heaven, Molly?"

"What?"

"I probably shouldn't ask. I didn't mean to."

"I have a friend—not a really best friend, but I like her—Alice Curtz, and she talks about heaven all the time. She talks about it like she's been there. It sounds nice, too, but I don't know if I believe her."

"You don't?"

"No. A little, I guess. I don't think she's lying. But it sounds ordinary when she talks about it. Her grandmother died and Alice came to school every day for a while crying. We started getting worried about her. Even the teachers."

"Well, it's sad."

"I know. It's sad about Marie."

"Yes."

"And Van Gogh, too, maybe." Though she kept her eyes downcast, he felt how strongly she wanted to see him. "I think about Marie, sometimes, and I have sad thoughts, too."

"Do you?"

"When she visited, you know."

"But she liked it here. It was a fun time for her, coming here."

"Oh, sure. I liked it, when she visited—when you guys visited. But you would go away and come back and it was like I could see her dying. I didn't like that."

"What do you mean?"

"You guys would visit and go away, and then come back,

and—or even when she was here for a little bit—some days, I felt like she was dying right in front of me and I could see it. That made me sad."

He stared at her, as if she had changed size or undergone some other unnatural alteration. "Life sucks," he said.

She peered at him, her countenance reflecting the pressure of multiple questions, and then she turned to her drawing, both hands outstretched over it with her palms turned down. They floated back and forth as if riding a vibration, or stroking the fur of an animal.

"What I don't like is people suffering, people in pain." He waited then, wanting her to look at him, but she didn't. She reached for a red marker, and then traded it for green. "I probably shouldn't have said that, either."

"I don't know," she said.

"Maybe not."

"Why, do you think? Because I'm little?"

"That would be one reason."

"Timothy Gibbons says that life sucks every day. He says it about almost everything. If he strikes out in baseball. Or if we get an assignment he doesn't like. Or he thinks it's too hard."

"I'm starting to keep you from your work. Maybe I'll check back later on."

"Okay. You can stay if you want."

"I'll come back." He stood.

"That homage thing is a big, big help."

"Good. I'm glad."

FOUR

With the day mostly gone, and the afternoon sunlight struggling in multiple colors, he stood at the kitchen sink looking out the window as he rinsed the bowl he'd used to snack on cereal. Kathy was at the far end of the lawn, where she bobbed about in a wide-brimmed straw hat, working in a patch of fenced-in vegetable garden. She was on her hands and knees, pawing at the dirt dappled here and there by snatches of green. He moved to the dining room, where a larger window gave a fuller view. Earlier she'd asked him to join her if he wanted. He didn't have to do any work, unless he chose to. She wasn't trying to get him to work for her. Just to keep her company. He could plop down in one of the lawn chairs she kept close by. He had given a fairly automatic response, shrugging off the idea as one with little appeal. He'd lazed around, getting restless. Both kids were on play dates and Robert was off playing tennis at a neighbor's. Lots of playing, he thought.

After a while, he set out on a walk. The dirt road, humped in the middle, was a shortcut known best to locals, and so cars were rare. He'd walked it with Marie before she was sick. When a squirrel bolted across his path and froze on the side of a tree, as if burdened with thought, he felt Marie watching with him. A second squirrel, unseen in the higher branches, spoke up briefly.

The rich green flooded the fields on either side of Thomas, one a sizable pasture with cows grazing in clumps or pairs, the other weedy and wild. In emphatic contrast a tree flowered in white, an oblong pillow leaking feathers.

He walked for nearly an hour, circling and returning to find Kathy still in the garden. The gray of oncoming evening fell through the tall trees over her. Perhaps it was this haze stealing the color that had been so vibrant and varied as he walked that led him back to his father and their luncheon. Benjamin's bitter accounting of Kathy that day had quickened the sense Thomas carried of having failed his sister at the memorial. He decided to go down to her, to thank her for her hospitality, maybe just to keep her company, as she'd asked, maybe help her with her work.

He was barely in the yard when a station wagon wheeled up the driveway, and Kenny barged out, carrying a soccer ball. As the car full of boys reversed and sped away with whoever was behind the wheel waving, Kenny shouted at Thomas, "Kick it!" and he booted the ball. Thomas danced sideways before popping the ball back at an angle. Kenny sped to it, dribbling to his left and then right before sending the ball back. Thomas glanced at Kathy, who was watching. She waved. Kenny scooped the ball into his arms and ran for the house. "We won, Mom!" he shouted.

"Good," Kathy called, waving both arms in a celebration, before returning to the dirt at her feet.

Thomas approached slowly, curious about what she was up to. Kneeling and patting soil into place around a knot of green, she smiled up at him. "Broccoli," she said. Her gesture indicated a row of similar protruding tufts. "I've got kale over there." She stood and arched backward, stretching before using an old yogurt container to scoop water from a large bucket fed by a hose. She bowed to one broccoli plant after another, pouring thoughtfully. Small black plastic pots lay in a pile where they'd been collected. "Cucumbers over there," she said and pointed without looking. "Cabbage, too."

"Who put the fence up?"

"Robert and this guy we know. You don't know him. The deer and rabbits—there's no stopping them without a good fence. I'm just about done." She came toward the gate, and then stood smiling down at the dazzle of tulips at her feet. "Every spring. Hard to believe, huh? What have you been up to?"

"Went for a walk."

"Where?" She tore open a small paper packet, dumped

the contents into her palm, and scattered the seeds, little more than dust into a trough already prepared. "Lettuce," she told him.

"Looks like you know what you're doing."

"Almost."

"Nature's girl."

"Little Miss Fecundity." On her knees again, she shoved in loose soil to cover where the seeds had fallen. She patted the dirt tenderly.

"I'm just going to jump in," he said.

"What?"

"I guess you didn't squeal on us, did you."

"Say what?"

"Squeal. You didn't. On Agnes and me. You didn't rat us out."

"Should I have? About what?"

"I had lunch with Dad."

"Oh, my. Poor you."

"A couple weeks ago. It wasn't so bad."

"Well, you get along. You find a way."

"Does that mean what I think it does?"

"Probably. Depending."

"There's nothing wrong with getting along."

"I suppose not."

Her taunt triggered a slighted feeling that he tried to by-pass by looking off at nothing. "We were talking."

"Well, of course. It was lunch. People talk."

"Are you aware that every time I pause to think or breathe, you interrupt. Are you trying to keep me from going on?"

"I think I am. Or could be. I think I may not care for what's coming."

"Oh." Deflection had its uses, and she had a right to them. The issue was slippery and he was shaky enough.

"So do we have to?"

"Well, I don't know. But we should, yes. We should get there. You should let me. I think I should persist anyway."

"Is there a point to it—to where you want to get to?"

"I think so. I think there is."

"Something worthwhile?"

"This is about your good—for your good. At least it could be. Your welfare."

"Really? From Daddy?"

"It's been bugging me that I haven't gotten this out. That we haven't talked about it. That I haven't brought it up. But you haven't, either."

"Bugging in what sense? The guilt sense?"

"Largely. Yes."

"Or do you want something?"

"I don't know what I could want."

"We all want things." She toed the dirt, levering up a clump of soil to reveal a worm that squirmed for cover. "Even that worm. He wants something."

"Probably not to be a worm. But in my case—the bugging I refer to is guilt. That sense. Or concern. That neither of us have brought it up."

"How could I bring it up? I don't even know what it is." She sagged down in one of the nearby lawn chairs.

He paced away a few yards. "When I was on my way over for that lunch, you should have seen me. You would have enjoyed it. I got there and I couldn't go in. I went around the block. All the way around Gramercy Park. More than once."

"And then stopped off for a drink."

"No. I didn't do that. I should have, but didn't. Just stalled. And then I finally went in."

"And there he was. Daddy. Doing what?"

"Reading *Time* magazine. But we got talking, eventually, and I realized something that I should have known, but I didn't. I guess I knew it but I didn't think about it. You know that moment outside the restaurant?" He waited, hoping she would signal welcome and permission, perhaps even interconnectedness.

The breath she took suggested a gap of some magnitude lay between them. "I think I do. But let's be certain."

"After the memorial."

"Not likely I'll forget that one."

"Well, he was going on about it."

"Of course he was." She made a small noise meant to inform him that her understanding of the matter needed nothing more from him or anyone.

"No. I mean, really," Thomas said. "On and on about everything you said and he said, and what you were up to—at least as he saw it. And I realized that you never told him that the idea wasn't yours. That you never told him that the whole thing about reconciliation with you and Melanie had been hatched by Agnes and me. Is that right? You didn't tell him?"

"Why would I?"

"That we put you up to it."

"No."

"Maybe you should have."

"It didn't occur to me. And even if it had—what's the point. He's such a dick."

"It was a big part of how mad he was at you. That you were trying to take advantage of Marie. That you were conniving. But you can't be conniving if you didn't come up with the idea. I guess I was thinking he should know that and see that you couldn't be conniving if you were following orders, and maybe then—"

"You should have told him then. Did you tell him?"

The search required to answer her question felt inexplicably large and complex when the answer was obvious. "No."

"Why not?"

"I should have. You're right."

"I didn't say you should have."

"Yes, you did. I thought you did."

"I don't know what I said, but whatever it was, I meant that if you felt you should have said something, then you should have. Not that I thought you should have, or I was telling you that you should have. Why didn't you?"

"I wish I had."

"Okay. Maybe. I guess. But you didn't, and do you know what? Then what? So what? Maybe what? He would have changed his point of view on what happened? On me? I don't think so. You have got to be kidding. You know that, right? You have got to be kidding. You see what I mean? Even if that was the case—even if I'd told him—even if you'd told him—then what? Maybe he'd have gotten mad at you, too. But I doubt it. I actually doubt it. Give up this fresh new justification to condemn me? No, no. He would have made an excuse for you. You were grieving. For Agnes, too. You both were grieving. Do you follow me here? And then I stepped in and I took advantage of the two of you in your grief. I took advantage of your plight."

Her short laugh made its ironic point, though what else she felt, other than smart and bitterly confident, escaped him. "No thanks." She repeated her unhappy bark. "This way—the way it went—I think I got to find out what he thinks about me. Once and for all. And it's about time. You know. He came after me with a butcher knife when I was fourteen. That's what he thinks about me. You know that."

"I know the story."

"It's not a story. It's what happened."

"It's still a story."

"What does that mean?"

"It's a story. You tell it."

"But what the heck does that mean—your saying that, Tommy?"

When he thought she might actually turn and walk away, he said, "You know. I wasn't there. It's a story. I heard it. People tell it."

"Okay. That's true. In that sense, it's a story. But in this case it's true. Not all stories are true, but this one is. He's dead to me. Already dead. Long dead. That's the way I'm thinking of him now."

"You're off the deep end here. I don't want to go off with you."

"Am I?"

He shook his head and exhaled, looking at his shoes. "Yes. So I'll just stay put, if you don't mind."

"Well, I think I kind of do mind."

"Sorry."

"I mean, why not go with me?"

"I have my own deep end, you know. It's deep enough."

"True."

"What is that anyway? It's a swimming pool metaphor. Right?"

"Or river. Or lake. Or pond."

"And somebody who can't swim."

"Right."

"They should be wading. But there they are. In over their head. Same thing with off the deep end. In over their head."

"Except if it was a river or pond or lake, there would be no deep end. No end at all to speak of. In that sense."

"So then it would be out too far. In too deep."

She presented an exaggerated frown, as if thought were ex-cruciatingly difficult and the matter very important. "In over your head would still work. That would be okay. Do you think it's about the money?"

"What?"

"I think it is."

"What?"

"The shit we take."

"I don't know."

"Why else? And it may not even be there. Or in any amount that amounts to that much. But whatever it is, I have to say—well, I'm done with it. He's done with me. So it's over. And sure—I'd like my kids to see something of whatever there is. From their grandpa. Sounds nice, doesn't it? But it's not going to happen. Not now. Not that it ever was. He's done with me. He's dead to me."

"You said that already."

"Do I need to say it again?'"

"I don't think so."

"For all that it matters, I've been dead to him most of my life. I'd have to say as long as I can remember." Her glance skyward felt pertinent enough that he followed to where the glint of a cruising airliner appeared to interest her, surprising him, the contrail breaking into fluffy sections. "Do you think that he's dead to himself?" she asked.

"No," he answered, both knowing and not knowing what she meant and feeling that same ignorance about the response he'd given, or could still make. But then he figured confirmation might be useful. "Who? Dad?"

"Yes. Dad. Our dad."

"No."

"Are you sure?"

"What do you mean?"

"Think about it. Take it in. Let the words sink in. Breathe with them. Do you think our father is dead to himself?"

"No. I know what you mean. But no. I think not."

"But you do know what I mean? Because to come after your own daughter with a butcher knife. What is that?"

"You were driving them nuts."

"That's not a good solution. A butcher knife, I mean. I had boyfriends. I got pregnant. I was heartsick day and night. I had an abortion." She stood up and walked to the bucket, which the gurgling hose filled to overflowing.

"I don't know. I was about six."

"I'm telling you. I did."

"I know you did. But at the time—at the time I was about six."

"But not oblivious." She turned the faucet with some violence, shutting off the hose. "You were six but not oblivious. At six we're like magnets—little magnets—little kids—like flypaper. Everything sticks to us. If it's in the air, it sticks to us, whether we know what it is or not. Whether we want it or not. So you were there."

"I didn't say I wasn't there."

"So he thinks, Oh, I know. I'll take a butcher knife to her." Looking toward the house over the expanse of lawn darkening in the twilight, she appeared surprised. "We should go in."

"Maybe he didn't mean it. Maybe it was a demonstration of some kind. A demonstration of something."

"Of what? What the heck could he have been demonstrating? Help me out."

"I don't know. How awful he felt."

"Oh, I see. Sure. He felt awful and words failed him."

"I mean, he was in World War II and a lot of those men— you hear about it all the time—they came back with PTSD, even though nobody had a name for it. They kept it all locked inside them. He never said a word about it, I don't think."

"He wasn't in D-Day, for god's sake, Tommy. He wasn't in

Normandy or Iwo Jima. He was in the navy. On a ship. He was on an aircraft carrier."

"That's right. And it sank. They sank it. The Japanese sank it."

"I don't care."

"I think you do."

"Think what you want. But let me ask you—Do you care? Did he ever say one word about it that you know of? To you, I mean. Because he didn't to me."

"I was a kid. We were kids."

"We're not kids now and haven't been for a long time. But he's never said a word to me. Do you think he talked about it to Mom?"

"I don't know. How am I supposed to know? Somehow I doubt it."

"I doubt it, too. So we doubt it. We agree." She scooped up water in the yogurt container.

"That's a lot to keep bottled up. Over a lot of years. Sixty or more. Seventy. Maybe he's managed to tell Melanie."

"Oh, for god's sake. Why would you say that?"

"People get older. They get older and things that didn't come out start to come out."

Ready to distribute the water onto the waiting seeds, she stopped. "But why would you say it? Just say it. So he doesn't tell Mommy—he doesn't tell you or me, but he tells Melanie?"

"Time is running out. That's' the feeling. He's older. That kind of feeling."

"Oh, now that's a pretty picture. Daddy confiding in Melanie. Is that want you want me to consider? Is that where you want to leave me? Is that friendly? I don't think so. With the two of them in bed, Daddy murmuring his secrets at last. Pillow talk in the dark deep of the night and Daddy unburdening to her. Whispering the horrors of his youth to Melanie? "

"Now you're being mean. You're just being mean."

"Why do you say that?"

"Because you are, and there's no point in that. I'm not going along with just being mean. He had friends die. Buddies. That had to be the case. It was an aircraft carrier and it sank. That has to have an effect. And he keeps it all locked up. He can be hard, but—"

"His heart is locked up," she said, as if she were the one breaking out of confinement. "I know that. You're right about that. And then his parents divorced when he was little. I mean, before the war, before the Japs. When he was little. Obviously, it was before the war. He was little and he never saw his mother again. Never saw her once. Or his brother. Not once. Not either one of them ever again. And that's inside him, too. Locked up in him, too. You're probably right about the aircraft carrier sinking and it being horrible. You're no doubt right. But do I have to admit it? I just don't want to admit it. But I feel sometimes—I can feel it sometimes—this isn't the first time I thought of it—the secrets—the hurt and the secrets that must be locked up in his heart."

"You're getting too complicated for me."

"You brought up the aircraft carrier."

"I'm regretting it. Reconsidering it."

"You brought up his goddamn heart."

"No, you did. I think. One of us. Does it matter? Maybe, maybe not. But if it's sympathy you're going for—"

"Stop being so urbane. Can you do that? So goddamn witty."

"You were. A minute ago you were the queen of it. The queen of urbane."

"Well, I'm done with it."

"You should have let me know you stopped. Maybe given me a heads-up."

"How's this? How's now? Heads up! Look at me. Look closely. Something happened to me. Something awful. Look at the mess I was. The things I did. The way I chased that god-damn prick of a boyfriend and let him do whatever the hell he wanted—fuck anybody he wanted behind my back. Flirt with them right in front of me. As long as he didn't leave me. As long as he didn't leave me. Don't leave me, Dougie. Don't leave me. Was I a bad seed? Like they thought? Maybe. I don't know. I'm not the one to ask, I guess. But was I? I know they thought it. Very convenient, that bad seed idea. Okay. Sure. 'I'll fix her with a butcher knife.'"

"I don't know anything about that. I told you. None of it."

"You knew."

"How can you say that? Eight years is a lot. You were four-teen and I was—"

"But you knew. If you're there, you know. You're there and you know. You're in the home and you know."

The moment whirled him, a spinning ride he wanted off of. They'd been at this juncture before, some of these same words. Looking around the strange light and the sharpening shadows of dusk surprised him. "I guess."

"There's a vibe. That's my word for it. Another word could do, but that's my word. There are vibes in families, and kids pick them up. They pick up the vibes."

"Right. I guess."

"It is right. Look at us. Out in the dark. Standing in a beau-tiful garden. Trees over us—the sky, the sky beyond. I see it. I feel it. The breeze. I have a life now. I have a life. I have the kids and Robert, and thank god for him. He's obsessive and distracted but he's tender, too. He gets angry, and maybe it's too often. But then I'm no walk in the park. As we both know. I'd say that's the topic of the moment here—between us—at least to some extent—'Kathy is a handful.' So he gets angry.

He carries some anger, and I can stick a pin in it. I mean, in the scar, knowingly or not. But sometimes for sure knowingly, or half-knowingly. And we fight. But the tenderness is always there. Why would I do that? Strike at a soft spot? Take the risk. Well, I mean, Daddy wielded a butcher knife at me. And so I make the misguided step of poking Robert where it hurts. But do you know what? There's glue. We are still here. We have glue. I don't know what it is exactly—he thinks of it one way, I think of it in another. His way is almost spiritual, and I don't know what my way is. I can't say it in the same way he can. I mean, he has clarity. One word. And he can try to describe it. But we both know it's there. And I have no idea why I'm telling you all this—I'm way off message—which is—or at least was—the kids and what they mean to me. Not mean, because that sounds mental. But are. What they are to me. I wouldn't have them without Robert. We have the kids. And they nourish me. I have this feeling I never had before. I love them—I'm learning what love is and learning that I never knew before. But I have it now. I'm learning it by doing it. I'm learning love by loving."

He turned and marched away. It hurt, something hurt and he couldn't stand it.

"Where are you going?" she said behind him.

He kept walking, eyes fixed on the silhouette of his sister's home in front of him. Three floors with banks of windows afloat in the nightfall, illuminated more at one end, the kitchen end, than at the other, more on one floor, the ground floor, than the two above it.

"Tommy?"

"I have to pee," he called back.

He heard her footfalls on the grass, a scampering, rapid patter that he wanted to hurry away from, but knew he couldn't without betraying the scope of his anger. This delay and confusion, along with her urgency, brought her close, first her breath loud behind him and then her presence alongside him. "What's wrong? Are you okay?"

"I have to pee, I said. And I do. I waited as long as I could."

"Was that too much? Did I go too far?"

"No. No." How easily he lied, and he went on for more. "I wanted to hear."

"I unloaded. I'm sorry. I got wired and then there was all this momentum to what I was saying, this gush that got going and when it got going it just kept going. I'm sorry."

"You didn't do anything wrong."

They wheeled around the corner of the house, mounting the steps into the mudroom, startling the dog.

"I think I did. I went beyond what was needed. That's not why you're here. Not why I wanted you here. Not why you wanted to be here. Not what we should be talking about. It was too much and I'm sorry."

"It's okay," he said. "Honest." He looked at her intently, hoping to convince them both that what he said was true. "We talked. You know? We talked." Hoping to appear at least witty, he mugged a face of abject desperation, as if his bladder were shrieking at him. "Gotta go."

"Sorry," she said. "Go, go."

The nearest bathroom was in the hall by the front door. She could be cruel, he thought. Talking that way to him about how her kids nourished her, the fulfillment they gave, when she knew that he and Marie had hoped for children. It was nasty of her, oblivious at best. He didn't want to assign intentionality to her carelessness, but he knew her well enough and long enough to recall the wreckage she left too often. She had to bear some kind of responsibility. As he stood at the toilet peeing, he wondered if there were any late trains back to the city. It was that business about their dad in bed with Melanie that had pushed Kathy over the edge. He didn't care much for it, either. Their dad in the dark whispering to Melanie all the things he'd never said to Kathy, or their mom, or to him, either, for that matter.

That night after everyone had gone off to their rooms to sleep, and the house was quiet, he sat up in bed with his computer on his lap, and tried to imagine his father in a sea of drowning men. He sat erect with his back against the headboard. He knew enough to imagine human screams, the agonized shrieks of suffering metal, rivets popping loose and huge slabs twisting as the water in heaving tons tore everything apart. Think Bedlam, he told himself. Imagine hell.

The site he'd pulled up contained a list of all the aircraft carriers the Japanese sank, along with short narratives detailing each loss. The USS *Langley* and the USS *Lexington*, the USS *Wasp* and the USS *Hornet*, and still others. Many more than he'd anticipated. The heading of the article said that twelve had been lost in battles fought at the Solomon Islands, the Coral Sea, or Guadalcanal. Iwo Jima was famous, but two ships had been destroyed in two days in the Battle of Leyte Gulf, a place he'd never heard of.

But where had his father been? On which of the twelve carriers had he served? It had to have been on one of them.

The ordeal of the USS Wasp, he read, *occurred on September 15, 1942, during the Battle of Guadalcanal. Torpedoes fired from the tubes of a Japanese submarine in a "spread" had searched it out.* He'd seen this in movies and imagined them streaming silently through the ocean, deadly and cunning, little propellers turning in the back to drive them on. They were Type 95 torpedoes—whatever that was—fired from a Type B1 submarine I-19—same question.

The *Wasp* altered course, working hard to starboard, but the warning was too late. "Spread" meant that the torpedoes traveled in a wide formation, maybe at different levels and slightly varied intervals in order to limit the chances of evasion. Two or three torpedoes hit the *Wasp*. The report said two at one point, and three at another. Those that missed glided on until they lost momentum and sank. Fire erupted. Given the amount of fuel and explosives aboard, the flames doomed the ship quickly.

This wasn't true in each case, he learned, though fire was a constant. Sometimes the sailors contained the fire and saved their ship, at least until new attacks came. He wasn't exactly looking for mention of his father, and yet the hope, however preposterous, was there as he studied the accompanying black-and-white photos. Huge swirls of inky smoke swallowed the sky, dwarfing one ship or another as the destruction was described. And always these ships were referred to as "she." He knew the practice was common, and yet the designation increased his experience of poignancy, as if they had been drawn unprepared into battles where they did not belong. The *Lexington* was a "she" known as *Lady Lex*. The *Yorktown* was a "she." The *St. Lo* was a "she," as were the *Princeton* and the *Hornet*. Torpedoes were the primary assailant, mostly fired from submarines, but they were also launched from torpedo planes. A dive-bomber that had been struck and was falling into the sea became among the first kamikaze of the war, when the pilot managed to crash deliberately into the bow of the *Hornet*.

The *Wasp* burned for three hours. Finally, a US destroyer, the *Lansdowne*, received orders to sink her. Almost two hundred men died and over three hundred were wounded. During her struggle, other US destroyers hunted the submarine that had attacked her, preventing a second assault and allowing many of her aircraft to be transferred to safety on the *Hornet*.

And then a month later in a different battle, the *Hornet* went down.

The photo of a burial at sea captured him. Generally, the photos were taken at long range, but here sailors in work clothes and officers in uniform packed the decks around a flag-draped coffin. It was intimate, offering distinct human faces. He considered searching for a magnifying glass to examine each one closely. But then he wondered, should his father, in defiance of all probability, be there, would he even recognize him as he was in his youth?

He imagined the house with the room where he lay suddenly quaking and tilting, cracking apart, the lights going out then flashing back on, the walls collapsing, the noise incomprehensible. He lay quietly. And then the brownstone of his childhood began to suffer, the four floors where he'd lived crumbling, each falling out from under the other, repetitive explosions bringing repetitive concussions. The stairs collapsed, the elevator stalled and went dark. He was smaller than any of them, and if he was on a different floor from everyone, or asleep in his room—he swore he knew only what Kathy had told him about that butcher knife craziness, and only because she told him.

His father had been aboard a ship that the sea swallowed. What of his friends? Who were they? Whom did he lose? How old was he? He was an officer, that much Thomas knew, so he was probably twenty-five at most. A young man, he would have had young friends. What was his rank? His job? How long had he been at sea? On which of these ships? He could have died, as so many others did. Two hundred on the *Wasp*. With his next breath, Thomas sank among them. He began to check out other casualty counts. Two hundred and sixteen on one. Six hundred and forty-four on another. And Marie was but one. He felt ashamed of his grief. Death was everywhere and always. It made him feel small and childish. So many deaths. Did every one of them have someone like him missing them? They had to, didn't they? And then there was time, all time, and history. He felt dwarfed and petty. He saw the tilted corridors filling with water, the walls against which men pounded for escape. One hundred and thirteen. One hundred and forty.

Before him on the computer screen, where his scrolling had stopped, images waited. Black violent turbulence covered a carrier. A different carrier, facing doom, tilted and nosed into the waves. Lastly the deck of a crippled ship pitched dangerously under skies pocked with swatches of anti-aircraft fire.

FIVE

His horse was broad and dark and Thomas wanted to gallop. The narrow trail twisted through congested woodland dictating they ride single file. Where the trunks and outreaching sprawl of branches had thinned, underbrush pressed in. He wasn't an experienced rider, like Kathy, and yet he repeatedly fought the impulse to slam his heels into the animal's haunches and pound past the string of riders in front of him. Greta, the teacher, was in the lead, followed by Molly on a pony, and then Kathy, who rode with carefree elegance, as always, perfectly at home in the English saddle.

"How are you doing back there?" she called to him.

"Good," he said. And it began to rain. The first few drops, rattling leaves and dotting his hands, gave way to a downpour. His horse snorted, shudders running through him. The darkening sky thundered.

"I thought it might hold off long enough for us to make the whole circuit," Greta announced. "But we better take the cutoff and head back in."

"How much more to the whole circuit?" Thomas shouted.

"The cutoff is only about fifty yards more."

"I'd like to keep going."

"No," she said. "We need to go in."

"It's not raining that hard."

"Just follow when I turn."

"Is the trail obvious? I could go on my own."

"We came out together, and that's how we're going back."

"I want to keep going. I can do it just fine."

"Not on my horse. Do you hear me? Not on my horse. Tell him, Kathy."

"C'mon, Tommy!" his sister coaxed, peering back at him over her shoulder. "We can come out again. Later if the weather clears. Or tomorrow, if you stay on."

Greta slowed and veered slightly into a bend that curved again before linking up with a wider path. She annoyed him, this Greta, big and broad, a kind of tree stump on a horse giving him orders. The rain was harder now, dripping in a veil over his eyes.

"Are you okay, Molly?" Kathy called to her daughter.

"I think Donnybrook is getting cold." Donnybrook was her pony.

"Not long now," Greta advised.

The woods ended near a wide field, clearly associated with a building he recognized as a school. With the next turn Greta took, he saw that this new route would carry them across the school parking lot to the paved road, significantly shortening the time needed to get back to the stables. "It's Saturday, so we can go through here," Greta informed them, confirming his deductions. "It's quicker, and school's out."

As the distance diminished, and the stables promised to appear, he surveyed the grassy expanse of the athletic grounds to his left. The steady rain beat on his head, drenching his shirt.

He tugged the reins hard to the left. When he felt the horse resist, he increased his force and the big head angled where he steered. "Just once around the field," he shouted, banging his heels into the animal's ribs.

That the horse hurtled into a nearly instantaneous gallop delivered a shock. The big body sprang, the powerful legs slamming the soggy ground. Thomas bounced off center and grabbed at the front of the saddle, where he wished for a pommel. In danger of tumbling with every lunge the animal took, he suddenly knew that he'd bounded off this way because he wanted to feel what it would have been like if he and Marie had made their trip out West, and he rode under the big sky.

He heard shouting behind him, where he didn't dare look, his name over and over, Kathy and Greta yelling. "Damnit, I told you," one of them said, and the other cried, "What are you doing?" He knew which was which, but was too busy to sort them out, gasping and fighting to get centered, as horse and saddle went out from under him and then slammed back to the accompaniment of great heaves of breath.

The clamor of animals in distress chased after him, horses and humans, the rattle of bridles, whinnying, and the crack of hooves on concrete. Cries of "Whoa," and "Easy," and "Are you all right?" continued, all of it growing louder, though the loudest sound was the thudding under him as he headed straight for a tree. "Whoa! Stop, damnit!" he yelled.

He jerked back on the reins with little effect. He knew only to get ready, bowing as close as he could get to the horse's neck, eager for chaos, disruption, even ruin if it came, as long as it emptied him of everything he knew and felt, and could not stop knowing and feeling. Leaves and limbs grabbed at him, clawing his arm and back. His guess that the animal wanted to scrape him off but not damage his own head saved him.

The tree, he realized, as the horse slowed, was not out in

the field as he'd imagined but close to the parking lot where Greta, Kathy, and Molly waited, and where his horse stopped and stood, huffing, perfectly content now that he was back with the others.

"What the heck happened?" said Greta. "Are you all right?"

"I don't know. I mean, I'm all right. I know that. But I don't know what happened."

"Did you do that on purpose?" Kathy asked.

"No. I mean, yes, but—"

"You scared Donnybrook," Molly told him. "She didn't know what was happening."

"I was having fun. And I didn't want to go in. I thought I'd just take a quick romp around the field, and then—I don't know, he—"

"You can't do that," said Greta. "Once we were in this field, Remington knew we were headed back. He wasn't about to go waltzing around this field in the rain just to suit you, while everybody else went back to the barn. I guess you don't know too much about horses."

"Maybe you should have told me."

"I did tell you."

"He tried to knock me off."

"That's right."

"You're okay, though," Kathy said in a tone meant to dictate calm.

He stared up, blinking into the rain, which had slowed to a drizzle. The clouds seemed lower than was natural, thicker and blacker than they should be.

"You could have been hurt. You're sure you're okay?" Kathy asked.

"I got scratched. Sorry, everyone. I'm sorry," he said.

"You're lucky scratched is all you got." Greta's irritation, previously muffled by her alarm, had emerged. "Let's go in now. Together. The way we should have."

They clip-clopped in a docile line through the parking lot, across the back road, and down the driveway to the stables. Greta took charge once they'd dismounted, gathering the reins to all four horses. It appeared to Thomas she had worked her way into some ultimate form of surly indignation. On the other hand, she was right. The trouble he'd caused could have gotten Kathy, or even little Molly, hurt.

They were okay, though, headed for the car now, jabbering excitedly. Greta, framed in the open barn door, unbuckled the cinch from the saddle under the belly of the horse he'd ridden. Remington. The moment flared back, the boom under him, the onrushing tree. He was pleased by what he'd done, proud of some hidden success. With a saddle and blanket draped over her arm, Greta stepped close to the rail of an open stall.

"Greta," he called. "Thanks for everything. See you soon."

The slow revolve of her grudging response conveyed indifference at best. "Next time, pay attention," she told him.

"Okay." Watching her shake her head in disgust, he felt the guilt her indictment demanded along with resentment that he was bothered by anything she did. He'd apologized. The hell with her, if that wasn't good enough.

Back at the house, the first order of business for Kathy was to get Molly out of her wet clothes and into a warm bath. She advised Thomas to do the same. "You have a change of clothes, don't you? I could get you something of Robert's if you wanted. He wouldn't mind."

"Thanks, but no thanks. I'm good."

"Take a shower, though. For sure. And then I want to look at those scratches."

He undressed and sat naked on his bed with his eyes closed for a while, watching thoughts ping about, until they took him around a dark corner, opened a dark drawer, and pulled out the details of an article he'd read about the strangeness of death—physical death—and the fact that there were cells that lived on in the body sometimes for days after the person was a corpse. Sometimes for two, three, four days. Even for weeks. There were examples of cells that actually increased their activity. Fish were electrocuted and mice had their necks broken in the experiments that produced this data. There were variables. Temperature was important. Refrigeration. He couldn't recall the jargon, but did remember a metaphor about an astronaut abandoned in space. It was used to animate the assertion that not only did certain cells survive, but they fought to live. They tried to connect with their lost organism. As if experiencing the effects of a distant disaster coming toward them, they tried to correct whatever had gone wrong and awaken the corpse before it was too late.

He took his time in the shower, and felt vaguely that he delayed something unpleasant but necessary. Downstairs he stuffed his wet clothes in the dryer and sat with a gin and tonic in the library, where Kathy found him. "Well, I have to say Molly thought it all pretty exciting. She'll be Facebook-ing and IM-ing her friends about her cowboy uncle. Can I see where you hurt yourself?"

"It's all right. I washed it out."

"Do you need peroxide or anything?" Simply by drifting as they talked, she'd enticed him to follow her to the dining room. At the liquor cabinet, she opened a bottle of red wine. "'What is he doing?' I thought. We were all startled, especially the other horses. Even Donnybrook looked like she might buck."

"I said I was sorry."

"I know. I'm just saying."

"What are you 'just saying'? What's the train schedule tonight? Do you know?"

"What do you mean?"

"You know. The train schedule. I'm thinking of heading back."

"Tonight? Are you talking about tonight?"

"I feel like maybe I should."

"No, no. Let's not even think about that. No need to rush."

"I don't know what I want."

"Then let me tell you. I would feel awful if you went now. Honestly awful. After what happened. Because of what happened."

"I don't know what happened. I had an idea and I went with it. An impulse. Something about the rain."

"The rain? Really?"

"Yes. I think. And a book."

"Well, what about the rain?" She eyed her wine as if a portion of the pleasure she anticipated was visual. The drink she took, curling in an armchair with her legs folded under her, produced an appreciative murmur. "Did you say 'book'?"

He wanted to answer, but then he couldn't, worrying that he would not find the right way to say any of it—the markings in the margins, Wyoming, Marie, Remington. His silence went on, while she waited good-naturedly.

"Well, all's well that ends well," she said.

"I think maybe I'll go upstairs for a while."

"Now?"

He was on his way out of the room. "I just want to rest a minute. Maybe nap even."

"Will you come down later? Robert and I were thinking of going out for dinner."

"That sounds nice. Have a nice time."

"Thomas. Come on now. You, too. We want you, too. With the kids. All of us. Early."

"I'll see."

"You have to eat."

"Not unless I'm hungry." He was on the stairway and she was at the base looking up at him.

"I'm not mad at you, Thomas. Nobody's mad at you. I didn't mean to scold you before. Did it feel like I was scolding? I didn't mean to be, but it was scary. I got scared."

"I know. I know." As the stairway curved, he hesitated for the seconds it took to process an impulse to roar or shout, maybe put his fist through a wall. He hurried on, and by the time he reached his room, the wildness had leaked away. In its wake came embarrassment, as he lay back on the bed, and shame. Maybe he shouldn't even be with people for a while. He would go home in the morning, back to New York. But first he would go out to dinner with Kathy, Robert, Kenny, and Molly tonight. He would do his best to appreciate their company, make sure they understood his gratitude, and even have a good time.

He hurried downstairs to find Kathy and tell her that he wanted to go out with them. He was sorry, sorry, sorry. What kind of restaurant did they have in mind? He could talk to Kenny about soccer, and to Molly about her poster, and the good taste she had shown in singling out Van Gogh.

SIX

He awoke, or thought he did. Uncertain that he'd actually been asleep, he had to wonder if he'd merely slipped through one of those fantastical gateways, where rumination grew impossibly disordered as it transitioned to sleep. He couldn't settle, and the fuzzy half-lit cavern of his brain offered little that might serve as clarification.

He sat up on the edge of the bed, and slipped on his T-shirt. He reached for his trousers dangling over the chair. Barefoot, he went down the stairs to the kitchen. Maisy, asleep on her circular bed in the mudroom, rose up as he passed the open doorway. She stood beside him as he drank a glass of water. He patted her head, and prowled the length of the first floor, unsure of his purpose, trading the kitchen for the dining room and then the front hall, and the library, which ended with two steps down into the large living room, where he considered the gray expanse of the TV screen. He listened, standing motionless and attentive, to the silence, realizing that in compliance with an earlier impulse, either dreamed or met in the twilight prior to sleep, that he listened for ghosts, that he hoped to detect any spirits who inhabited the house, if they were willing to be found. It was late. Two twenty-five. The house was old enough to be haunted, not that ghosts had ever specified a necessary age. Anywhere there had been life and loss would do. He believed that the central section, expanded over the years, had originated in the early nineteen hundreds. The night, visible through windows on either side of the room, was black and forbidding enough to chase any sensate beings indoors.

Walking again, on his way somewhere, he paused in the library, alert to the books on their shelves like rows of entrapped humans in strange boxes, their sensibilities transported through time. As he sat, Maisy wandered in, and climbed up on the couch to join him. She licked his arm, and he lay back, stroking her head, which she nestled on his hip. "You're a sweet dog, Maisy. Have you heard that before? You probably have." He rested a moment, setting his mind free, wondering where it might go. "Do I dare watch *Wings of Desire*?" he whispered. "It's a movie." He felt Maisy would know and advise him wisely. "I've been thinking about it. Dead people. Angels in overcoats."

It wasn't long before he heard them outside. Different words and different voices. His sister, her husband, and Grace

Tolber, who was his sister's old friend visiting from the city. They were talking about ghosts, telling ghost stories about plates that moved without being touched, chairs that rocked with no one in them, loud footsteps on the stairs where no one walked. They were reverential, the experience of one person opening the way for others to share what they had witnessed.

He shifted, sitting up, and Maisy grumbled. This was memory, he knew, not a dream or an actual occurrence, though it felt that vivid. It had happened nearly a year ago, when he and Marie visited, and in the summer night people sat outside in lawn chairs and on the stone stairs and the ledge around the patio. It was after dinner. And Molly's teacher, whose nickname was Houdini, was with them, a kind of guest of honor, and another couple Thomas hadn't known well. Marie lay flat on one of the lawn chairs, wearing a sweater, wrapped in a blanket. The tales were straightforward, not intended to arouse fear, but simply to give an honest account of an inexplicable event, possibly bearing witness to the supernatural.

Marie started coughing. It felt intrusive, as if she wanted to disrupt them by calling attention to the unkindness and insensitivity they showed by talking about ghosts in her presence when she was so close to death, and they all knew it. In all likelihood, she would be a ghost soon. Thomas had been about to scold them, or at least shift the subject, and he felt like it again. It all sounded so distinct in memory, and physically alive, their chatter, their hands lifting wine to waiting lips, as if they were still in the night outside the glass doors beyond the desk in the room where he lay surrounded by books. He'd been with them then, not lost on the couch with this dog in his arms, half asleep. He'd listened to the stories and to Marie's cough. Her gasps had knifed into him, breaking apart the stories, imposing gaps, after which she had struggled not to cough again.

Their hushed, semireligious tones tinged with enough

irony to protect them from ridicule were gone now. The world outside was silent, the patio empty. He tried to hear the wind. He wanted that lost moment and the people in it back, that summer evening, all of it, all of them, and then he wanted only Marie. He searched for her, looking into the folds of his mind that appeared to him like shifting curtains of tissue parting to reveal the narrow hospital bed where she had died in their apartment. There had been instants in a series. One before and one after and one when it occurred. The minutes before had been prolonged, each suspenseful because the end was approaching, but only approaching, still approaching, always approaching, and the question was, when would it occur? Marie's pain had been extreme in the preceding days. Agnes was there with a friend who was a nurse. They'd been dosing Marie with morphine, pills, and shots, fear of needles or not. Marie had receded with the effects, swaddled in a haze of unrolling gauze within which she lay as remote as a mummy. He hovered near her, hoping that she was as removed from the pain as it seemed she was, from the room, from the world, from him. And then it came. The instant after which Marie was dead. And the next seconds, though opposite in nature, were as suspenseful as those that had led the way. They dragged him onward and left him looking back. Had it happened? Was this it? Was this death? Only the next seconds would determine it, granting her one more breath or leaving her breathless and still. He wanted to shout, "What just happened?" Had they given her too much morphine? Had they done this to her? After so much pain and struggle, had there been nothing at all in the end? Had there been something to see and he'd missed it? Had his mind wandered? Had he daydreamed?

Agnes and her friend announced their plan to leave quickly, after calling the mortuary. "No," he told them. "Not yet." He wanted more time. How much did he want? An hour seemed a lot, and at the same time it seemed nothing. "Tell them to come in an hour. At least an hour."

"All right," said Agnes, while the friend stood nodding.

"No," he said. "Tell them two hours. Two. Do you hear me, Agnes?"

In the next minutes, he was startled to find he was alone. He kept waiting for something. For Marie to do something. At least to speak. Or breathe. He stared at her. He called their friend, Paul, a doctor who had been helping with Marie's care. "Paul," he said. "She's dead. Marie is dead." Paul said he would rush over. Thomas wanted Marie seen as she was now by others, as many as possible, and he telephoned Kathy and Robert, who were in town, having visited yesterday. They arrived before Paul did, and Thomas paced, watching them observe the stillness Marie had become. But warm. He couldn't believe how warm. Kathy grabbed him unexpectedly and held him, though he didn't want to be held. Robert murmured and put his hands to his face. He touched Marie's arm and nodded, confirming that she was so warm.

Agnes returned, and Paul walked in the door, and so they were all there to hear the two mortuary attendants announce their presence over the intercom. The elevator hummed and the two men entered, one wheeling the gurney, which was folded into an upright position. The other carried a body bag. They conferred with Paul, who signed some forms, and then they zippered the black rubber shut over Marie, before opening the gurney, carefully transferring her to it, and then strapping her in place. Thomas hovered, his hands fluttering in gestures of miniaturized assistance. Only as the men attempted to leave did they realize the trouble they faced. The hospital bed had been located in the kitchen against the wall for convenience, and now the bed frame, the wall, and an odd angle in the entrance to the kitchen combined to block their departure. The gurney couldn't make the turn. Their failed attempt led the two men to whisper and then manipulate the undercarriage, raising the wheels and converting the gurney into a stretcher. But the exit remained too narrow, if only by inches. They conferred further, and then with unhappy, contrite, almost shamefaced expressions, the burly Italian and the diminutive Hispanic turned the stretcher sideways, hinging it and hinging Marie upon it, as if they would fold her in half, creating a right angle that allowed them to clear the corner. Thomas gestured more emphatically than before, as if to lessen these contortions. But then it was over, and the men released the wheels, locking them in place. They hastened into the hall. Thomas rushed to the window and out onto the fire escape. Kathy and Robert accompanied him, while Paul and Agnes lingered. When Kathy took firm hold of his arm, he felt the thought pass through her mind that he might jump. "I'm okay," he told her, looking down on the blue van stationed in front of a fire hydrant. The gurney emerged from his building, Marie a tiny black lump somewhat crooked from her journey in spite of the straps.

Soon the van was gone, along with everyone except Paul, and then he and Paul had had that crazy conversation. Thomas kept thinking how warm Marie had felt. "It was like she wasn't really dead," he'd said. Panic had seized him, the air in the room robbed of oxygen. "What if she wasn't? You checked, didn't you, Paul?" Paul had said, "No, but she was dead." And Thomas had said, "You didn't check?" And Paul had said, "No, I took your word for it." "Don't tell me that," Thomas had shouted. "You're the doctor. You signed those forms. I saw you. But you didn't check?" "Thomas, Thomas, she was dead. She was."

He'd thought the lead room was their last resort. It had

to be, didn't it? The lead room in a children's hospital in New Jersey with a viewing window for Marie to look out and Thomas to look into where she lay in a bed alone in a room encased in twenty-seven thousand pounds of lead, a stuffed animal in her arms, a gray rabbit with floppy ears and big feet. The treatment was an IV delivering an antibody tagged to radioactive iodine. It took about an hour and a half to administer, but Marie had to remain in the room isolated with her rabbit and limited contact for the next three days, and then the rabbit had to be destroyed.

Half asleep, or maybe deeply asleep, but aware at the very least that he inhabited sleep of some kind, he started to fill with a cutting, helpless emptiness of understanding that memory was the last resort. Not the lead room, but memory. And hope. Because she wanted to come back. No, he said. You can't. Please, Marie begged. Her cells were fighting to live and she wanted him to help them. And then he knew what to do. He knew what he needed to do. He would do the visualizing; he would start working at visualizing. He peered into the dark, rich core of her bones where the marrow was concentrated, where her cells had once been born in a ceaseless succession, almost wasteful in their abundance. He was doing the visualization as he had never done it before, with a fanatical faith and determination. And they were stirring. It was working. He saw the dull dormancy tremble with the first pulsing of some deep activity that erupted almost before he registered its existence into a flowering of rejuvenation. The marrow began to bloom with T cells sprouting amid neutrophils whose fledgling appearance ripened, each triumph generating others, and he could see that she was coming back. It was working. It was going to work.

Except he had made a mistake. He had made a terrible mistake. He had burned her. He had cremated her. If only he hadn't burned her, it could be done. If only he hadn't let them thrust her into that furnace. Her bones. Her bones. The flames had seared and tortured them, as they sparked and spit in protest against the fire turning them to ashes. It was unforgivable that he had allowed a workman at a table to take a hammer and pound those stalwart chunks of her that had defied the force of the flames and remained, trying not to be battered into dust. How could he have let them escape from his care?

He was lying on the couch in his sister's house, wanting to sit up, fighting through sleep like a drowning swimmer stroking to climb up from an infinite depth, and Marie was there, too. She was coming with him. You can't, he said. You can't come back. Please, she said. And she told him that what he was saying was silly. It didn't matter, because there was no difference really between him and her, between the living and the dead. Not really.

But there is, he said. There is.

SEVEN

Two years later, Thomas rode another train through another late afternoon. Any train seemed to bring back the sensation of all trains, not directly or specifically, but generally, their rumble and rattle with him inside. He wasn't reading a book, though he had several in his satchel. Rushing to depart his apartment, he'd worried that he would miss the train, if he took the time to collect his mail from the tiered boxes in the vestibule. Still he took the risk, and now he sat sorting through all but the obvious flyers and catalogs he'd tossed into the recycling bin before hurrying out the front door.

The blue envelope with the delicate lace trim stopped him. It belonged to Crystal, the wife of a dear old friend, Gregory Cantillon. He recognized it as one that she'd customized and started using, both envelopes and stationery, several years ago.

The return address was theirs, though it bore only her name, Crystal Cantillon. He read her note slowly, not savoring so much as absorbing. As he'd expected and as the tightening in his chest had warned, Gregory, who lived in far-off Phoenix, had died. The details she offered were few, but his illness was known, his battle long. Thomas glanced out the window at the dancing trees, the flash of a small wooden building, then more trees, as Gregory and the trees in the window flashed and blurred, and Thomas thought of Crystal. He would compose an email as soon as he arrived and had Internet access. But then the letter in his fingers corrected him with her example, which seemed to request that he use paper, a pen, stamps, and an envelope. Email felt thin, skimpy, even stingy, somehow; brusque and impersonal. In the days after Marie's death, it had been letters, real letters that offered comfort. His satchel held folders containing both lined and unlined paper. He withdrew an unlined sheet and a pen. The binder offered a flat surface that would serve as a table. He began deliberately, alert to the intermittent shudders of the train on the old track.

Dear Crystal,

Your note with the sad news of Gregory's death has reached me. I cannot deny that in spite of all I knew of his illness, your words came as a shock. Let me say that from the letters I received after Marie's death, I realized that however difficult it was for me to believe that anyone really knew what I felt, I sensed also that they were making the effort. That was what mattered, I think. Simply knowing that others were thinking of me, and of Marie—most importantly of her.

I hope that knowing that I'm thinking of you and Gregory brings you some comfort and support.

My deepest condolence at this difficult time.

Thomas

He folded the paper into thirds, calculating the proportions to match so that the ends were even, the overall impression neat. He fit the letter into the largest of his books, a hardback which would offer the most protection. Whoever picked him up at the station could run him by the pharmacy to purchase envelopes and then on to the post office, which would still be open. With that, he closed his satchel and sat back to the degree the rigidity of the seat allowed.

It was Robert who waited, and though he appeared harried, he put forth a convincing smile as he agreed to shepherd Thomas around on whatever errands he needed. "Absolutely," he said with what could have been undue volume. "No problem."

Thomas dashed in and out of the pharmacy and then, sliding from the car at the post office, he said, "I won't be a minute." When he returned, Robert had traded his harried manner for that of someone with a secret. "All set?" he asked.

"I'm good."

With a nod Robert changed again, this time exuding not exactly relief, but a definite release of tension. "Okay then. I need to tell you something. Your dad's here."

"What?"

"Your dad."

"Where? Here?"

"At the house. I wanted you to get finished with whatever it was you needed to do before I said anything. He just drove up."

"Why?"

"Why did he drive up? I don't know. I had to leave almost immediately to come get you."

"So you don't know why? Had Kathy said anything?"

"No, no. It was out of the blue as far as we could tell. Just somebody at the door. Dog barking. Doorbell. 'Who could that be? Are you expecting anybody, Kathy?' 'No.' 'Me neither.' 'I'll get it.' 'I'll get it.' And there's Ben."

"He didn't say why?"

"Not that I know of. But I barely had time to say hello."

"Did he know I was coming, do you think?"

"I don't see how, unless you told him. Did you tell him?"

"We haven't spoken for a couple weeks at least."

"I know I didn't tell him. No chance of that."

"I'd been thinking of calling him, but I didn't. And today, as you know, I decided to come up spur of the moment, so I don't see how he could know. I guess it's all right, though."

"Sure."

"When did you guys see him last?"

"It's been a long time for me."

"Same with Kathy, don't you think?"

"Absolutely. I'd know if she had any contact, and I don't."

"The memorial, then?"

"I think so."

"And he just showed up?"

Two large, gray, weather-worn stone lions guarded the driveway. Formally posed, they contemplated the road with a sense of duty and calm behind thoughtful, possibly philosophical eyes. Gliding between them, the Volvo took the gradual climb of the long straightaway and then the gentle curve to the house. Robert slowed and stopped at the front door. "I think they're in the library. I'll be in in a minute." He walked off toward the back of the house.

Stepping in the front door, Thomas faced the library entrance, and as Robert had predicted, Ben was there on the couch. His back was to Thomas. Kathy sat across from him in one of the big leather chairs with her arms around Kenny, who wasn't exactly in her lap, because his feet were on the floor.

"Hi, Uncle Tommy," said Kenny.

"Hi."

"Look who's here," Kathy said.

"Robert told me."

"Grandpa," said Kenny.

"Just barely. And not for long," Ben said to Thomas, who came around the edge of the couch, searching for a chance to read his father's expression. "Have a seat," Ben told him in a way that conveyed, as much as anything, his wish to keep Thomas from getting any closer.

"Sure."

"Big surprise," said Kathy.

"Me or him?" Ben asked, nodding at Thomas.

"Well, you, Dad," Kathy told him.

"Not really."

"Almost the same for me, Dad. I decided this morning. I phoned this morning to say I'd like to come up."

"Nice place. Big. Lots of rooms. Pretty countryside."

"I know."

"Tommy, why don't you see if you can help me talk Dad into staying for dinner. I've been trying."

"Not going to happen." Ben shook his head and made a huffing noise. "Don't bother."

"C'mon, Dad," said Thomas. "C'mon."

"Not going to happen. Waste of breath."

"It'd be nice. You're here, now. I mean, you're here. Why not stay?"

"Not going to happen. I have to get home." He raised his arm, adjusting the distance from his eyes to his wristwatch, which he considered with a deepening frown, as if the device and its information were preposterous. "I have to go. I was driving. Had some work in Boston and then over by Albany. I saw the sign. I was on 684 and I saw the sign. So I took the exit. I thought I'd stop by. Although I almost couldn't find the place. Thought I was driving in circles. I probably was. Tried one road and another, and I was about ready to give up when I saw something that reminded me. I pulled over and studied it, this other house—red—kind of a ruin, really. Not the way I remember it. But I got my bearings there anyway, though I'm not sure how. Served at least that purpose. I can't remember the last time I was here."

Thomas pictured the red house his father had referenced, while sorting through the half dozen questions the story prompted. He didn't know where to begin, or whether any of it was worthy of mention. He tried to check out Kathy's expression without being noticed by his father. He hoped for guidance of some kind. Or perhaps, having a better perspective on Benjamin, who sat straight across from her, she would know to do or say something helpful. But she was blank-looking, vacant almost, captive to a sense of distant focus that had carried her far from the room. "Dad," Thomas said. "What are you driving? I didn't even look."

"Rental. Not bad."

Kenny, peering back and up over his shoulder at his mother behind him, began to hum tunelessly. Soft for a breath or two, he became discordant, jarringly loud and nonsensical.

"Okay," Ben said and moved to stand up. Balance eluded him, and he landed back where he'd started. "That's my cue. If he's going to start with that kind of thing." With some calculation and an increased determination, he got to his feet.

"Dad, listen," said Kathy. "You have to stay. You have to. I have meat loaf in the oven. I can throw together a salad. Molly will be home any minute."

"C'mon, Dad," said Thomas.

"No, no, no. How many times do I have to say it? I've got to get back on the road. What's wrong with you people?"

"We want you to stay."

"No. I don't want to. I can't. Let's not ruin a good thing. All right? I have to be on my way. Where's the bathroom?"

Kathy indicated the general direction. "It's right there."

Kenny jumped free of her and raced into the hall, pulling open the bathroom door, which was to the right of the main entry. He stood almost at attention. Ben paused to look down at him. "You're hyper. Take my advice. You better learn to slow down."

The rental was a deep blue Chevy sedan. Ben walked around the front, pausing to study the car, apparently making certain it was the one he'd arrived in. He'd barely shut the door and started the engine when Kathy said, "I'm going down to the garden."

She was slightly behind Thomas, both of them in the open doorway.

"Okay," he answered.

She swept her palm across her brow in a caricature of wiping away waves of sweat. "Close call," she said, turning to go.

Kenny ran up the stairs. By the time Thomas had reached the window, Kathy was in the yard. The Chevy, almost creeping, was still in view, though an approaching cluster of trees would blot it out in the next several instants. Kathy carried an old-fashioned watering can, gray metal with a wide spout for sprinkling, and her straw hat, which she placed on her head. It startled Thomas when she bolted toward the trees where the Chevy had vanished, appearing to want a last glimpse, or perhaps even intending to wave their father down. But her chase, if that's what it was, lasted only a few strides. Her hat flew off. She grabbed for it, twisting and bending, but it eluded her,

99

fluttering to the ground. She still held the watering can, which he realized must have been empty. She retrieved the hat and placed it on her head, adjusting the fit, using both hands. She started for the garden, and then stopped, looking back toward the house, as if wondering if he or anyone watched.

UNCLE JIM CALLED

A week ago Thursday, my uncle Jim called. When I picked up the phone and said, "Hello," he said, "Hello." The voice was familiar and yet I didn't recognize it. "Who is this?" I said.

"Jim," he told me. "Uncle Jim."

"What?" I was very surprised, because I thought Uncle Jim was dead. "Who is this?" I wanted to know. I really wanted to know.

"I just told you. Jim. I'm here with Hank. Is your mom home?"

"No," I said. I thought Uncle Jim had been dead for years.

"Where is she?"

Now, the Hank he'd just referred to was probably his older brother, and my mom was their sister, Margie, and the thing of it was, the bewildering thing of it was that I thought they were all dead. "Is this some kind of joke?" I asked.

"We're not laughing," he said.

"Look," I said, "I was in the middle of something here."

"Oh, yeah? What?"

"Well, cooking. Dinner."

"What? Is it dinnertime?"

"Yes."

"What are you cooking?"

"Stir-fry. You know, vegetables in a wok."

"You never did have time for us, did you?"

That was a new voice, a different voice.

"Hank?"

"Yeah."

"I'm not sure I know what you mean by that."

"Oh, I think you do." He was right. I did.

"Anyway, Glenn."

Now Jim was talking again, and he said my name as if it were a window into countless flaws inside me. As if it revealed my essential weakness, grossness, as if it were the name of a fool. I imagined the two of them somewhere handing the phone back and forth.

"Okay, Glenn. We were just hoping to get ahold of Margie. If that wouldn't be too much trouble."

"Look," I said. "Look. I don't know what you think you're doing, but—"

"I just told you, Glenn. We're looking for Margie. That's what we're doing."

"Stop saying that. Just stop it."

"Stop saying what? Where's Margie?"

"No. My name. Stop saying my name that way."

"What way?"

"The way you're saying it."

"I guess you don't like it, huh?"

"No. I don't."

"Don't like the sound of it."

"I just said I don't."

"Or is it us you don't like?"

"We're your blood, you know. Bloodline. Blood relative."

"So why wouldn't you want us to find Margie?"

"What?"

"She's our sister."

"She's dead! You're all dead!"

"So?"

They seemed to know something that I didn't, some inherent mistake in my assumptions about what I'd just said.

"Where are you?" I asked.

"What?"

"Where are you?"

"Why?"

"I'd just like to know," I said. "I'd just like to know, okay?"

"He wants to know where we are," one said to the other. I think it was Jim to Hank, though it could have been the other way around. Whoever was speaking, his report of my question made them both laugh. They found it very entertaining. I looked out the window, half expecting to see them prowling about in the October air. A mist, on the verge of freezing into snow, waved under stressful crosscurrents. I could see rows of lights defining buildings. It was a certain kind of heavy black night, blotting out the stars that I knew were up there, twinkling like the last of something. It wasn't that I didn't understand the strangeness of their call, as I hung up and walked down the long corridor to the kitchen, because I did. I just didn't know what to do about it, or even what to think about it, and I was hungry for the vegetables I'd left on the stove in their pool of oil. Halfway down the hall, I became afraid that I'd neglected to turn off the burner under the wok when I'd gone to the bathroom, only to be interrupted by the ringing phone and my uncles. But the fire was off, the kitchen safe.

That night, they were on television. I was up late, restless, alone, because my wife and daughter were in California, celebrating my mother-in-law's birthday. I sat with a bottle of Scotch and a glass, into which I poured and from which I sipped as I channel-hopped. I don't know what I was searching for. I never do. And there they were. I hopped right past them, and then sprang back. They were sitting at a kitchen table. They had coffee cups and were leaning toward each other. Hunched over and talking, they appeared earnest and thoughtful. Their voices were very low and hard for me to follow. I held my breath, trying to hear. But I couldn't understand a word. Or rather, a word here and there was all I could understand. The sense eluded me. The subject matter appeared to be, if their postures were to be trusted, of the utmost importance. I had my suspicions about what it was and moved closer to the set. But tilting and arranging my torso so that I pressed my ear against the speaker brought no improvement. The obvious thing to try was turning up the volume. Something about this choice worried me, as if it might signal my presence when they were clearly being secretive. I lightly tapped the little arrow on the remote. But what my action prompted was a hum that further muffled my uncles' conversation. It was as if wherever they were, the signal was weak and couldn't quite reach me. The quality of the image was sort of like in the early days of television, when signals searched out antennae on rooftops. Hank and Jim were in my grandparents' kitchen, I realized. The layout was one I knew. I'd been there many times, sitting in those exact chairs while something went on, or I waited for something. Maybe my grandmother was cooking, or maybe she and my mom were talking while they cooked. There were times when I sat at that kitchen table while the adults, Jim and Hank and my mom and their sister, Amber, and my dad, Matty, and Jim and Hank's wives, Kate and Gayle, and Amber's second husband, Harold, or her first husband, Arnie, played cards at the dining room table, which was only a few feet away and visible through an open doorway. The rooms were small, the ceilings low. Everything was small there, the houses squeezed together on little square blocks bounded by narrow streets, as if there weren't miles of open land, farmland, and woods all around. They would play poker sometimes, betting nickels and dimes and quarters, shoving their coins into the kitty, which was the name they gave to the spot at the center of the table where the money collected. They talked to their cards, asking for good ones; they groaned at bad luck or barked happily when the cards they needed came to them and they felt blessed, as if something somewhere cared about them, and for a second they'd been given proof.

But they weren't doing that now; they weren't playing cards. They were huddled together, talking in low voices, just Jim and Hank, as if they were worried that someone would think they were up to no good, even if they weren't, or maybe they were. So they had to be careful. The static or snow on the TV screen thickened over them and then blew away, and I saw them clearly, Jim and Hank with their special faces, their one and only faces, the features of brothers. Perhaps they were worried about everyone else. Perhaps they were wondering where all the others were, Margie and Matty and Amber and Arnie and Harold and Kate and Gayle, along with their mom and dad, my grandma and grandpa, Dorothy and Sam. Or maybe they were worried that someone would catch them in that house and throw them out because it belonged to somebody else now. It belonged to the strangers who'd purchased it. It had been sold long ago, right after Grandma died, Grandpa having passed before her, which was years before Jim and Hank themselves died.

It seemed important that I hear what they were saying. I tried the volume again, touching the remote stealthily, my fingers like feathers, the tips tapping with shyness, tenderness. One of my uncles was shaking his head. The snow on the screen was so thick, suddenly, that I couldn't tell which of them it was. Their features were distinct, yet similar, and the snow, or static, call it what you will, was expanding, the flakes getting bigger, their wild movement driven in swirls, rising while falling, and sweeping in from both the left and the right, obscuring everything, the table, the window, and Jim and Hank, too, as if they were being swallowed up by a blizzard, while the humming noise intensified, grew shrill, and started to stutter with a kind of Doppler effect, pulsing louder at a higher and higher frequency. I thought I heard a word but I wasn't sure, then I heard it again. "He." The pulsing gave way to a vibrating drone that stopped for an instant and I heard, "He's watching."

"No, he isn't."

"I think he is."

"He doesn't care. He isn't interested. He never cared."

What came next was a hiss that evolved rapidly into a buzz that somehow contained their voices, compressed and distorted. It sounded as if they were screaming. The pang I felt was of such magnitude and loaded with such aching potential that I turned the TV off. I reacted without thinking. I was hurt by what I thought they'd said. I acted impulsively, not taking even a second to reflect on what I was doing. The silence felt abrupt, almost shocking. I was sitting on my couch. My TV was dark. They were gone. My apartment was dim. I could hear the wind outside, blowing through the high corridors formed by the streets in the geometrical patterns of the city where I lived. Fearing that Jim and Hank would be gone when I turned the TV back on, I sat there for a long time in the gloom, wondering, but unwilling to test my theory. From where I sat, I could see the front door of my apartment. Beyond the door was a hallway, small and straightforward, with a wrought-iron bench against the wall, facing the elevator door, so that weary people might sit if they needed to rest while waiting for the elevator to come clanking and moaning up, or if they needed to pause for a moment as they tried to decide what to do next, whether to attempt to rouse me by knocking on my door or ringing my doorbell. Visitors to my neighbor, whose apartment door was directly across from mine, had equal access to these options. I imagined them out there on the bench, Jim and Hank, both nicely dressed, both handsome men, trying to determine their next step, wondering if I would let them in if they knocked, if I would walk over, turn the knob, pull the door open, and stand before them. I sat in the dark, waiting. When I turned the TV back on, what appeared was perfectly ordinary. The screen offered a smiling woman with a bright, eager, vaguely sexual manner, gesturing at a map to explain the weather, which seemed to excite her. The picture was clear, the weather not promising. Her every word was distinct. I turned her off. As I lay in bed that night, I tried to forget what had happened. It was over. There was nothing I could do. But trying to forget something is a fairly futile enterprise, because, in order to succeed in forgetting what you're trying to forget, you have to keep remembering what it is. My window blinds were open, and the moon was big and pocked and glaring. It seemed grudging and annoyed, looking down without seeing, stranded somehow way up in the black, where it was frustrated by something it couldn't understand but had to contend with nevertheless, a puzzling, incessant pressure that would not reduce either its constancy or its impenetrable, insolent obduracy.

I had the feeling that Jim and Hank were in a bar somewhere nearby. They had always liked to drink; I thought maybe I should go looking for them. Their complaints about me were more or less familiar, in the sense that I had a pretty good idea what they were. That is, it would have been easy to guess them, the way one can surmise with certainty, or in other words, intuit, others' estimations of oneself—their impressions, attitudes, opinions—though more often than not, unless people lose their temper and erupt in raw confrontation, these estimations go unspoken, at least between the people directly involved, though other people, those with similar opinions, such as Jim and Hank must have held about me, might speak to each other, privately, offering observations that confirm flaws or recalling anecdotes that give clear-cut support to a common judgment regarding a specific failing.

Still, why had they called? What was it that they wanted? They were looking for Margie, my mom, their sister. That was their ostensible purpose. And there was no reason not to believe them. It might be odd that they were together but didn't know where she was, but there was nothing odd in their worrying about her or looking for her. They had been a passionately connected set of siblings. A high romance of charged emotions, expectations, disappointments, and competition bound them. But if they were all dead, why weren't they together? Or, at least, aware of one another's whereabouts? It made me uneasy. Not that this seeming incongruity was the only aspect of the night that deserved such a response. Certainly, I was aware of the larger concerns, the irrational, irreducible elements. I recognized them for what they were, irrational and irreducible, as uncanny as they were compelling. But that didn't help me with them. Why had my uncles called? Why did they think I might know where Margie was? Their concern about her whereabouts made me worry, too. Was this what they wanted? For me to think about her, worry about her?

I went for a walk. I peeked in bars. I went into a couple. I had a few drinks. People were laughing. Televisions were on, playing mainly sporting events. The people got louder as the night wore on. They were howling, some of them, their faces red, eyes glazed with thickening moisture, as if they were drowning. But Jim and Hank were not to be found.

In the morning, as I sipped coffee, I was surprised that I had slept at all. But I had, waking and dozing repeatedly, until I'd jolted awake to the ringing of my bedside phone. I was in my underwear and a T-shirt. Certain that it was Jim or Hank, I grabbed the receiver, but was greeted instead by a pushy, motor-mouthed telemarketer that I didn't immediately realize was an automated voice. I hung up with a groan.

I needed to talk to someone. I went online and started searching for help, perhaps a therapist of some kind. Maybe a psychoanalyst. Someone with whom I could establish a professional relationship. Professional boundaries would be useful. I started jotting down names, phone numbers, addresses. When I had a list of ten, I stared at it, as if each name might emit a signal, a subtle vibration that would guide me to the correct choice. On the basis of what I experienced as delicate sensations somewhere just behind my eyes, and interpreted as a kind of acceptance or its lack, mainly its lack, I started crossing off names. One after the other, the black slash of my pen like a sword lopped them off. I ended up with none. When I left my apartment, it was to visit the office of a private detective.

My elevator ride down led to a cab ride and then an elevator ride up in the detective's building. When the elevator door opened on one floor to release a pointlessly smiling girl wearing a beret, and on another a hunched-over old man with dandruff on his shoulders and a faint odor of urine, I caught sight of shabby hallways in a state of disrepair, the name of a dentist gouged into frosted glass on the first and a lawyer on the next, his long foreign name nothing but consonants. The elevator door screeched while closing, as if wounded, and the hallways I left behind, as I rose in a series of shudders, reverberated with a sound that was almost gleeful.

On the phone, the detective's secretary had said that he'd had a cancellation and if I hurried I could see him almost immediately. As it turned out, this was true, but the minute I saw him, I knew I'd made a mistake. His hair was stylishly coiffed and his suit, double-breasted and buttoned, struck me as all wrong, a kind of elaborate deceit implying fabled expertise and dark competence. When we shook hands, I found his skin distasteful, the palm soft and moist, the pads of his fingers too smooth. He smelled of aftershave, some aggressive assertion mixed with flowery scents. Someone had trimmed his nose hairs. I shook my head.

"Sit down," he said.

I shook my head again.

"Why not? What's wrong?" He urged me to tell him the details of whatever had brought me there. I couldn't remember what I had said to the secretary over the phone. I started rehearsing the facts, as best I knew them, cycling them through my thoughts, as if to find their most useful order, testing out phrases, but I was reluctant to speak. Something inside me knew better and would not allow it. I shook my head.

"You've come all this way."

I wanted to tell someone, to unburden myself, to get it all off my chest. But why? Why should I want that? It made no sense. His phone rang and he answered and started talking. "Who is that?" I asked him. He smiled. Why was I even in such a room with a man who looked like he did, had hair and socks and pretensions as he did? "Who are you talking to?" He held up his hand to soothe me, an apologetic palm that became his forefinger, meant in its solitary extension to tell me that he would only be a minute.

"No," I said.

"What? Wait!"

I was going. He could say "Wait" all he wanted. I was out the door. The secretary looked up, smiling. I shook my head. "He's a terrible man," I told her. "How can you work for such a man?"

"What did he do? Did he do something?" She beamed at me with a diffuse innocence, the glow of her computer screen a haze in which she had become difficult to see. But there was more to it, more than the strange effect the lights in the room had on her: She was obscured by her habitual practice of deception, most glaringly manifest in her conviction that she knew of nothing unsavory about her boss.

Outside, I began to worry that my behavior had been counterproductive. Not so much that my actions had been wrong but, rather, that I'd enacted them with insufficient cunning. My concerns had been blatant when they should have been sly. This whole situation was getting to me. I was acting as if I could figure it out, when I couldn't. At least, not now and perhaps not ever.

Exiting a cab in front of my building, I met a steady, almost silent downpour. The doorman looked out from the protection of the vestibule. He didn't like me. He glowered at me, and then he nodded in greeting as I entered. It was his job, but he did little to disguise his distaste. He was from one of those Slavic countries, angular and crookedly handsome in a broad-nosed, corpse-like way. I stood waiting for the elevator, and he came up and put his big palm on the wall, leaning there, looking at me. His brother was the super of the building and he had another, older, heavier, even grimmer brother, who also worked shifts as a doorman.

"Some men were to see you," he said.

"What?"

"Two men. They look for you. Your name."

"What did they want?"

"They don't say."

"What did they look like?"

"Older. Older than you. Older than me. They both older men. Plain in their clothes. From some other town."

I described Jim and Hank, their hair, dark on the one, sandy on the other, thinning on both, at least when I last saw them, but still healthy, with a light dance of gray, and both with small, tender bellies, middle-aged bellies, crinkling skin around their eyes when they looked at you with their bright, bright smiles. The doorman stared at me as if he hadn't understood a word I'd said.

"Did they leave a message?"

"No, they laughed when I tell them in so many words you are not at home. They laughed and shook their heads like this was what they know was to happen. They would come here and you would not be home."

"What happened then?"

"They go. Out the door. What else? I don't see which way. After a while it rains."

By going to look for them or, rather, by seeking someone else to look for them for me, by searching in the most roundabout way, by acknowledging my yearning only grudgingly, I'd missed them.

I turned on the television as soon as I got to my apartment. I channel- hopped. I had to calm down. My wife and daughter would be home in a few days. This was how it was going to be, I realized. I'd have to get used to it. Go on with my life. And I did. Or tried to. Other people seemed to go out of their way to say "Hey" to me, because I said "Hey" to them. Or "Hi." "See you." "Stay in touch." Other people said, "Hello. I think we've met before." Niceties, pleasantries.

My wife and daughter walked in the door. Soon they were floating around the apartment, passing before me, bouncing down the hallway, settling in chairs. Hovering near the windows, like helium balloons. Drifting in and out of doors. We chatted, and I tried to do whatever my daughter asked. I wanted to meet all my wife's needs, both those she expressed and those to which, although they were unstated, she gave clues.

"You're in an agreeable mood these days," she said.

"Am I? Good."

Every now and then, I saw Jim or Hank rounding a corner,

getting on a bus, riding in a cab, or looking out the window of a car driven by somebody I didn't know. I can't say that they ever acknowledged me in a way that confirmed my belief that they were who they were. I thought about my mom a lot and wondered where she was. And my dad, too. It didn't seem right to think of one without the other. But then, none of it did. Seem right, feel right, that is. And then one night I was at my kitchen table watching a bug that I couldn't identify crawl along the wooden tabletop and up the steep slope of a newspaper crumpled into creases and canyons, a sheer bluff from the perspective of the bug. Brown, with six delicate legs, like threads, really, the bug had feelers coming out of its head, pawing the air. Its wisp of a body appeared to defy gravity, poised upside down on a white slant of newsprint, its back legs bent like reverse elbows, as the other four legs danced and the feelers explored for something to sustain it. Though it wasn't a spider, I worried that it would bite like a spider, like a certain brown-bodied spider I'd heard about whose name was, I thought, hermit spider, or maybe recluse spider, and whose bite was painful. When the phone rang, I grabbed the receiver.

Jim said, "It's me, Jim. Uncle Jim. You got a minute?"

"I'm here, too," Hank said. "I'm on the extension."

"We've got some questions, Glenn. We just need a couple answers."

I knew what was coming. It was what I'd been waiting for. I started describing the event they were calling about. It had taken place years ago, in a large Midwestern industrial town where we'd gathered for what we called a "family reunion." Hank named the city, pressing against my reluctance. "All right," I said. "I know. Grand Rapids." I went on, laying out the details of the reunion, how we'd traveled from a variety of towns, smallish to larger in size and flung across the map. A combination of unacknowledged and forgotten impulses had scattered us in this way over the years, like the proverbial ripples radiating out from a stone tossed into still water. We balanced our push and pull, our repulsion and allure, through distance. Though most of us had remained in the Midwest, the complications of multiplying generations had spread us even to the East Coast, where I lived.

"Planes," Hank said. "Cars. Trains. Buses. It took every kind of conveyance known to man to get us together."

"Some of us got by using only one or the other," Jim added. "Most of us had to use two or more kinds of transportation. I know I did. Cost me an arm and a leg."

"For the food," Hank said, "for the hot dogs on a barbecue. Burgers. Potato salad. Corn on the cob."

"And the singing," Jim added. "You remember that."

"Yes," I said. They loved to sing, the four of them, Jim and Hank and Amber and Margie, and they were pretty good. They harmonized, played different instruments.

"You remember that time out East? Near your place?"

Now they were pushing me to remember something else.

"You remember. The four of us in New York City."

"The Big Apple."

"And us together under that street sign for Broadway, the streetlamp lighting us up like a spotlight."

I didn't want to remember any of it, but mostly I wanted to forget my embarrassment at the intimacy of their embrace, arms looping around waists and over shoulders, voices harmonizing in a shameless performance of "Give my regards to Broadway, remember me to Herald Square," for the night, the stars, and all the passersby.

"Why didn't you join us?" Hank said. "You just stood off to the side and looked at us."

"Stared at us, really. You kept your distance."

"That's what we want to know."

"That's our question."

"It was like you didn't want to be seen with us."

"We wanted you to sing with us and you wouldn't."

"We weren't doing anything wrong," Hank said. "Just singing. Having fun. But a person would have thought we were committing a crime."

"And not just a crime," Jim said. "But something really bad. Dastardly."

"And another thing," Hank said. "This has bothered me for a long time. We were all together for that family reunion in Grand Rapids? You remember."

"We were just talking about it," Jim said.

"Yes," I said.

"This was in the living room," Hank said.

"Yes," I said.

"Your dad and I were talking. You were there. But off to the side again. Always off to the side."

My dad had spent a lot of the reunion in the basement, which had been turned into a recreation room and where, in fact, we were all sleeping on cots for the weekend. So there was nothing strange about his being down there. But he was down there a lot. Except when there was a card game. For meals, too, of course, he came up. Everybody ate together and ate heartily. Off and on, there was singing upstairs in the living room, with instrumental accompaniment. Amber, whose house it was, had an organ, which she played with big florid hand gestures and a big florid smile; Hank had a trumpet, and Jim a ukulele. My mom contributed mainly with her pleasant singing voice, though she struck an occasional note on a violin. They sang and made a tape recording that was somehow too slow, so that when they played it back, everything was elongated, the words dragged out and in a melancholy minor key, a spooky chorus, as if they were ghosts lost in a hauntingly gorgeous foreign movie.

"That was so stupid," Hank said. "Stupidest thing I ever heard."

"Complete waste of good tape," Jim added.

I worked up the nerve to tell them, "I thought it was beautiful. Surreal."

"You would," Hank said in that scornful tone I hated. It was his way of reminding me of what he really wanted to talk about. Which was the question he'd asked my dad during the family reunion, the three of us, Hank, my dad, and me, ending up somehow alone in the living room, while Hank practiced a little on his muted trumpet. Light seeped through the cracks of the closed blinds, and only a single floor lamp had been turned on. The wallpaper had a flowery pattern and there was some kind of plush rug in a dark color. Maybe it was already early evening and everyone else had gone off to get ready to eat. Hank blew the spit out of the release valve in the horn's tubing and smiled over at my dad, who seemed to be daydreaming. "You like music?"

"Oh, sure."

"Yeah, I really like it. It's a lot of fun," Hank said.

"I like classical music."

"Oh, sure. But that's not as much fun, I don't think."

"I prefer it."

"It's good. It's good. That's for sure. No argument here."

"It's called classical for a reason. It endures. It has endured. It's classic."

"You're not going to get an argument out of me on that one. So what do you like to do for fun, Matty?"

"Fun?"

"Yeah. You know."

"Well, I like to read about the Black Death. It decimated

Europe. The plague. It all but wiped out Western civilization. It was a horror story. No one knew how to stop it. It spread like wildfire. The corpses were stacked in piles. And Hitler, too. I like to read about Hitler. The camps."

I pressed back into my chair, as if retreating into shadows could change where I was, and I watched shock give way to puzzlement on Hank's face. It was understandable for Hank to be perturbed, though he tried not to show it. "Oh, sure. That could be interesting. I was in the Battle of the Bulge, you know. The Germans were some tough SOBs. I saw piled-up dead. Mud. Snow. Planes high up letting out long ribbons of bombs. But they were tough SOBs, those Germans. You can take my word on that one."

"He was a history teacher, remember," I said. "Remember that, Hank."

Because they never did. They never remembered that about him. Like Jim, he had ended up working to make ends meet at the John Deere plant, and that was all they cared to know. But I knew he felt a darkness in the course of his life that those terrible historical events confirmed. They reflected something tragic and lost in his inner world. My hope here was to excuse my dad, to exonerate him of the stain of his brooding, and I wanted Hank to speak, or perhaps laugh in acknowledgment, possibly even in agreement, but only silence answered. I waited before saying, "Hank? Are you there? Jim?" I lowered the phone and looked at it, thinking that I might discover the cause of our interruption. It squawked at me, the disjointed alarm of a failed call. Ordered by a punitive automated voice to hang up, I obeyed. I discovered that I was seated at my dining room table. The nearby windows offered a view of lighted apartments in layered tiers streaked with hints of a moon somewhere. There was more to it, we all knew, Hank and me, and my dad, too; more than history lurked in his dark interests.

The next time the phone rang, it was the middle of the night. I was restless. I'd been that way for days, sleeping in strange, deep blocks of solitude, and waking at the intrusion of a hand that was never there. My wife breathed beside me. I tried to sleep and succeeded, only to jolt awake in alarm. On this particular night, I'd risen and peed, then wandered down the hall into the living room, thinking I might have a drink. The moonlight startled me with an unnatural sheen, as if it were filling the room with ice and snow. I poured some Maker's Mark and sat with my back to the windows. The ringing phone did not sound normal, and the caller ID was a series of signs and letters, more like a scientific formula, or perhaps a code, than a standard telephone number. When I answered, bringing the receiver slowly to my ear, the grumble of static seemed devoid of anything human, though I knew better, and my patient attention and increased effort drew out from the mystery faint squeals, like the protests of drowning men fathoms deep. Then all grew quiet and the doorbell rang. It seemed softer than usual, suggesting concern about the late hour. I peeked through the peephole and saw our doorman scowling back. When I opened the door, he said, "They were here again."

"Where?" I asked.

"In lobby and then outside. I ask them if they want me to go up and find you and they say no. But then I remembered what you had told me."

"Shhh," I said, thinking I'd heard sounds from the bedroom.

"Sorry." His apology twisted him with regret. He shook his head in misery, responding to invisible slaps. I peered back into the apartment, but saw nothing moving, no one coming.

He was still shaking his head with his nearly crippling remorse. I stared at him, and he said, "You told me to tell you if they are back. I remembered and came up."

"Where are they now?"

"Outside when I take the elevator. Near the curb. One stood with one foot in the gutter, his other foot on the sidewalk. The other stood in the street. They probably know I came up to tell you."

I grabbed a coat and we rode the elevator down. When the doors slid open, I saw my uncles through the glass of the lobby doors. They gestured in my direction, as they no doubt caught sight of me, then moved off. I thanked the doorman and hurried out. They were rounding the nearest corner, or one of them was, Hank, I think, lagging slightly. After a few blocks of hasty pursuit, I was close enough to see them, in a mix of milling bystanders, as they conferred, glanced toward me, and ducked into a bar. I was certain I would find them sitting at a table, or perhaps at the bar, but a quick scan left me frightened and alone. A bathroom door opened, but the man coming out was a stranger. Only strangers stood around me, their chatter bringing confusion and noise. Then my haphazard glance through the large front window found them, scurrying across the street. The cineplex they entered felt conceived to keep them from me forever. Long hallways awaited me, and escalators leading to at least a half dozen auditoriums. I had no idea where they might have gone. Why wouldn't they let me catch them? I ached to know, realizing then how strongly I wished to join them. I wanted to have fun. Wait, wait. Please. I wanted to explain. I could have sailed with Hank on the lake that was like his backyard, holding the rudder, if he let me steer. I could have worked with him in his business, selling musical instruments, making millions of dollars. I could have gotten drunk in the desert with Jim, trudging at his side over the rough roads, the beaten-down sand, joking with him, elbowing his ribs as he elbowed mine, weaving through patches where rattlesnakes lurked on our big adventure across the desert to play cards or bingo in a bar and drink. I could have gone to prison with him, when he was sentenced for drunk driving, wearing a colostomy bag and pushing a drip stand through clanging corridors. I could have died with him, drunk in his little room. But my father had kept me back. I did not dare to join in with the singing and leave him alone in his mind, wandering that medieval landscape where corpses festered. I could not leave him to stand without me at the concentration camp gates, sniffing the air, eyeing the macabre chimneys. He needed me close, so I stayed, hovering nearby, silent, stolid, his grim little angel. If Hank and Jim had known him better, if they'd been forced to flee his big hands in the kitchen, if they'd heard his howl, so lonely and sad, they would have understood. I would have died if I'd betrayed him. He would have died. We all would have died.

I begged them: Let me find you. I have questions, too, things I'd like to ask of you, and Amber and Harold and Arnie and Gayle and Kate and my mom, Margie, and my dad, Matt or Matty. You weren't perfect. Not that anybody is. But you were giants with your singing and your laughter, your epic wounds and your colossal grudges that would not heal on the battleground of love. That was where we all were, where it all happened. That was where we all won and lost.

When my surrender to hopelessness returned me to the street, they were waiting half a block away. I called to them and waved, and they hastened off, leading me into Central Park, where they hid among the trees, and I plunge in after them.

My daughter answers when, like my dead uncles, I call. "Dad, please. Dad, Dad, Dad."

And then my wife is on the line, too. "You can't do this. You can't treat us this way."

"Don't yell at him, Mom."

"I'm not."

"You are."

"Where are you, please?"

Their worry concerns me; I feel cruel, and I don't want to be, so I tell them, "Listen. I don't want you to worry. I had help. I was led."

"Led where? By whom?" Home, home, home, I want to say, but I don't dare. I've wanted it for so long and now I have it. "Home, home, home, home." It bursts out of me. When tears claw their way out, I allow them to take hold of my words with the relief I feel in this moment of release, fulfillment, confession, hoping that my heartbreaking stab of expression will convert my wife and daughter to understanding.

"What are you talking about?"

"Dad. This is your home."

"Stop it. You have to stop this."

"We're home. We're here." Her voice sounds little, like she's little again. "We're all so worried, Dad. You're not home. Where are you?"

"Don't worry."

"But we are worried."

"It's been weeks, Dad. Nobody knows what to do."

Just this phone call and I will be finished. I'm far away. It's colder here. "I want you to know how to live," I tell them. "I want you to know that I love you and you must go on, as I will. But with diminishing expectations that we will ever see or hear one another again. I see no other way. Though one day perhaps everything will change for you, as it did for me, and there'll be a shift of some kind, a stepping from one place to another, a change in how it all appears, as you enter a different way of seeing, as you and your mind step out of one mode of sensation into another, and you will see where you are. Or maybe this shift will bring the opposite, and when you step through into the new place or plane, there will be nothing. Not the perspective I just described but an emptiness where you must learn that none of this happened and I never called, never mattered, perhaps even that I never existed. Nor did you. In the meantime, you must keep going, aware that should you feel chills every now and then, or an uncanny tingling in your blood, goose bumps, you must look closely at whatever might be advancing in whatever form, as those waves of irreducible longing wash over you.

SUFFOCATION THEORY

Amanda surprised me when she said we had to move. I'd barely got in the door, barely been in the hallway of our apartment a second, when she passed in and out of my peripheral vision, catching sight of me, I guess, and making her announcement. I'd been planning to take off my shoes and flop down on the couch with a cup of coffee to watch the news on TV—one blast of terrible news after another. I didn't know what the terrible news would be today, but I knew it'd be terrible. Car crashes would be the least of it. Accidental ones anyway. It had become common for people in cars to mow other people down. But that wasn't the only thing. There were terrorists and gun battles in shopping malls. Locals and tourists in Malaysia and Mali and London and Paris fleeing, stampeding, as soldiers ducked behind jewelry displays and fast-food counters, hunting down militants in one boutique after another. Bombs were often involved. We'd all become familiar with acronyms like IED. Long guns—that was another term we were necessarily familiar with. Boom, they'd go, these IEDs, in churches, synagogues, mosques, concert halls, and the aforementioned shopping malls. Movie theaters, too. Strip malls. Scattered and maimed bodies, an outward gyre of victims propelled from the explosion. Or the perpetrator (or perpetrators) might arrive with military-style weapons loaded with clips or magazines of hundreds of rounds. Like that goofy-looking white kid who went to a church meeting, where those prayerful African Americans welcomed him, and he listened to them read the Bible, and then he stood up and started shooting them.

Something is up. That's what I think. Something is up.

Anyway, back to the cars. Or maybe not. I don't want to forget the pundits, who come on right after the shootings or the bombings, as regular as clockwork, these experts, talking heads, network contributors on national security or terrorism or profiling the criminal mind. Lone wolf or affiliated? A bomb goes off and these experts weigh in, a banner below them broadcasting their names and specialties. I find the fact that they show up consoling, the way they chart a course through the mayhem.

Anyway, I came in the door eager to get settled in front of the terrible news. I'd grown addicted, you might say. "Dependent" was probably closer. I had come to feel that it was important for me to pay attention to it all. It seemed the responsible thing to do.

A gun, a bomb, or a car, the instrument was always in the hands of a person or people overcome by the power of this very powerful idea, this irresistible idea—at least to them— that killing a bunch of strangers would solve whatever problem they thought they couldn't solve in any other way. The problem might be personal—a lost job, a failed marriage. Or it might be cosmic, with supernatural imperatives. Some astrophysical battle between light and dark. This religion or that one. Or this one over that one. But the solution was always the same. Dead strangers. Sometimes these terrible news events were deemed to be terrorist events—bloodshed with a political motive. Sometimes the deaths were the result of rage or simple insanity. Not that the factors couldn't be combined. And then there were storms, floods, tornadoes. Those received some attention, too. Entire small towns wiped out. Overturned double-wides. That kind of thing. But I have to say that bad weather was a relief when compared with all the other pieces of terrible news, because it didn't have a human behind it. Unless it was due to our ignorance, greed, indifference, self-delusion. Everybody argued, "Climate change this and that." But not this one environmentalist. With dark, stricken eyes, he said that calling it "climate change" was wrong, because it should be called "climate suffocation." That was what would happen once the oceans stopped making oxygen, which was already happening, with dead zones and oxygen declines. The oceans were suffocating. And after they stopped producing oxygen, the trees would stop, too. And the fish and sea life would suffocate; the animals would all suffocate.

When I caught up with Amanda, I told her that I liked our apartment. I hadn't known we were thinking of moving. But she had everything arranged, she said. The movers were on their way up. I went to the window and there were cars and people on the street, but no moving van. Then I heard loud knocking, and she yelled at me to "let them in," and when I failed to move, pretending I was captivated by things outside, she ran past me, shouting that she didn't understand why she had to do everything. I said I didn't know why, either. They came in, six big men in uniforms, with their names embroidered on their shirts in red stitching, right above the chest pocket—Brett and Tom and Buck were three of the names. Actually, it was seven men. And when I counted again, there were eight. There was a logo of a truck on the back of their jackets. They were laughing and pushing one another, like cowboys or football players. They started taking our furniture—two of them to the armchair, three to the couch. Several were dismantling the television.

Grabbing my shoes before one of the movers took them, I headed for the door.

The new apartment was a big disappointment. Too small

to be a real warehouse, it had that feeling of vast emptiness one finds in a warehouse. Amanda kept saying that it was perfect. She ran from room to room, shouting, "I like it! I like it! It's perfect!" I still didn't understand why we'd had to leave our old place. I really didn't like the new neighborhood. And we had this new roommate. I could tell the minute I saw him that I disliked him and he disliked me. Amanda said that we'd get used to each other. She said that it would work out and that it would save money. We'd been living frugally but nicely, I thought. Money didn't seem to be a problem. At least, not more of a problem than it was for most middle-of-the-road people. So I was completely confused by what she said. I could tell that the kids were unhappy, too, wandering about barefoot, in clothes that needed to be washed.

I told Amanda that I didn't like the new apartment or the new neighborhood. She gave me her patented fed-up headshake, which left no doubt that I'd just confirmed something she knew about me and could barely tolerate. The point here was that, although the new neighborhood wasn't that far from the old one, it was drastically different. Our old place was on a wide, beautiful street running along the crest of a hill. Below it was another street running parallel to the crest of the hill. And below that another parallel street, and so on, for five streets down, each one getting narrower, more potholed, and dirtier. Desolate and chaotic would be a good way to evoke the lonely, abandoned mood of the last street, the fifth street, where the new apartment was. Almost no one had a car and nearly everyone you saw was bedraggled and despondent. The amount of trash adrift in the wind and kicked by these dispirited people steadily grew. It wasn't a class system, Amanda said, but just the way things were.

I'd gone out to look around and get a better feel for the new neighborhood when it suddenly got dark, and there were no streetlights. I was on one of the side streets that ran up and down the hill. It was an irritating feature of the area that the street signs disappeared as you got lower. I couldn't remember how to get back into the new building. The door in front of me didn't look right, but I went in anyway, and started to climb the stairs. Usually, in this type of building, there's a door on each landing, marked with a number to indicate the floor. But this stairway didn't offer that kind of exit or information; nor did it switch back the way most stairways do. It just kept going straight up, which meant that the building was very, very tall, and unusually wide. At last, I spied a door very far above me, a hundred yards or more. It seemed too far to go without knowing if I was in the right place. After backing down a few steps, I turned and hurried the rest of the way until I was outside, where I recognized the shabby façade of our building across the street. I didn't have a key to the front entrance yet, but one of the movers held the door open for me.

The new roommate was the first person I saw when I got to the apartment. Blond, younger than me, muscular across the shoulders, which was all I could see of him, except for his calves and the lower portion of his thighs, he trailed water on the floor, his hair sopping. He had wrapped a beach towel around himself and tucked it high under his armpits, the way women do, so the towel covered him from his armpits to his thighs. In one hand, he held a sandwich that looked like ham and cheese on white bread, gobs of mustard dripping out, and in his other hand he had a pistol, and he was walking around the way people do when they're looking for something.

"Did you lose something?" I asked.

"Why?"

"You look like you're looking for something."

"No."

"Where'd you get that?" I nodded in the general direction of his hand and fixed my eyes on the gun.

"It's mine," he told me. "Don't worry."

"I don't want guns in this place."

"It's just one."

"I'll get one, too. If you have one, I think I'd better have one."

"If you want."

"That's what I'll do."

"So right now the one I have is the only one here." He smiled icily.

"But I'm going to get one."

He pointed the pistol at me. It was silver-plated with a long barrel and a white pearl handle.

"Don't do that."

"Why?"

"I don't like it."

"Why?" He put the gun against my temple. Then he pressed the barrel into my cheek. He stuck it against my stomach and my chest. He bumped my cheek with the tiny tip thing on the end of the barrel—one, two, three, four, five, too many times. He tried to poke it into my mouth. I pushed it away.

"I don't like it here," I said.

"I do. It's nice."

"I don't like the neighborhood."

I don't know how long we talked like that. Amanda came back from wherever she was, and I said I needed to take a shower. She pointed me to the bathroom, and that was when I discovered that there was no shower. Just this old bathtub full of scummy water, which must have been left from the new roommate's bath. There was rust on the faucet handles, and the tub had old-fashioned legs, like chicken legs. I started shouting that I needed a bathroom with a shower. We argued for a while.

Amanda looked hurt and angry, but she kept yelling, so I kept yelling. I don't know for how long. But when we stopped, the President was on the television, shouting. He wanted revenge. He wanted to get even. He started reading from a list of names of people and countries that he liked. He had a second list of people and countries that he hated, and it was long, and eventually some of the names from the first list started showing up.

Then the front door buzzer buzzed, indicating that somebody wanted to be let in, and when I went down and pulled the door open, there was Amanda, with dirt smeared on her face and a thick black hose thing in her hands. "I got this for you," she said.

At that instant, I heard cursing. A large, lumpy man in a ripped shirt jumped out of his car and threw open the hood. "It's gone, goddamnit!"

I looked for Amanda, but didn't see her. Something tugged at my pants leg. She was down on her belly, and I realized that the dirty tube thing was a car part that she had stolen. "For the shower," she said.

"What?"

"For your shower."

That was her way of saying that she'd taken the hose because I'd been upset. She explained that she hoped to rig a shower by running the car hose from the tub faucet up over this kind of towel rack thing sticking out of the wall, so the water could pour down.

"But it will be filthy, because it's a car part," I told her. "You have not really thought this through."

"No. The water will clean it out." She looked scared, and I wanted to help her, although I was mad. I inched the hose in through the doorway, so as not to draw attention from the owner, who stomped around his car, screaming and slamming the hood.

I'd barely shut the door, with both of us safely inside, when my cell phone dinged. It was a text from PETA:

"Friend—we have heartbreaking news: Slow lorises are threatened with extinction. But instead of being protected, they are trafficked, because people want these cuddly creatures for pets or as status symbols."

A photograph presented a tiny primate, its furry face contorted by a yearning to be friends with everyone.

Amanda and I were reading to the kids. It was a children's book, and we all four nestled around the open pages with their energetic illustrations. A man came in. Sports coat, linen slacks, top three buttons of his shirt undone. He carried a bottle of wine. For an instant, I didn't remember that we had a new roommate, but even when I did, I had to ask what he was doing. He shook his head and complained about his inability to find a corkscrew. What the hell did he have to do to get along in this place? The children were waiting for the story to continue. Amanda watched the new roommate, her eyes full of concern. And then I remembered. They were having an affair. Amanda and Reed. How had I ever forgotten? It had been going on for a long time. He was over by the window looking out. His baggy trousers had baggy pockets, and there were other pockets in his coat. His pistol could have been in any one of them, and I didn't know which, but I did know that it wasn't in his hand. I sprang on him and got him in a choke hold from behind. He wanted to grab for his pistol, wherever it was, but he couldn't make his hands do anything but fly up to claw at my forearm, which I'd locked around his throat. He was gurgling with a kind of pleading sound that might have been his attempt to say "Please" and "Don't" and "Stop." I constricted every muscle I had, so that he'd never get away. I could feel the life going out of him, and I could see the light in his eyes dimming in the full-length mirror that Amanda held up. He was too heavy for me to keep upright, so we sank to the floor, where his life continued to slip out of him.

Amanda said, "What are you doing? Let him go."

I asked myself if I dared to do as she wanted. Or did I really want him dead? He would be my bitter enemy for as long as we lived now that I'd done this. I wished Amanda weren't holding the mirror, because then I wouldn't have to see his eyes. They were so lonely and hopeless. But she made sure I saw.

I collapsed off him. He flopped onto his back. Amanda hurried to him. She brushed his brow tenderly and placed her mouth over his. She pinched his nose shut and blew into his mouth, and I knew I'd made two terrible mistakes—one in attacking him and another in letting him go. She peeked at me out of narrow, hate-filled eyes as she established a rhythm for puffng the life back into him, until he let out a growling cough full of tears and then curled into a fetal position. After a minute, she helped him to his feet and they went off.

I'm not sure where the young woman came from. She might have come from another apartment, or from one of the many rooms in the new apartment that I hadn't been able to look into yet. She was animated, talking to people I didn't know, who I assumed were Amanda's friends, or maybe the new roommate's. There was a circle of four or five men and three women, and they talked excitedly to the young woman. They were fascinated by her, though I could tell they didn't know why. And then she reached for some chips in a bowl. As she ate, her eyes came to rest on me. She didn't say a word, just crossed over to where I sat in an armchair and lowered herself onto my lap. She took my hands and put them on her waist. I didn't care if people stared at us. An elderly man in a vest and bow tie approached with a tray of party snacks. She asked for a glass of water and rocked her hips a little forward and back, causing a shiver in me, and then in her.

"Where did you come from?" I asked her, thinking I'd make idle conversation.

"Troy." Her dark eyes had a fathomless quality, with flickering light in the irises.

My cell phone dinged, and though I didn't recognize the organization that was texting, I did see what it wanted to tell me: "Rabbits are screaming." I said, "Troy? Really? The city?"

"Troy. Yes."

"The ancient city?"

I imagined her ship at anchor outside, where the dirty street contended with wind and debris, its square sail furled, its oars pointed skyward.

It was dark now and some men were gathered at a table in a little room off the kitchen. They were bunched around a light, and the biggest of them glowered at me. I didn't recognize him, or any of them, but when I got closer, I saw the smallish television that entranced them, their bodies warped by their angry, worried concentration. The volume was low, but I heard two somber voices, before I saw the team of male and female newscasters.

"The President is unhappy," the sharp-faced female anchor said.

The men at the table conferred in intense tones. "The President is unhappy," read the crawl across the bottom of the screen.

"He imagines himself happy," the male anchor declared. "He imagines himself young. He imagines himself handsome. He imagines he is well-liked by everyone in the world. He imagines he is omnipotent."

"Day after day," the woman said, her lucidly intelligent eyes blinking. She had straight brown hair. "Night after night. Prowling the halls."

The men at the table were solemn, nodding at the screen and then at me in a uniform way that made me uneasy.

Duppedee-do! went my phone, delivering an email with a yellow Labrador and a golden retriever looking at me mournfully, each trapped in a structure of metal rods that immobilized its head, as text explained, "These innocent dogs await the pharmaceutical experimenters who will drill holes in their skulls, in order to inject a deadly virus into their brains to kill them slowly."

"We're trying to help the President," one of the men said to me. "He needs our help. No one understands him. He wants people to understand him so that they'll like him. So we're trying to understand him, and then like him, so we can teach everybody how to understand him and like him."

"Oh," I said. The man who was talking turned away, and so did the others, except for one who stared me down, his spiteful eyes full of plans. Suspicion clouded the air between us, like an oil spill.

I went off down the hall and in a door. Amanda and the new roommate were in bed. Just lying on their backs with their eyes open. They seemed to be staring at the ceiling.

"What do you want?" he said.

"Nothing," Amanda answered.

"Not you." He poked her. "Him."

"Who?"

"Him."

I left. Behind me, Amanda kept saying, "Who? Who?"

"Open your eyes, Amanda. For god's sake, open your eyes—he was just here."

Sinister men were waiting for me. They wore dark suits. They circled me and then moved closer. "You're in danger," one of them whispered. His eyes shimmered, like broken glass.

"I know," I told him.

"We want to help you."

"We want to warn you," a different one said. He shoved me.

"We want to protect you," the first one said, and he shoved me harder. I staggered back a few steps.

"Don't trip," another one said.

"There's a border," one said.

They kept shoving me every time they said something.

"There's a border that is a boundary."

"Don't cross it."

"It's a boundary that is a border."

"I understand," I said. "Now let me alone."

"We're done anyway." They tried to speak in unison, creating noise like an out-of-kilter engine ready to explode.

I went toward the television I heard blasting. Not the little one in the room off the kitchen but the big one that I usually watched. The little one was gone. The men who'd huddled around it must have taken it. It seemed they'd taken the room, too. The kitchen was there, but the small room off the kitchen was gone.

Duppedee-do! went my phone: "Help. It's up to you." I hit Delete and walked away. I didn't know where I was going. When my phone dinged again, I knew better than to look, but I did anyway, and I learned that a man, infuriated by his crying infant daughter, had stuck his finger down her throat to make her be quiet. I kept walking. I don't know for how long I walked and walked, but I came to the small room off the kitchen. It was back, as were the little television and the men watching it. A beaming, impish man identified as a Presidential adviser announced, "The President knows more than anyone about everything."

The interviewer, a woman with a quirky mouth, asked, "More than the scientists, who—"

"Absolutely."

"You're saying he knows more than the scientists, who—"

"Yes, yes."

"Wait. I'm speaking of people who are experts in their particular field, such as climate change. Let's talk about that."

"Cassandras. All of them."

"Cassandras? Your position is that the experts on the Intergovernmental Panel on Climate Change are Cassandras? That those predicting disappearing glaciers, rising sea levels, and—"

"Cassandras, Cassandras, Cassandras."

"But she was a prophetess. You know. She told the future."

"Exactly." His face formed a childish, doll-like grin, while his eyes disclosed cold-blooded desires that he believed no one could see. "A prophetess people didn't listen to. If you're a Cassandra, nobody listens to you. That's the great part, that's the fun part, the thrilling part—they know the future, and they tell us, but we don't have to listen, because the President is smarter than anyone."

Duppedee-do! went my phone: "Australia is on fire!" Images flashed: The sky blazing with supercharged pillars of twisting flame. People retreating to a beach. A woman spraying water onto frightened alpacas, their long necks pivoting between her and the burning world.

Amanda and the new roommate were throwing my things around. Into boxes. Into piles on the floor. I didn't know what was going on. When I first came upon them, I was too startled to speak. I stood off to the side, hoping they'd explain without my needing to ask, but they just kept throwing my things. Finally, he looked at me, clearly thinking I was the stupidest person he'd ever seen in his life. "Amanda," he said.

"Oh, I know, he's utterly useless." She looked at me. "You're in the way." And then, to him, she said, "Don't pay any attention to him."

I couldn't take it. I shouted, "What are you doing?"

"We're throwing all this junk away," she said.

"Those are mine," I said.

"It's all junk."

"I want it. I like it."

They laughed. "We're getting new things," they said, one after the other.

I picked up a short-sleeved shirt. "This is a good thing." I grabbed a coffee cup. "I really like this. I've had it all my life."

They laughed so hard, they started to gasp. "He likes it. He likes it."

"We're getting rid of it. All of it. It's old."

"Her, too," one of them said.

"What?"

"Her, too," the other one said.

And I realized that they were talking about my mother, who I remembered was in a room at the very end of the hallway, a little room you reached after almost doubling back. I'd hidden her there so they wouldn't know, but they must have found her. "No," I said. "You will not!" I hurried toward the hallway, aware that they were laughing uproariously behind me.

"We've already done it," they shouted. "She's gone."

It was maybe the worst laughter I'd ever heard. This was what they'd been thinking about when they were in bed, looking at the ceiling, and I walked in. "We can keep the reading lamp," I said, rushing back. "I think the reading lamp and some books."

"No, it's all going."

"We're moving," he said, and she said it, too.

"But we just got here!"

"No, no, not you."

"You're not moving. We are."

The moving men walked by with their stitched names, all nine of them, going into a room and shutting the door. I saw how big their feet were.

"If you're moving," I said, "if you're—"

"That's right."

"Why take my things? I like them."

"I hate them."

"Amanda hates them."

"But they're mine. And you're moving out."

"You're such an idiot," Amanda said. "You don't understand anything."

"Just leave my things, goddamnit!" I screamed.

She ran in, the young woman. She searched wildly, perspiration on her brow. She had something to tell me, and her mouth was open with fear that she was too late.

Other people walked and talked all through the apartment. It was a party of some kind. Amanda and the roommate laughed, welcoming their guests. They were hosting. When Amanda gestured at me, the guests regarded me with the dismissive, intolerant attitude she modeled for them. The party guests shouted, drinking rabidly, grabbing goblets off trays. The young woman disappeared in the ribaldry, everyone smelling of perfume and drowning one another out in their hysterical good time.

"It's a housewarming. In reverse," Amanda said. And the way she howled, and everyone howled with her, made it clear that this was the wittiest comment ever made by the wittiest woman ever to live. "The end is here," she added. "The absolute end."

"Of everything," the new roommate said.

They howled even louder. The young woman whirled back

into view. Several men jumped in front of her. They grabbed at her arm. The women stayed aloof, behind blinding veneers of gems and furs, jewelry storming their ears, hair, and necks. But the young woman escaped.

It seemed impossible, but she did it, and she came straight to where I sat in the big armchair. Her eyes affirmed that, as I'd thought, she did have something to tell me. Out of breath from wrestling free from the party guests, she sank onto my lap, and leaned close, whispering so softly I didn't understand. "What?" I asked. "What did you say?"

She threw her head back in a way that suggested anguish. "Mankind is suicidal, I'm afraid—a suicidal species."

"Is that what you said?"

"I thought you heard me."

"Oh, I hope that's not true. It's just too hopeless to think that. I want to have a little hope."

"But what if there isn't any?"

I stared into her profound eyes, following their dark invitation to consider her wide forehead, her high cheekbones, the depths she had yet to reveal. "Troy?" I said. "That's where Cassandra lived, isn't it?"

"Yes. I am Cassandra, the prophetess, whom no one believes. Cassandra, full of mourning and prophecy."

Like the horizon, her eyes went on, until they could go no farther. I was so relaxed, so dreamy, she could have said anything.

"It's your body," she said. "And my body. We're animals. Two animals."

I just wanted her to keep moving, and letting me fill with that bewildering syrup for which I felt only love and gratitude. "Are you Cassandra? Are you really?" I wanted to hear her say it again, but I couldn't wait for her to respond. "I like to think that people are good at heart, Cassandra."

"We all do, but unfortunately they're not anything at heart." She closed her eyes and chanted, "Thus said the hawk to the nightingale with speckled neck, while he carried her high up among the clouds, gripped fast in his crooked talons, and she cried pitifully. To her, he spoke disdainfully: 'Miserable thing, why do you cry out? One far stronger than you now holds you fast, and you must go wherever I take you, Songstress. And, if I please, I will make my meal of you, or let you go. He is a fool who tries to withstand the stronger, for he does not gain mastery and suffers pain in addition to his shame.'" For a second of enigmatic sorrow she paused before explaining, "So said Hesiod, the Greek, of the fast-flying hawk, the long-winged bird."

I groped to keep my hands on her waist. "Doesn't it make you sad?"

"That people are not good at heart? Of course it does."

"No, no. That no one believes you."

"It's a curse." Again, she closed her eyes. "We possess in full bounty all that animals need to live, any animal, all animals. Of which man is one. Except he has decided that he isn't."

"Because mankind has a spirit," shouted one of the party-goers celebrating the end of everything. Amanda handed him a megaphone, as if she were dissatisfied with how loud he'd been so far.

"Mankind may or may not have a spirit," Cassandra roared. "But either way, our bodies are animals and that's true of me, you, Amanda, and the hawk."

"Oh, Cassandra," I said. "Why are you doing this?"

"Bodies," she sighed, and shivered. "They want things. We're so ignorant, and we hate being ignorant, and we hate being told we are ignorant. But we hate most of all being told we are animals. Especially when we are tall men, or short men, or fat men, or balding men, or gray-haired men in suits who believe that we eat, shit, and breathe money, and so we don't need food, water, or air. Here is my prophecy: Breath after breath, the air insults us by saving us, by letting us live a few seconds more. But only a few, before another breath is needed. Twenty-three thousand and forty times a day." Her lips exhaled her vision: "I am Cassandra and this is my prophecy: To prove that we are not animals, that we are above and superior to animals, we will destroy everything that an animal needs to live, and thus obliterate our world and ourselves."

Color and light shift inside me. I'm a landscape before a storm. I've assumed that all those men and women with their guns, cars, and bombs—I've assumed that they don't really solve their problems. That the solution of dead strangers doesn't work. But what if it does? What if the mayhem they cause, the bloodshed and slaughter, in fact solves their problems, and could also solve mine? They don't know until the last minute. I can know only at my last minute. I begin to feel it. Holding the long gun. Watching the world flee before me, the blood on the pavement, the raining flecks of gore. I'll never know unless I try. It's happening already, just by thinking, just by considering, a strange but powerful sense of completion. There are gun shops not far from here. I'll go to one. I'll tell no one. I'll go about everything as I always have, quietly, privately. It seems obvious now. Dead strangers solve everything. "Mankind is a suicidal species." The evidence is in. And so what could it matter, even if I'm wrong, and the problems remain, and the only thing that's gone are a few strangers and me?

I make excuses to Amanda and the new roommate about my travels. I tell them that since they are thinking of moving, I am thinking of moving, too. The way they smirk and roll their eyes tells me how much they underestimate me. I imagine Amanda's shock when I shoot her. I'll start with them. Him first, one in the chest and one in the head, before he can move to get his pistol. Then her. I'll go on from them to strangers. To the fat men in suits, the balding, or gray-haired, or sleek-bodied men. But first Amanda and the new roommate. "I'm not moving again," I'll scream. "Where did you put my mother?"

I start evaluating fat men on the street. I need to pick the right fat man to make it worthwhile, and there are so many of them. Maybe a bald man. But there are lots of them, too.

In a nearby state, I find a gun show in a defunct supermarket with GONE OUT OF BUSINESS painted in white on its windows. The inside is an expanse of arid deadness, where I wander about, hoping to blend in with the men and women in sneakers and boots, T-shirts and jeans, sports coats and camo clothing. They munch chips and hot dogs, gulp soda and coffee, looking awestruck as they shoulder a weapon and peer down the sight.

Driving home with an AK-47, a twelve-gauge shotgun, and ammo for both, I begin to worry that I might have betrayed my intentions somehow. Churning anxiety advises me to act more swiftly than I was thinking.

At the apartment, Amanda and the new roommate pass me in the hall, smug and dismissive. I start to think that it may not matter which fat man I shoot. It's probably not a matter of getting the right one. Any fat man, or balding man, in a suit. Or maybe not in a suit. Or maybe not even a fat man or a balding man, but just someone.

But then I wake up in the dark, knowing that my Dear One is dying. I feel stricken and alone with the force of this knowing. I want to escape it, but it takes me into the blackest of nights. I'd forgotten her, and now she is dying and she's looking for me to say goodbye. How could I have forgotten her? My Dear One, my Dear One. She's down by the sea. She's standing at a harbor, or a dock, or a port, or a waterfront at the edge of dark water, and she's looking off into the dark water. For an instant, I think she's Cassandra. But I know I'm only thinking this because I want to understand more than I can. She's older and deeper and more loving than Cassandra. My Dear One is everything to me, and I want to say goodbye to her, too. I want to tell her that I love her. I have always loved her.

I start down toward her, because the gigantic lightless vessel coming to carry her off is crashing close through the waves. I'm sorry I forgot her, and I have to get to her before she is gone. I'm running, but trying to conserve energy, because I don't know how long it will take before I reach her. Strangers start coming from the opposite direction. They don't mean to block the way, and yet they do, because they're frightened, and their fear makes them clumsy. First a bearded man, and then a trio of men and a gaggle of women, panting as they go up the hill I need to go down. Some carry babies or drag children. I dodge and shove to get through them, but it's almost impossible, and I realize from the wild look in their eyes that they are almost blind with fear.

Suddenly someone pushes me out of the way, wanting to get past me. He's shouting for my Dear One, trying to get to her, too. He announces that he's near, begging her to answer if she hears him. He's taller than me, with unnaturally thin, expressive arms and legs. He's graceful, and his voice is cultured. He shoves people aside, and through the jumbled bodies climbing toward me, I see him reach her and take her in his arms. She's slight, a wisp, looking up at him, but so precious. He loves her, he tells her. He is shameless in his passion, pointing to the sky to invoke it as his witness. He has come to say goodbye and she must know that he loves her more than anything or anyone else on earth ever could.

I have to turn back. I cannot go to my Dear One now and

say the things I want to say, because he has said them all. My words will ring hollow and insincere, like I'm imitating him.

I join the rabble laboring up the hill, and now that I am in their ranks, I understand that they are fleeing the dark water below, where burning boats inflame the rolling waves and the sky, as far as anyone can see.

Men and women flow on, lugging boxes, bags, and children, the sound of their breath like a growing wind. When I nearly stumble over something, I look down at one of the big fat men, who has fallen, his suit in tatters. The wheels of a cart grind over an old woman who barely responds. And then I hear my Dear One behind me. I see her fighting to reach me. She calls to me that she wants me.

When my Dear One reaches me, we both start to cry. She says that she had to find me. She could not go out onto the dark sea without telling me she loved me. Without saying goodbye. She must say goodbye to me. All the things I wanted to say to her she wants to say to me. As I hold her, she is as slight as when I first saw her, barely there in her clothing. People bang against us, and then part to go by, sweeping on in two streams that rejoin in one ongoing throng.

After a while, we begin to walk with them, and we are refugees, too.

I HAVE TO TELL YOU

ONE

There pennies, two dimes, four nickels, and two quarters formed a nest of coins on the cutting board balanced on her lap. She had to strain against the fog deep inside her hand. It muffled her effort to work the penny across the faded brown surface, the poor old wood almost worn blank. But she concentrated and managed, the coin traveling like this little nomad, this little child, and she was helping it along, holding its hand. It was terrible the way it had all worked out. All of them dead. Even little Teddy. Dead in the desert. An old fat man. Not a dime to his name, nothing to leave behind, but the clothes on his back. Nothing to call his own but a six-pack of beer and half of it gone. Found by strangers in his little one-room rented apartment, probably a shack. A bunch of rented furniture. The last letter he'd written to her had joked about the way he had to be on the lookout for rattlesnakes when he trekked through "this no man's land," as he called it, until he got to the road, where he could walk to the bar. Just like her penny, he walked for miles. It was three, if she remembered right—three miles to the bar/restaurant kind of hangout where he could play cards or bingo. She could get the letter out and reread to be sure, if she cared to. As if it mattered how far he walked to get to that joint way off in the desert, so far from home and family. All of 'em dead anyway. What was he even doing there? Arizona, for god's sake. She'd stayed home, all her life, while the rest of them left and came back to visit and left and died. Just like him, walking that Arizona desert road. No car for him. Drunk behind the wheel, one too many times. Put him away in a California prison. She hadn't really believed it was him, her baby brother, dead when they called. She'd wanted to go see the body. But how could she do that, going on eighty years old herself. It felt wrong, almost impossible to take on faith. Just a phone call like that. A stranger's voice on the other end. It could have been anybody. It wasn't, of course. And she knew that, too. Just wished she didn't. He was nice enough, that stranger. A policeman trying to answer all her questions about the body, the way they found him, this corpse alone in his bed. Little Teddy. The baby of the family. Stinking of beer and worse, for sure. The TV on. Dead for days. So five years younger than her. She knew the tally, but wanted to work it out anyway, like it was something hard to be sure of. Little Teddy, born in December 1923, would have been seventy-two if he'd hung on one more month until December 11, 1995. But the poor kid didn't make it.

After the penny, she did the dime. Dr. Cameron believed the trouble she was having with her fingers was most likely caused by a pinched nerve up around her neck. Where she felt it, though, was more under that wing bone. What was it called? It nagged like a saw blade in the hands of a little gremlin. Ache, ache, ache, morning, noon, and night. Sure, she knew she was riddled with arthritis, but this was something else.

The quarter was easier than the penny. The little extra thickness gave her just a shade more to get hold of. That perky little pregnant physical therapist had explained each of the exercises for her. Talked her through them. It was some kind of finger aerobics. That was the way she should look at it, and she was more than willing, scared as she was darn near to death of not having her fingers working. She needed her hands to take care of herself, especially her right hand. Needed it for darn near everything. Doors. Shoes. The TV remote. Had to be able to wipe herself. Pee anyway, if not poop. Poop was a matter of changing her colostomy bag. Not that she wanted to give that a try with her left hand.

The dime was tougher than the quarter, tough like the penny, and she should have expected that and been prepared, but the difficulty annoyed her. She was determined, though. She needed her right hand. She'd been right-handed all her life. Always a right-handed person.

The minute hand of the regular clock on the wall gave a nudge and twelve noon arrived. A minute or so more and the cuckoo clock, hanging nearby, would let go, the white bird carved with folded wings, jumping out on his platform and then back in the door that was stuck wide-open and wouldn't budge. Twelve whole times he'd pop in and out, a little late, but dutiful as all get-out, his wooden beak wedged open wide as if he really announced the hour with his cuckoo noise. Well, at least she could count on him, she thought, reaching for the radio that her son had fastened to the table with these Velcro strips the last time he visited. The idea was to give her more room on the table by putting the radio close to the edge but to fasten it down so she couldn't knock it off. The idea was a good one, even though the location made it hard for her to reach the on-off knob without all kinds of contortions, or what felt like contortions. She wanted to hear the obituaries. They came on WDDQ at twelve every weekday. It was the way she kept track, or tried to, of who was gone and who was still around, names she didn't know, and some she knew in passing, acquaintances, you might say; and other times somebody she'd known in the past, maybe even known them well. And every now and then there was a shocker. Somebody, who for one reason or another gave her a jolt, either because she knew them well, or had seen them the other day waltzing around the mall, or Eagles Market, shopping cart jam-packed with what they thought they needed, or maybe they were the child of somebody she knew well. Dying young and tragic. Car crashes, more often than not. So she bent and strained to get her arm out where she could give the knob the little twist it needed. And just like she'd hoped, the radio popped on—still kind of amazing if anybody wanted to know what she thought—this man she couldn't see miles off somewhere talking and yet she could hear him without budging from her recliner. Douglas Wenke, the local radio personality, had a rich-sounding radio voice, respectful and familiar laying out the souls gone as of the hour, and his tone, so somber more or less, put them in their caskets, where she saw them floating. The poor deceased fools. She was half holding her breath waiting to see who would be next. Here yesterday, but gone today. It was as if Douglas Wenke saying their names finished them off.

The knock on the door made her jump. Given her rueful thoughts, her mood almost suspenseful, she felt intruded on. She didn't have time to move, let alone think who it might be, because she sure wasn't expecting anyone, when the knocking came again, the bossy insistent impression even stronger this time, unmistakable really, of somebody standing out there who meant business, and expected to be answered. Like maybe a police officer or a salesman, or one of them Jehovah's Witnesses who got in the halls somehow.

So she was surprised to find a bunch of her neighbors all huddled together. It was clear Elroy Kane from upstairs had done the knocking. His wife, Connie, was behind him with Maggie Ouderkirk from across the hall pressed tight to her, and May Brenner and Clara Luzum from the building next door hovering, the three of them widows same as her.

She gaped at them, tongue-tied, trying to transfer her mind from the dead to the living, where it was needed now.

"Can you let us in?" Elroy said. "We'd like to come in."

"What the heck is going on?"

"Just let us in."

She'd already backed up by way of invitation, opening the way for them to march in, but they seemed to need something more from her. "You bet," she said. "Sure, sure."

The women trekked past, Elroy waiting and gesturing for them to hurry, looking right and left, maybe out the windows at either end of the hall, like he was a lookout scanning for danger. He slipped in then, and shut the door.

"What the heck is going on with the bunch of you?" Emma said to him. "Did somebody die?"

"No, no," said Maggie.

"You want to sit?" She couldn't help staring at Elroy's big feet. They were size fifteen or more. He'd been a farmer, owned hundreds of acres before he retired, and she had to say he still walked like he plodded around in furrows, only his floor was her ceiling. She couldn't see him without thinking how mean he'd been when Charlie, her husband, had asked him to walk more quietly, poor Charlie barely able to walk at all after the accident, and Elroy stomping around overhead, and acting like such a bully. Iowa was full of oafs like Elroy, farmers who stopped farming but couldn't get the hang of living around people.

"There's something going on," he said. "And we think you ought to know about it."

What the heck could it be that it took the whole bunch of them to tell her? "Okay," she said, watching the women perch in a line on her couch against the wall. Elroy stayed on his feet, the general, commander in chief, or whatnot, banty rooster with his gaggle of hens.

"It's about Bud," he said, his eyelids half lowered, ominously.

"Okay." She searched the women for a clue. She was stirred

up, no doubt, her heart quivering in a mix of fear and worry, a feeling of being overwhelmed already, even though she didn't know what was going on.

Bud was the landlord of the apartment complex in which they all lived, five buildings with four units situated on MacDougal Road at the corner of Johnson Boulevard, the main road in their part of town, so it was heavily traveled and noisy but convenient to a heck of a lot, drugstore across the way for example, Eagles Market just a couple blocks on, and the mall a straight shot. Bud managed things, a hired hand with not ten cents' worth of ownership; he took care of maintenance, made sure the garbage was picked up, the lawn mowed, that kind of thing. She figured he got a salary of some sort and his apartment rent fee.

"He's pullin' a fast one," said Elroy. "Or tryin' to. Excuse my French, but it's BS. Only we caught on. So now we got to put a stop to it."

Bud was a nice enough fella, she'd always thought. He didn't seem capable of anything bad enough to rouse this bunch into such a suspicious, indignant mood. He'd always been okay with her, friendly enough, taking things into account, civil for sure if she saw him outside somewhere, even considerate during one or another of her trials. Sending flowers when Charlie died. "What the heck did he do?"

"I'm the one who caught on," said Maggie, hunching forward. "Blind luck. I was talking to that little chubby thing, who just moved into the corner building with that guy she's living with, who's maybe her husband."

"I'd say he isn't," Clara chirped in, which got May nodding.

Taking in the three of them, powdered and rouged, their hair done up, Emma thought they'd gone to a lot of trouble just to drop in on her. At least she was dressed so they hadn't caught her sitting around in her nightgown and robe like she did some mornings.

"I almost did a double take," Maggie went on. "We were just passing the time of day, the way you do, especially with somebody new, making them feel welcome, and she let it slip."

"She's not playing with a full deck." May sounded assured, like they'd all been waiting and kind of almost lost without her assessment. "Cute sure. But, I mean, good lord." She was shaking her head.

"What?"

"Well, lettin' it slip. Not knowin' to stay buttoned up on something like that. And living with that walleyed one. What more do you need to know?"

"I guess."

Elroy cleared his throat in a big, showy way. He shook his head as if the disgusted curl to his mouth wasn't enough to make clear how useless and female he found them. His head-shake got wider the way a voice might get louder, until finally they were all looking up at him, and he could drag them back to the point of what mattered. "The thing of it is, are you for us or against us, Emma?"

She scrunched up her eyes and looked out the window, feeling somehow incriminated in god knew what before she admitted her confusion. "I'm sorry? What?"

"We got to organize, don't you see? Present a unified front when we call for a meeting with Bud and go to confront him. All the tenants who have been here for years. And that includes you."

"Well, it sure does." Her mind sprang backward, as if from an insult, bounding past events she'd survived in that apartment, like living on the ground floor with her poor crippled husband and then without the poor guy. It was some kind of endurance contest she'd triumphed in. She'd been there the day everybody else in that room moved in, Elroy and Connie the most recent to show up, Maggie the furthest back. She had seniority and it needed recognition. "I been here longer than any of you, I'll have you know, Elroy," she told him.

"That's right."

"We know that."

Fixated on Elroy, she didn't know which of the women had said what, but she thought it had been May first and then Maggie, though she didn't much care.

"So your participation matters," Elroy told her, as if she hadn't just told him.

"I think I said that."

"We got to know if you are with us or against us."

She'd asked it before, but it seemed the time had come to ask it again, and this time she knew to make her question forceful, like one nobody better disregard it. "So what is it? What the heck did Bud do?"

It was a kind of grab bag, potluck explanation that came her way then with everybody pitching in but Maggie and Elroy doing most of the talking. It turned out that what the little chubby thing had let slip was the amount she and the man she lived with, whose name nobody could remember, paid for rent. Maggie admitted to actually gasping when she heard the figure, because it was thirty-seven dollars less a month than what she paid and what she got Elroy and Connie to admit, paying, Clara and May, too.

"Good lord," said Emma. "You're sure?"

"Oh, yeah," said Maggie. "I double-checked. I covered up that gasp with a cough and acted pleased and impressed that they had such a good deal. I kept her talking, and one way or another the figure popped out of that pert little mouth again. I ran right home to write it down before my short-term memory fogged it over."

It made no sense, they all said, one after the other, each in their own way. It was "morally reprehensible," Maggie told them, nodding for emphasis, the wealth of her vocabulary part of the point she wanted to register. She let it be known whenever possible that building up her vocabulary was something she pursued. And why not? It kept her mind sharp and helped everybody out in circumstances like these, where understanding was bettered by precise expression.

"Well, it sure is," said Connie, her squirrelly little eyes impressed behind her big glasses. "And Elroy when he found out—well, you should have heard him. 'No sir,' he said. 'No thank you. Not on my watch.' Isn't that right, Elroy?"

"Not while I have breath in this body. I had a shady feeling about Bud the first second I looked into his eyes."

"Yes, he did." Connie turned from one woman to the next, as if to remind them that the man talking was her husband, and so she could assure them that he was the kind of man they needed in charge.

The other thing Emma saw in Connie's glance was pity meant to express her sorrow that she alone had a living husband, as if this was her special accomplishment. No need for that, Emma thought. As far as she was concerned, Connie and her pity were nauseating and totally misplaced, because if having a husband meant being married to Elroy, she could do without.

"It didn't take long. The second my Connie told me what Maggie told her, I let it be known, 'No how, no way.' I put my foot down."

And I probably heard it land, Emma thought, imagining his gigantic shoe rising and falling on her ceiling. You and your size sixteens. She couldn't help herself. She didn't like Elroy and never would. The way he'd treated her and Charlie that time. Couldn't forget it. Why should she? But in this instance, he was right. Darn that Bud. It was wrong in every way. If anybody ought to have lower rent, it was the ones who'd been there the longest. The ones who'd been loyal and steady. Never causing problems. If the rent needed to be lowered to get new tenants, which might well be the case—they all knew a number of the units were empty—well, then, the right thing would have been for him to tell the older tenants and offer to lower their rents, too. Why not? Maybe not good business in the short term, but in the long run it'd pay off. The least he could have done was inform them. Not try to pull the wool over their eyes, so cocksure they were too old and stupid to ever catch on. And all this while she'd thought Bud was on the up-and-up. When would she ever learn? Maybe never. Old as she was, there wasn't a lot of time left. It hurt. It really did. Just hurt. That was the truth of it. In more ways than she could count. She hated using Elroy's phrases, but in this case he'd been on the money. She remembered seeing Bud the other day as she was on her way back from the drugstore and he was going over, and they'd said Hello, and he'd asked about her arthritis, like he cared. And all the while he was doin' dirty sneaky business behind her back.

"You bet you can count me in," she said, feeling her stomach tighten and twirl and a wave of these completely out-of-place tears rise up to push from behind her eyes. But she fought them, keeping everything roiling up inside her, the hurt and all, hidden away. Anger was better.

It was like she'd shot a gun to start a race the way everybody started yammering, with Elroy trying to keep them "on target," as he called their plan to meet again on the day after tomorrow in order to plot out what they might say when they confronted Bud. They'd have to decide who went to him. Maybe they should all go, strength in numbers; or it could be better if everybody signed a letter and then only a couple of them delivered it, acting as representatives.

They wound down, starting to talk about maybe getting together in the afternoon to play some cards at Maggie's apartment. Elroy and Connie were the first to leave—he sure wasn't interested in playing any cards with them, he told them—which gratified Emma, because after a few minutes she got to roll her eyes with Maggie, May, and Clara, the three of them laughing and shaking their heads at the sound of Elroy and his big feet clopping about over their heads.

TWO

Her belly gave a twinge, and she told herself to calm down. It was the middle of the night, and she was dog-tired but scatterbrained. So much on her mind. Bud most of all. It rubbed her wrong. It was insulting and that was all there was to it, that these kids were getting treated better than her, for no good reason other than the fact that they were young. For crying out loud, she'd been young and nobody gave her a hand out. What had this bunch done to prove they were worth a darn, let alone deserved special treatment. Just born later is all. Like that mattered. All they did is run in and out and have loud parties that she had to call Bud about, and the others had, too, she knew, Elroy and Connie for sure, complaining about the noise on a Friday or Saturday night. Bud had to go down and knock on the door and ask them to be quiet. Not that it did much good, because it all went on, maybe even louder, cars pulling in and out of the parking lot everybody shared, music so loud a normal person would have thought they were deaf. Good lord, that was another thing she couldn't stand about Elroy. The way he acted like Napoleon about his parking space. That time her friend Mary Beth stopped by, only going to stay a second, so she parked in the first spot she saw, which happened to be Elroy's. She wanted to drop something off—Emma couldn't remember what—she'd be darned if she could. And it just so happened that Elroy came back then and stomped up, banging on her door, like he did today, only worse.

The need to pee had gotten her out of bed a bit ago and now she crawled back, wide awake and staring at the dark. Her insides hinted that everything wasn't right with them, this knotted-up feeling shooting out faint spasms of threat every few seconds. It was a miserable sensation, because she knew what it might turn into if she didn't stop fussing and fuming. She took a deep breath, and the tangled-up squeezing grabbed at her belly so hard, she winced, just the opposite of what she'd hoped for. "Oh, no," she whispered, turning to get a look at the bedside clock. A little before three in the morning. "Please," she said. "Come on, now. Not tonight." The diverticulitis had been so bad, she had to have surgery and then the scar tissue afterward was so tough that when McNamara went in to reverse her, he had to back out. All she wanted was to be able to go to the bathroom like a normal person, like she'd done all her life. But the scars were like cables, McNamara told her, and steel ones, too, leaving her like she was, with a bag of poop on her side, and these darn miserable cramps every now and then, no matter how often she flushed everything and kept it all clean. And they were coming now. She had to admit it. The pain had been remote and threatening, like something that might blow past the way storm clouds did sometimes. Up till now it had been like listening to distant thunder that might roll off in another direction, but this ache wasn't going anywhere. It was rising up in terrible clouds pouring hurt down on her, and she let out a moan, which sometimes helped but it didn't this time.

Far off and like some lonely friend who knew of her plight, the cuckoo clock called to her. She didn't have to be in the living room to see him, his little beak wide open like he hurt, too. One, two, three cuckoos and then he fell silent. Three o'clock in the middle of the night and she was moaning now, over and over, the cramps increasing, like somebody in there was twisting her guts into knots. She had to get up and walk. Just change her position. Sometimes they went away, even after they got this bad. Fighting to find her way into her robe, she dropped the darn thing, and bending to pick it up made her yelp. What a dirty trick. It wasn't leaving this time, unless she puked. Maybe then. Sometimes that helped. Or pooped. One or the other. The last time she puked and it went away, and she was weak for a day, but that was all.

She didn't recall getting back into bed, but there she was rolling around, and then she was walking again. Prowling through her apartment. The cuckoo went off, calling out four times, and she saw him in the shadows like he was coming out of the wall. She went through the kitchen, and around the table. She thought about sitting in the recliner but was scared to try. By now she had her rosary in one hand, her fingers fidgeting over the beads, her mind squirming over the words, her voice joining in when she could manage a sound that wasn't a groan. "Hail Mary, full of grace . . ." She had the little trash can she hoped to puke in, having picked it up along the way, and she held it tight with the hand that didn't have the rosary. She looked down at it, feeling almost worshipful, and praying just as hard to it almost that it would let her puke, as if it was somehow in charge. It glowed just then in the excess of the streetlight out on corner of Johnson Boulevard pouring in the window, where a car went by with a whoosh, the headlights washing over her and her bucket, too. It was terrible.

Back in bed groaning, she got up and started walking, keeping her rosary and that bucket close, one in each hand, and the cuckoo clock cuckooed but she couldn't keep the count. Fingering the rosary and praying when she could, a word here and a groan there, looking down at the trash can, concentrating on her insides like they were behind a door she was pressed up against listening to hear who was coming because maybe it would be poop. She didn't know which might come first, poop or puke—didn't know where she was going or what she was doing—dropping into bed, where she couldn't rest so she got up again but she couldn't be up, either.

It was seven when she called for help, tearful and shaking so bad, she worried she wasn't working the right push buttons on the phone. She stopped and started over, still worried. She hoped she didn't sound too pitiful and useless when Maggie picked up. She was an early riser so the one Emma tried first, asking for a helping hand, if it wasn't too much trouble. Could Maggie give her a ride up to the hospital? "Cramps . . . colostomy bag . . . up all night . . ." was about all the explanation Maggie needed to hear. Emma hated her situation and everything it indicated about her life, her need and all for her neighbor, the way her kids lived so far away, the mess her bowels were in, all of it. But she was at her rope's end, and knew she didn't dare try to drive. She'd kill herself for sure, and probably take a bunch of other poor souls with her.

Maggie kept her little Honda spic-and-span, seat covers on the seats, the dash and windows spotless. Emma couldn't help but notice. And as they made their way through the hilly streets that rolled up and down, some of them way too steep, Emma tried to sit still and straight. As much as she'd prayed to puke all night long, she prayed now for the opposite result. It would be the height of ingratitude to make a mess in Maggie's sweet little car, immaculate as it was, her pride and joy. Just thinking about it made her burp, the burn in the back of her throat bringing up hot tears.

But then the hospital was in sight and then they headed for a stop at the emergency door. Maggie ran in and out, came with an orderly pushing a wheelchair. He looked familiar but she couldn't place him. But then she realized it wasn't him she knew, but the blunt forehead and something in the nose spoke of a family resemblance she knew from somewhere. But she couldn't think who they were, either.

The doctor on call, whose name tag was crooked, said, "Well, now what did you do to yourself?"

"Not a thing," she told him, way beyond finding jokes of any interest, particularly ones at her expense. He was scanning her chart and taking much too long, kind of bouncing from one foot to the other, like maybe somebody had told him to keep moving to burn calories. He was flabby enough for layers of belly to bulge, his checkered shirt showing under his open white coat. He resembled somebody, too, she thought, though whom she didn't know. She wondered if lack of sleep was getting to her and she was kind of hallucinating this sense of widespread familiarity. She'd read that happened when people got sleep-deprived. Hallucinations. Not familiarity. "Morphine," she said. "It's all that helps me. It must say that."

"I see." He smiled, something narrow and unhappy in his eyes, like maybe his belly hurt, too. "It's right here in your chart."

"Good. It should be."

"Well, that's why we're here," he said. Nothing about him was real, especially not his smile. It looked like something he thought a doctor should have, so he'd practiced it in front of a mirror, which put him face-to-face with his deficiency and left him lacking confidence. He turned to the nearest nurse and said whatever mumbo jumbo was needed to get her scurrying off. "Is she going for the morphine?"

"Won't be long now."

"I been up all night, I have to tell you," she said. "Miserable."

"I'm sorry to hear that."

Maybe she was wrong about him. He seemed nice saying

that. His name tag had been straightened. His last name was Paisley. Cute, she thought. Just knowing the morphine was on its way let her relax enough to look around for Maggie. They'd rushed her inside some kind of tent with curtains they'd pulled shut. "Where's my friend?" she asked. Dr. Paisley was slow to respond, dialing a phone, and the delay gave her time to answer her own question by searching around until she spied Maggie's pink shoes in the gap between the curtain and the floor.

"I don't know where your friend is," said Dr. Paisley. "Did she come with you?"

"She's right there." Emma pointed. "Those are her shoes."

"Oh. Good. Would you like to see her?"

"I can see her."

He started talking to whomever he'd called, who she realized was her surgeon, Dr. McNamara. Maggie's legs were bare all the way up to her knees, kind of startling, all that skin, like she was naked out there except for her pink shoes and white socks, making Emma uncomfortable and embarrassed that she would have such a bawdy friend, until she remembered Maggie explaining on the way over that she'd been up early and just about out the door for a golf outing when Emma and her emergency call brought her plans to a screaming halt. She'd been wearing navy blue shorts and a lighter blue blouse, and one of those sun visor hats, which might have been blue, Emma mostly remembered now. The trip over hovered behind a haze of fogged-over pain, blurry and thick, giving up only the facts she could wrestle out of it, and surrendering those stingily. They hooked her up to the IV, the nurse telling her to squeeze a fist and look out for a pinch. She watched the plastic bag beginning to drip, the doctor, breathing hard, she thought, bumping his stethoscope around on her chest, looking into her secrets.

"I checked with Dr. McNamara, and he said the morphine was just fine."

"I told you. But I don't want that stomach pump business. I don't want it in my nose. It hurts too much."

"We'll just wait and see."

"No, thank you."

"I can't promise."

"Okay." She closed her eyes and took a deep breath. "How'd my heart sound?"

"All right."

"People say I got a good heart. That I'm good-hearted."

"I'm sure you are."

"Sometimes too generous for my own good. That's their opinion."

"Sure," he said.

"I don't really see how that's possible, though, if you know what I mean."

"I think I do. I bet I do."

Maggie's pink shoes struck her funny the way they poked in under the curtain, like she was trying to eavesdrop or maybe peek. Or else she was just out there with her face pressed up against the curtain, which would be a peculiar way to stand, if standing were all she was up to. "That's no way to stand," she said.

"Sorry," said Dr. Paisley. He looked hurt and ready to change anything and everything if he had somehow offended Emma.

"I like your name. Dr. Paisley," she said, thinking he was doing his best and could use a little help, awkward as he was, almost too awkward ever to be good at what he wanted to be good at.

"Well, thank you."

"That's a nice name. Is it your real name?"

"Well, yes it is."

Didn't hurt to compliment the poor fella some, working so hard the way he did to have a good smile, which he did his best to come up with right then.

"I'll be back to see how you're doing," he told her, retreating with a hand extended out blindly to feel for the curtain behind him.

"Better look where you're going," Emma said, hoping to get a laugh out of him. "I'm countin' on you, you know."

She wasn't sure he got the joke. Well, she could only do so much. The nurse who came in as he went out could have done with a few less donuts, but both her eyes and voice were soft and caring. "How are we doing here?"

"Okay, over here," said Emma. "How about you?"

"No complaints here." She fingered the tape securing the IV in Emma's arm. "You're all hooked up nice and good here. How are you feeling?"

"My friend out there in the hall was headed out to play golf, but she stopped everything and brought me over. What do you think of that? No questions asked." She felt like she announced meaningful information, a kind of credential that would leave no doubt about her value in the world. "She's dressed the way she is because of the golf. She was on her way. That's how they dress."

"Do they?"

"She does."

"Actually, do you know what? I play golf."

"You don't."

"Yes, I do."

"Real golf?"

"That's the one."

She stared at the nurse, cumbersome and thick and hard to imagine stuffed into Maggie's dainty outfit. "She canceled

161

her game just to help me. Can you imagine? Four of them were headed out. But they're gonna have to play without her. She says they'll be fine."

"That's a good friend," said the nurse. "She can come in and visit with you in a minute, if you'd like."

"Okay. Sure. She came all this way." The cramps dissipated slowly but dependably, like black thick dirty water that the morphine washed away in a steady clean stream.

She dozed a little and woke to find Maggie sitting in a chair leafing through a magazine.

"Are you still here?"

"I'd say so."

"Looks like it from where I seem to be. Did you get something to eat?"

"I did. Had some coffee and a sandwich."

"Any good?"

"Not half bad. Grilled cheese. Coffee was a little weak."

"You oughta go, don't you think? Get some good coffee on the way home. Dunkin' Donuts."

"How are you feeling?"

"Better. That's for sure. I'm awful glad I didn't puke in your car."

"Me, too."

"That's a real nice car you got there."

"I love it."

"You really ought to go home, Maggie."

"I'm fine."

"How can you be? Just sittin' there like that. Time's awasting."

"I was readin' a nice article till you had to wake up and start bothering me."

"You've done enough. Go home. You go on now and go."

They went on like that for too long, almost getting really

angry, and then Emma dozed some more, and when she came to, she said, "Are you still here? Maggie? I wish you'd go. You go on and go, like I'm telling you."

"I'm not going to leave until you're feeling okay."

"I am feeling okay."

"I'm thinking until they admit you. Maybe you go up to a room. If I stay on, maybe I can take you home."

"They'll never let me go home tonight. They'll take care of me, and keep me here tonight. That's for sure."

The next time she woke up, she was all primed to say, You go on now, darn-it. She might have even said it out loud, though Maggie was nowhere to be seen. In fact, Emma was being wheeled into a room by an orderly who had the worst tobacco breath.

"Hello there," said the woman in the bed they passed by, the one closer to the door. The orderly went, taking his stinky breath with him, and his belly so big, it could have toppled him. Two nurses hurried to get Emma situated in bed. Between the morphine and her interest in the woman who'd welcomed her, Emma paid little attention to them. The woman wasn't as old as Emma, but not too far from it, and tiny. She was just this almost shocking little slip of a thing, smiling her big welcome amid the wide-open, white expanse of all those sheets and pillows. Two other women, both younger, sat in chairs pulled close where they visited. One was in slacks and a nice beige blouse. The other wore a simple, pretty dress and had a kind of seashell bracelet on her wrist.

Emma worried they'd grown quiet because of her. As the nurses left, she said, "Don't let me interrupt your good time over there."

"You're not. I'm Annette Olson." Her voice was big, considering how little there was of her. "Annette Olson."

"I'm Emma Skayhill," said Emma.

Annette introduced the other two women, kind of holding court, who were her daughter, Grace, and her daughter-in-law, Bonnie. Just then two young boys scurried in, herded along by a man. He was tall and rangy, you might say, in a white shirt, the tie loose, a jacket slung over his shoulder. The boys were both blond, one with about a million freckles. They were maybe five and seven.

"These are my grandsons, Annette said. "Paul and Brandon Kalisheck. She looked up at the tall man and asked, "How are you doing, Hank?"

"Fine, Mom."

Annette went ramrod straight, looking almost reprimanded by a strict superior. A person might have thought she'd forgotten something enormously important. "Now Paul. You and Brandon go on over and say hello to Mrs. Skayhill."

Before Emma could get a word out edgewise to say they didn't have to bother, they were on their way, two perfect little gentlemen, coming up to stand side by side in front of her. They put their hands out for her to shake one after the other.

"Hello, Mrs. Skayhill. I'm Brandon."

"I'm Paul." The little one blinked a lot and kind of wiggled his nose.

"Well, hello," Emma said. "Nice to meet you, Brandon. And you, too, Paul. I'm very happy to make your acquaintance." Past their somber little faces, she could see Annette looking on, a nice, smiling grandmother, and just like that, Emma was having a darn good time.

THREE

Annette. Such a little bit of a person. Emma couldn't get over it. Daughters and daughters-in-law coming in and out all afternoon to visit, and every one of them pleasant. That was the common denominator. They were nice. Grace, the first daughter she'd met, talked about her garden with Emma, pulling up a chair to sit beside her and ask real considerate questions about what Emma could and couldn't eat, given her problem. Emma had made a point of grabbing the first opportunity that came along to explain about her colostomy operation, and about living with that darn bag ever since. She even went into the cramps that had brought her to the hospital, getting it all out in the open right off the bat. Grace was real sympathetic and said she had the most wonderful string beans this summer. "I'm going to bring you some to take home with you when you're ready to get out of here, Emma."

There were interludes when Annette and Emma had the place to themselves, everybody gone off to the cafeteria, or on an errand, or home for this and that. She and Annette talked about their families—their kids and grandkids. Emma had three grandkids living out East with her son. She and Annette just hit it off. Just real good roommates. Annette's grandkids came over and talked to Emma whenever they visited, both the boys and the girls. Annette made sure of that. Emma enjoyed Paul and Brandon the most. Gwen, the last daughter Emma met, was married to a Denlinger. Tim Denlinger. Heck of a coincidence, if anybody cared to notice, because Emma had worked with Tim Denlinger's mom, who would now be Gwen's mother-in-law, at Sears for eight years. So there was all that to talk about. That's the way they visited. Friendly like they'd known each other years.

It went on like that, a steady stream of company, and they could have closed that curtain around Annette's bed any time they wanted, and they would have been within their rights. Emma would not have blamed them for wanting a little family privacy. But they always left the curtain open and did their best to include Emma in their conversations because she was alone a lot. Annette had all these children, all of them living close by. Her sons came after work, and their wives stopped by, too. One of her boys worked at Billings Lumber, another sold insurance, and one owned a gas station. Her husband drove a truck delivering oil. He was a big man. They were all big men, and they were polite and friendly. Emma said a little prayer of thanks, because it didn't have to be that way.

It took the end to visiting hours to quiet things down. Almost surprised to be alone, Emma wondered if maybe they might watch a little television. Annette turned out to be just as easygoing about picking a program as she was about everything else. Detective shows, or game shows. Comedies. It didn't matter. So it was all smooth sailing until they were ready to call it a day, and get some rest, when this ruckus started up in the hall. It was hard to tell what they were doing out there other than making noise. She and Annette rang a nurse to find out what the heck was going on, and get whoever was banging around at this hour of the night to quiet down. The nurse turned on her heel and left, and this big man came in. He wore a green work shirt and pants, grease-stained with tattered pockets, and big work boots, and he said he was sorry, though he didn't look sorry, but the hospital had gotten it into its mind to fix an electrical wiring problem that meant opening up a little section of floor and maybe the wall, and it was work that was best done at night. With the meat hook of his hand already clamped on the edge of the doorframe, he told them he was going to close their door so they could get some sleep.

"Oh, no you don't," Emma told him. "I got to say no thanks to that one. I'm so claustrophobic, I don't really like that door closed very well."

He looked at her funny, and then did the same at Annette, trying to get her to take his side against Emma was the way Emma read him. But Annette eyed Emma knowingly, and said, "I'm with her." The man did a kind of double take the way comedians do, like he had to make sure they understood how ridiculous they both were and where he'd like to tell the pair of them to go, but he left the door open when he went.

The nurse popped back in, looking disheveled, like someone had grabbed her and shaken her before shoving her in. She offered them sleeping pills, which, after a shared shrug, they accepted. She said she was sorry for the noise, though they didn't see how it was her fault. Her husky little voice sounded truly sad as she explained that nighttime was the only chance the workmen had to do the job, because there was just too much traffic in the halls all day long. She snapped up the guardrails on the sides of Emma's bed as she talked, and then moved on to Annette. "You understand, Mrs. Olson, that you must never, never get out of bed without one of us to help you."

"Okay," Annette said.

"If you need to use the bathroom, remember you must put on your light and wait, and never go until we get here."

"I know. Okay."

Emma thought Annette sounded embarrassed, even put upon, getting talked to, like she was a little slow or senile. Given all Annette's visitors and the free way they talked, Emma knew that Annette could see out of only one eye, and she had a heart problem, too, though it wasn't clear to Emma what kind. Not congestive, though. She hadn't heard that word.

When the nurse was gone, Emma said, "Reminds me of pulling up the side of that crib on my kids when they were newborns. Fencing us in like a couple of infants so we don't fall out of bed and knock ourselves silly."

"As if we ain't already silly enough."

"Speak for yourself."

"I thought I was," Annette shot back at her, cheerful sounding, her spirits lifted.

When Emma woke up to pee, the door to the hall was shut tight. The dimness felt spooky, only those artificial lights glowing from the machines monitoring her and Annette, this fluorescent slash creeping in under the door from the hall, the clock up on the wall blurry, but maybe about ten after three. She put on her glasses to be sure.

She felt lucky, because unlike Annette, she could get up and go to the bathroom on her own. She had to bounce to sit up, feeling a bit like a turtle on its back. After lowering the guardrails, she rocked back and forth to get her legs over the side. Her dangling feet searched for the floor and she was glad to find it. Pushing the IV tree along, she made her way through the blinking and beeping, some of it filtering in from the hall and other rooms. The workers must have finished up and gone home. The place was almost quiet. She felt sad for no reason she could name, and scared, like she was on another planet where human life was different and almost unwelcome. It made sense that they didn't want Annette trying this business on her own with one eye on the fritz. It was hard enough for Emma with her two good ones and her glasses on. She shut her right eye for a second, just to see how it would feel to be hampered that way. Pulling the bathroom door shut, she was grateful to throw the bright lights on. Annette's good spirits seemed all the more admirable, given her difficulties and how tiny she was, so darn near scrawny. It worried Emma a bit that Annette maybe had cancer. Skin and bones came with cancer. No wonder they didn't want her getting up alone.

Emma dribbled away, and finished, but she sat a second more, all of a sudden fretting about the meeting that would go on back at the apartment building without her tomorrow. She almost ached to be there, putting her ten cents into what they figured out to say so that Bud knew she was with them, and ready to fight tooth and nail to make sure the older tenants got a fair shake on the rent. Maggie would surely tell everyone who was counting on her what had happened, and how Emma had to get to the hospital fast. Maggie was a good neighbor.

She flushed and stood, getting a firm grip on the doorknob before throwing off the bathroom switch. The light rushing in under the door from the room she'd left dark startled her. Her feet looked pale and strange like fish. She opened the door to find Annette standing there, a nurse on each side, the three of them like cops with a prisoner ready to advance.

"Oh, sorry," Emma said.

"Monkey see, monkey do," Annette told her.

"Did I hold you up?"

"No, we just got here."

And they marched in.

FOUR

Emma was starting to feel halfway on vacation as the next day purred along, Annette's gang popping in and out. Emma was doing so much better, she felt ready to get out of there and back to takin' care of all she had on her plate. Mainly that darn rent business. She'd get a report from Maggie on the meeting, and that would put her up to speed. She needed to get up to the cemetery to tend Grandma and Grandpa Durham's graves, and her dear husband's, too. She should call her son out East and tell him what was happening, though she didn't like to worry him. Still he should know she'd been in the hospital.

Midmorning, both her GP and surgeon, Grennel and McNamara, came by. They checked her over and asked some questions, good ones, she thought. They ordered blood drawn to run some test they thought useful. After conferring right there at the foot of her bed, they decided they wanted her to stay on another day so she got good and rested. She was ready to argue when a spasm cut into her so sharp, she winced. They saw it and exchanged a smile they shared with her, like it satisfied them somehow, these bad cramps ready to jump on her, because even if they hurt Emma, they proved that Grennel and McNamara were good doctors, so she better listen to them. Grennel thought they should do an electrocardiogram, and McNamara thought that might be a good idea. They could do it right in the room.

When she wanted to know why, McNamara said, "Nothing to worry about. Just wear and tear on the machinery. You've been riding around in this car for a lot of years."

She figured she was the "car" he meant, her body anyway. He was an odd duck all right. "As if I don't know it," she said, figuring it best to show him she could make a joke, too.

As soon as they were gone, she called Maggie to explain she'd be stuck a bit longer than she'd first thought, and she was relieved to find out that Elroy, Connie, Clara, and May, the whole bunch of them, had agreed to wait for Emma to get out, unless her stay in the hospital went on too long.

"No how, no way," Emma told Maggie. "I'll be home tomorrow for sure. After they run these stupid tests."

"What tests is that?" Maggie wanted to know.

"Stupid ones."

The electrocardiogram proved simple enough on her end, though she couldn't understand why they needed to stick so many patches on her. Wouldn't a couple have done the job? Soft, gooey, and cold, every one of them. Arms, legs, chest, you name it. Then the machine started up, lights and a purr, showing this pattern on a kind of TV screen, while rolling out a strip of checkerboard paper. Her angle on the whole thing didn't let her see the details clearly, but there were lines, squiggly and dancing. "How'm I doin'?"

"This won't take long."

"Hot off the presses," she said. "Big news about Emma." She nodded at the paper spilling out. The nurse didn't seem to get her humor. When the end came and the patches got pulled off, she said, "What now?"

"The doctors will evaluate the results, and consult with you, of course."

She was a prissy one. Had to say "evaluate" rather than some simple word like an ordinary person might use.

The day wore on, with Annette's visitors starting up, the first being a woman around Emma's age who appeared in the doorway, leaning on a cane. Annette whooped at the sight of her. Irene Wurzer was a childhood friend from Rydersville, a little town maybe twenty miles east, where Annette had been born and raised. Irene had called Annette's house, hoping to stop by. The news that Annette was up in Saint Anthony's sent her straight over, like somebody shot her "out of a cannon."

"A sight for sore eyes," Annette said.

"You, too, Annie-bannie."

For the first time excluded, Emma turned on the TV with the volume low while Annette and Irene visited. Then that prissy nurse came in to tell her neither McNamara nor Grennel was satisfied with the results of the electrocardiogram, so they were going to take her down to the "echo chamber." At least that's what Emma thought she'd heard. "The where?"

"It's downstairs."

"What is?"

"An orderly will come for you when they're ready."

She was thinking, echo chamber, torture chamber? What the heck. Ohh, she felt so alone. She wanted to tell Annette, maybe crack a joke, but Annette and Irene were engrossed, chattering and gesturing with this bubbly laughter Emma could almost see. She felt like the smallest boat in the river, and the currents were spinning her off. The orderly who came was the same as the other time, his breath stinking of cigarettes in spite of the gum he chewed. The elevator shuddered several times on the way down and then made a grinding squeal as it came to a stop. The orderly delivered her to a young woman with smart-looking glasses and dark hair cut in a short perky style. "I'm your sonographer, Mrs. Skayhill. My name is Katie Shew." Her smile didn't amount to much, like she worried it made her less important. "You just need to open up your gown so I can get at you from the waist up, then we'll be all set."

It seemed pretty much the same routine to her, the cold sticky gel and way too many patches, but then Katie started moving this kind of TV remote control around right on Emma's chest. Her eyes were intent behind those glasses, staring up past Emma's head to where Emma had noted a TV screen as she lay down. "There," said Katie. "That took it. I got it." The way she spoke included Emma, but it would have been stretching the truth to say she was talking to Emma. "You're a hard one. Where did you go now?" Her expression reminded Emma of someone determined to win a game. "That little rascal, he's hiding on me."

"Who are you talking to, dare I ask?" Emma whispered.

"Hmmmmm?"

"What's going on?"

"Your heart is really hard to get close to—and to get a hold of and get good pictures of. Oh, there I got one." She was completely unwilling to look away from the screen. She moved the remote control thing, pressing a little hard. "That's a good one. That's it now, Mrs. Skayhill. Don't move. You moved. C'mon now, Mrs. Skayhill. There. There. Oh, I grabbed a hold of it that time."

"Of what? Could you tell me?"

"Your heart. But it's hard. It keeps hiding. Hold your breath. That's right. Keep holding. Thank you. Steady, steady."

Emma wondered if this Katie was one of the Shews from the west end of town. There was a bunch of them out that way. Some of them got in trouble every now and then, and you read about it in the paper in the Police Blotter.

"You're a tricky little devil," Katie said. "Yes, you are. I got you, though. Got him cornered, Emma."

What she meant, Emma didn't know and didn't much care. She didn't like hearing her heart talked about that way Katie Shew was talking about it, and she wanted to tell her there wasn't a grain of truth in anything she said. Emma had been good-hearted all her life. She knew Katie was talking entirely different than the way her words made Emma feel hurt, but the two meanings were stuck together, melted into each other almost, and she couldn't get them apart.

Once back in her room, Emma was glad to be with Annette, even if Irene was still there, because the regular visitors started to show up, opening Annette's world to Emma the way they had the day before. She tried her joke about the "echo chamber—torture chamber," a couple of times, and it seemed to go over okay, but not well enough to keep trying it. Paul and Brandon made an appearance. But then another day was over and done with, everybody gone except for Annette's daughter Grace, who hung on past visiting hours like she didn't want to lose sight of her mom. She told Emma that she'd bring those string beans she'd promised the next morning, since Emma had said she'd likely be discharged by the end of day.

Left on their own, Emma and Annette gave the television a try, more out of habit and stubbornness than interest, the both of them nodding off in spite of the squealing tires, gunshots, and angry faces on the cop show. They finally admitted that they were wrung out.

"Dog-tired."

"Probably because of all that ruckus in the hall last night, don't you think?" Emma wondered.

"Let's hope they don't have another shindig in store for us."

"All that banging and so on, and we're in here not getting good rest. That's what I think."

"I am bushed, I have to tell you," said Annette.

The door opened, bringing in the nurse who'd been on duty since late afternoon. She had a good way about her, Emma thought, friendly, but clear and firm, like a scoutmaster. A pregnant little redhead trailed her, the two of them talking about something that ended with a laugh, and then the scoutmaster said, "Well, ladies. Time for some shut-eye."

"That's just what we were thinking," said Annette.

The little redhead bustled over to the window, cleaning up Styrofoam cups and food trays from dinner that had been set on the sill. The scoutmaster snapped up Annette's guardrails and said, "If you want some good news, I have it. You can rest assured, ladies, they got that work all finished last night, so everything will be nice and quiet tonight."

The redhead set about checking Emma's pulse, while the scoutmaster eyed the monitor above Annette's bed. "Now remember, Mrs. Olson, no getting out of bed on your own. No matter what. Your night nurse will be on soon. Ask for her. Just put your call light on. You're getting a new night nurse, too."

"So not that blonde who was on last night?" Emma wondered.

"No," the scoutmaster chuckled. "You better believe this one is not a blonde."

They were gone only a few seconds before Annette sighed, "Darn it, Emma, the thought just came to me that you're not going to get to see Brandon and Paul again. They can't get by in the morning. School and all, you know."

"They're a good pair, those two."

"I'm a foster grandparent over at Washington School. You ever do that?"

"No. What is it?"

"Well, those kids that go there, you know, they don't have much. So I go over and spend time, as a foster grandparent. Those kids in that neighborhood, even their parents, half of them are cast to the winds."

"I don't know much about that place."

"I like helping them." They settled a moment, sheets rustling. "How are things going for you, Emma, them cramps and all?"

"Pretty good. You know what they say about getting old."

"Don't they now."

"How about you, Annette? How are you doing? They getting things figured out for you?"

"Oh, I wouldn't go that far."

Emma was sure it was part of a dream when she heard a whispering voice. The dream fluttered, pale and flimsy, all this fabric gathered into a curtain that she was on one side of and then on the other. *Emma, Emma,* the dream whispered. *He's got awful big feet, you know.*

What? Who? Elroy? Whoever it was had come to tell her something about her brother, Ted, who was a baby in the desert, sand drifting over him, wind and loneliness rising, rattlesnakes everywhere.

"Emma, are you awake?"

"I am now." She felt sad and lost, like the whole world was empty, but she sounded irritated, even angry. She was just this woman with this other woman in a hospital room in the middle of the night.

"I gotta go, Emma. I gotta go."

"What the heck are you doing?" If appearances could be

trusted, the pale blur that was Annette across the room was shuddering like somebody getting electrocuted.

"I gotta go. Bad. I got my call light on, but they're not coming. Nobody's coming."

"Is it broke?" Getting her glasses on, she had a better look at, Annette, who twisted and twitched.

"I don't know. How'm I supposed to know?"

"Maybe it's not working right. I'll put mine on, too." She flailed to press the call button, hanging on to it and feeling kind of panicky, as if the predicament was as much hers as Annette's. "Is it peeing you need?"

"No. The other. I mean, both. I can't wait. I can't."

"Keep tryin'." That it was her bowels gonna move was scarier still. At least Emma didn't have to worry about that kind of trouble, because she had her bag. And the next thought that came was to wonder what in the world is going on over there with Annette wiggling around in her bed. There was no way to think of her except that she looked like a little monkey, grabbing and shaking the guardrail. "I don't think you wanna get out of that bed, Annette, if that's what you're tryin'. Not if you know what's good for you."

"I can't get it down."

"You're not supposed to."

"I can't wait, I'm tellin' you."

"Hang on." Emma hit her call button over and over, turning it off and on rapidly in the hope that the blinking would send a kind of SOS.

Annette was crawling right out under the bars. She couldn't get the rail to lower, but she was escaping anyway. She was so darn tiny.

"I'd stay put, if I was you."

"I can't, and I ain't."

"Oh, be careful now, Annette. Hurry, if you can."

Annette landed, aiming for the bathroom. "I'm not going to go in the bed. It's their darn fault for—oh." Her little cry was like she'd stubbed her toe, but that wasn't what happened. She'd lost some of the poo on the floor. Even in the half-light, Emma could see it, wet and shiny, and she saw, too, the awful, appalled way Annette looked down at what she'd done. But she rushed on, grabbing at her behind, kind of packing her nightgown up against her bottom to stop what was tryin' to come out, and rushed on out of sight. And darned if the nurse didn't barge in right that second, this sudden blur of a blue shape. It was the scoutmaster, the little redheaded gal trailing her still like they were some kind of team. "What's going on here?"

"She's in the bathroom."

"Mrs. Olson?"

"She hadda go bad. You better help her."

The nurse started toward the bathroom, and Emma, picturing her slipping and falling ass over teakettle cried out in alarm, "Watch you don't step in it. There's some on the floor."

"What?"

"She had an accident."

"I'll be darned. I'll be darned and kicked in the head," said the nurse, grabbing a fistful of napkins, a couple wipes, and crouching. "Goddamnit."

Oh, now she was mad. But to hear a nurse cursing like that gave Emma a start. A nurse, for goodness' sake. At a patient. "You ought to know better! We told you." She was down on the floor, facing into the open bathroom door that the little redhead held open. "No! Don't you dare move. Didn't we tell you not to get out of that bed, Mrs. Olson? Now look at this mess. You just sit there," she scolded. "You're one of those thinks they know best about everything. Well, you don't. You damn well don't!"

She was shrill and wild, kind of rabid. It struck Emma that cleaning up that mess had pushed her round some kind of bend, and she was having trouble coming back, if she even wanted to.

"Well," Emma said, "she had her light on. And she couldn't wait. Nobody came." But Emma might as well have been talking to a post. That nurse was so far gone, she wasn't hearing anything, just ranting at Annette, like you would at a child who'd dirtied her pants. "I said, Don't you move. No, no. You sit there until your bowels move, because I'm not going to let you get back into bed and dirty that, too. Don't try it. Or I don't know what I'll do with you. Or you'll—if you fall, it's not going to be my fault. Because I told you to stay in bed. We all told you to stay in bed. What kind of a person are you? What kind of a person would do this?"

Emma figured Annette was perched on the toilet, agog at this onslaught, and she kept expecting Annette to stick up for herself, but the bathroom was quiet. Though she hadn't paid close attention, she had noted that the little redhead had retreated into the hall, out of sight for a bit, but now she was sneaking back. The scoutmaster had gone into the bathroom and was coming out with Annette, still scolding her. And Annette just took it, like a little lamb.

Emma thought she had to say something. "She couldn't help it. We did everything but call in the cavalry."

The nurse answered with a glare and squint as if she was surprised to find Emma in the room. But the threat was clear. Emma better hold her tongue, or she'd be next. The scoutmaster and the little redhead lifted Annette into bed and popped up the guardrails. Then the curtain moved to enclose Annette with the scoutmaster's fist on the rail like she might rip the whole thing apart. Annette started screaming as she disappeared. Just let loose a screech that turned into tears and blubbering. "I'm not staying in this goddamn bed. You can't do this. I'm going home. Or to my daughter's place. Get off me, darn you. You nasty shit. I'm going to my daughter's place on East Twenty-Third. She'll take me. She says I should stay with her."

Lord, thought Emma. Now it sounded like Annette had followed the scoutmaster nurse off the deep end. Her cussing shocked Emma, but at least she had a right, the way Emma saw it. Oh, she was so hurt. You could just hear it. The nurses might be trying to calm her down now, but they'd let loose a banshee. "I'm not sitting still for this kind of crap from anybody. I never took it all my life and I am not going to take it now. Not from the likes of you."

Emma could barely keep track, but she guessed the little nurse had run out and come back with other nurses and a big orderly. Some kind of struggle full of shadows and grunting was going on behind that curtain. Orders shouted, like parts of something once sensible that had exploded into jagged pieces flying every which way. "Her arm."

"Just grab her."

"What?"

"I don't know."

And Annette sobbing all the while. "You know what you can do, you son of a bitch. You assholes. You're all full of shit. All of you. You sons of bitches. I'm talking to you. You let me out of here, you bunch of goddamn stinkers."

"You're not going anyplace. You hear me?" The scoutmaster was still in charge. "You just settle down. We'll check on you in a minute, and if you have calmed down, we can remove those restraints."

Goodness, thought Emma. Restraints. The whole bunch of them, so clumped together, she couldn't be sure of the number trooping out, leaving the curtain shut around Annette, who wailed and sniffled, just heartbroken by the sound of her.

Emma was panting, too, her heart going full speed, as if she'd been battling to help Annette, the both of them in danger. If somebody had asked her, she couldn't have said whether she was more confused than alarmed. But the weeping and misery behind that curtain were just too awful to bear. She had to do something. "Now Annette. Calm down. It's over now." The blubbering came to an instant halt. "You can just go to sleep, why don't you." So far so good, Emma thought.

The secret space occupied by Annette filled with a kind of mystery. "Who the hell are you?" said Annette.

"What?"

"Who the hell are you? Shut up."

"I'm Emma. You know. It's me. Emma."

"I said, Who the hell are you? Damnit. Where'd you come from?"

"Well, I'm your roommate. We're in this room together."

"You're crazy. Who's your doctor?"

"What?"

"Do you have a doctor? Are you a doctor?"

"C'mon now, Annette. We won't pay any attention to that darn nurse from now on. You couldn't help what happened. Go to sleep now."

"Goddamn it." She was guttural, like a growling animal. "I asked you a question. If I asked you once, I asked you a thousand times—who the hell are you?"

"Emma. I told you."

"Are you a doctor?"

"What? No. I'm Emma. Emma."

"Do you have a doctor? It's a goddamn hospital."

"Yes. I have two doctors. My surgeon is McNamara, and my—"

"He's an asshole, that McNamara. I wouldn't let that rotten son of a bitch take care of my cat. He's a rotten son of a bitch. I hate them all, every one of the bastards. Because they're all bastards."

The scoutmaster nurse reappeared, only to vanish behind the curtain while the little redhead came up to Emma and said, "Hello, Mrs. Skayhill. Sorry for all this. So sorry. You need to get some rest now. Would you like a sleeping pill? You must be all worked up."

"What's happened to Annette? She was never like this before you. Two whole days we've been together. And she was so nice. Will she be all right?"

"Of course. But you need to sleep. Here." Both hands thrust into view, delivering a pill, which Emma accepted on her tongue, and a cup of water that Emma tilted and sipped to swallow. And then she was looking up into the eyes of the scoutmaster nurse, who smiled, and with ice in her eyes said, "Now go to sleep, Mrs. Skayhill."

"Okay."

They left. Annette wasn't making a sound. "Annette," Emma whispered. It was spooky how totally silent she was so all of a sudden. Emma wondered if they'd given her a shot of some kind, or just a pill like the one Emma had swallowed. Fearful that she'd made a mistake taking the darn thing, like a gullible dope, she worried that if she went to sleep, they'd come and do something even more awful to Annette, and maybe include Emma this time in whatever they were up to. I don't know what her husband does, she thought. What had Annette said? It seemed maybe lifesaving for her to remember. Annette really liked her daughter's mother-in-law. And the feeling was mutual, the two mothers-in-law both liking each other a whole bunch. We had so much to talk about, Emma thought. She was so nice.

The room was eerily still; no one else there. But something had happened. Emma was waking up. The door was opening and there was this huge, dark shape filling the doorframe, blotting out the light from the corridor. "Hello, Emma," said the figure, moving toward her, like a cloud or a shadow, gigantic-seeming and advancing. "I see you're awake. I'm Marianne."

She was a great big black lady. And Emma thought, Oh My God, what is happening to me? Am I dreaming or—? What is going on here?

The figure towered over her, smiling down with her eyes catching light, and she took Emma by the hand and found her pulse. Emma was sure there were no black nurses working at the hospital, but here was this one, doing like they do, finding Emma's pulse, taking her temperature, fitting that blood pressure cuff on her arm. She'd said her name was Marianne, and she was a little bit scary because she was awful black and awful big, and so strong. She could feel the strength in every little thing the woman did. She could just about pick Emma up out of the bed and go off with her, if she wanted, do anything she wanted to her.

"How are you doing, Emma? Sorry to bother you. But we need to make sure you're faring well, don't we? Through the whole night. And I'm the one here to see to it. And you are, Emma. In every department. You're doing fine. You go back to sleep now."

"All right. Thank you."

"See you in a little while."

"All right."

Marianne had an accent, her words oddly shaped clots put forth on a hint of singing. Emma had no idea where Marianne might be from, but she guessed somewhere nice. She must be the new night nurse those other ones had talked about. When asked about the new night nurse, the scoutmaster nurse had said: "Oh, believe me, she's not a blonde." Emma had missed their joke then, but she got it now.

She woke up because she heard so much going on, so many voices. She opened my eyes, almost talking in her sleep, "What's going on?" Blurry as heck, and like it was underwater, the hands on the wall clock looked like they were maybe ten after three. Nurses were huddled around Annette, who was whimpering in the littlest voice, though curses surfaced, like hot steam bubbling up in boiling water. "What's going on?" she repeated, and the nurses turned, all three of them, none of them Marianne, and none of them the scoutmaster, who of course wasn't there, who must have gone home by now. Thank goodness. Good riddance to bad rubbish. One of the nurses whom Emma recognized from somewhere, probably the hospital here, or maybe Eagles Market, approached and said, "Don't you worry. We've called her daughter to come. We just had to. She just wouldn't settle down."

"Oh," said Emma. She recalled a rumbling, quaking, storm-tossed presence in a dream. "Was there more? I was here for the first part."

"She just had this terrible reaction to her medication."

"I know. Is that what happened? It was terrible."

"It's good you were asleep, Emma."

"I didn't hear any more, I don't think."

"It's just as well."

"I was sleeping, I guess."

"And you should go back to sleep."

"How is she?"

"She'll be all right. We have the doctor coming soon."

"Oh. Good. Do you shop at Eagles?"

"What say?"

"For groceries. At Eagles Market. Do you?"

"Oh, sure."

This answer, as if it made everybody friends, smoothed out the jagged edges of whatever was going on. Emma dropped into the power of irresistible sleep, just slipped off the edge of the conversation, and didn't care. It was as if she was drugged. In fact, she had been drugged. I am drugged, she thought, surrendering to a force that inhaled her down into her mattress and through her mattress into some inky otherworld below the mattress, and on down past the bed, the floor, the other floors, the hospital basement, past everything to somewhere unknown where no one moved or spoke or thought, not even her.

When she bubbled back into the world, she was glad to find Annette quiet, and her daughters sitting with her, two of them anyway. Emma blinked, and because she wasn't hearing anything too much from over there, only the smallest whispering, she saw no reason not to let sleep have her again. The next time she looked, she couldn't focus. She peered groggily out of eyes barely able to get out from behind her leaden eyelids. It looked like Annette's whole family was over there, and Emma got scared. Is she gonna die? Is Annette gonna die? Is she dying? Or what is all this? "Oh, no," she said.

One of the daughters came gliding straight over. "Emma, dear, we are so sorry Mom made such as fuss as we heard about. It must have kept you awake half the night."

"Oh, that's okay. Is she going to be all right?"

"Well, I hope so. She better be. She was fine yesterday, wouldn't you say?"

"Oh, sure. But all of a sudden she didn't like anybody. I never saw anybody go off the beaten path the way she did from getting scolded." When the daughter, whose name Emma couldn't come up with at that instant, didn't react other than to squint and glance back at her sisters, like they might explain something, if she could get their attention, Emma said, "That's what it was from. That's what I think."

"What?"

"Your mom."

"Mom got scolded?"

"That's right. She got out of bed like she knew she shouldn't, but she had her call light on to get a nurse to help her, and nobody came. We both did—both had our lights on and nobody came. So she got up to go. Even though they'd laid down the law. But she had no choice. That's how I'd say it. Couldn't wait. Maybe she even waited too long, if you get right down to it. I think that's the truth of it, because this little bit came out of her. An accident, you know. And then this nurse who had to clean it up, well, she lit into your mom something fierce. The way you would a child. Just crazy and mean because she had to clean it up. But it wasn't a big mess—it was just where she dropped a little—and that goes with it, I'd say, being a nurse."

Listening had forged these big furrows in the daughter's brow, worry or surprise so extreme, she looked halfway cross-eyed. "That couldn't be," she said.

"What couldn't?"

"They're saying she was overmedicated."

"I don't know anything about that." With a wistful shake of her head, Emma added, "Annette just loves those little ones of yours. That Paul and Brandon. I hope they're all right. I keep thinking about them, and the way they marched up to shake my hand. I sure hope they don't have to see their grandma like this."

"They're my sister's kids. They're Grace and Hank's kids."

"Oh. Okay."

"Everybody's saying she was overmedicated. The nurses, and the doctor, too."

It occurred to Emma that maybe this daughter, who was

still close enough to touch, but somehow far off, too, didn't want to know about this nasty business with her mother getting treated that way; maybe none of them did. "How's she doing?"

"I think she's going to be all right. There are these other doctors who are going to come soon to check her out."

Darned if Emma didn't go to sleep again, and the next thing she knew, she was surprised to be waking up to the sight of Dr. Grennel coming in the door in what looked to her like early-morning light. She peered through eyes clouded over and blinking to focus, as he walked past the mob around Annette, the biggest gathering so far. He smiled. "How are you doing, Emma? Ready to go home?"

"I'd say so." She felt better, getting her glasses on so he looked like he was really there, sitting down on the foot of her bed.

"I like the way you're looking," he told her.

"Okay."

"Everything in the blood work was fine. The electrocardiogram was inconclusive, so we did the echo. There was a little something, but not anything definitive, if you know what I mean. Let me ask you a few questions."

"Okay."

"Would you say you've been feeling fatigued lately? Unduly fatigued?"

"I wouldn't say so. You mean more than normal? I'm tired, sure."

"But not so much you don't want to do things."

"How do you mean?"

"Well, things that you normally do, but somehow you don't want to."

"Oh, no. I'd say, no." All of a sudden Bud and Maggie and the plans to get the rent problem straightened out jumped into the forefront of her mind, and just thinking about all that made her ready to get up and go.

"Also, any swelling that you've noticed?"

"You mean in my feet. Ankles. Like that?"

"Any more than usual recently. That you've noticed."

"I always have a little. That's not what you mean."

He'd cleared away the blanket and sheets, and they both studied her feet, sticking up down there, her toes curled too much and a little crooked, the poor things battle-scarred as they were, callouses, bunions. "My toenails need a trim."

"That'd be surgery. Not my bailiwick. Should I let Dr. McNamara know?"

"No thanks."

"Getting up at night to go to the bathroom. How about that?"

"Well, sure. But not more than normal."

"No noticeable increase. No more often than you're used to?"

"I would have to say, no."

"All right then. But let me know if there are any changes. In any of these areas. Have you been able to sleep?"

"Oh, yeah. They gave me this pill."

He got jittery at that, looking at her like maybe there was more to her than met the eye, his glance skittering toward Annette, the four or five family members, and several doctors conferring quietly. "What's going on over there?"

"What?"

"Do you know what happened with her?"

It jolted her to have him ask. Shouldn't he know? He might as well have been turning into a scary stranger jumping at her from somewhere she'd always thought harmless, like her closet or a kitchen cabinet. Coming from him, the question felt dangerous. She couldn't say why it hit her the way it did, but she was scared. "I don't know. They gimme this pill, like I said, and it put me into the sleep of the dead. I kept waking up and sleeping and waking up. Didn't know where I was half the time. The sleep of the dead, let me tell you."

"What was it they gave you?" He glanced down at her chart, leaving her to think how maybe the smart thing was not to get any more involved in this mess than she already was. She could end up in over her head before she knew the first thing about what was really happening. As often as she was in this darn hospital, she could find herself at the mercy of these very same nurses, especially that scoutmaster one. She'd already tattled maybe too much, and if that nasty thing found out, she was the kind of person mean enough to want to get back at Emma.

"I think I ought to move you into another room," Grennel said, his attention fixed on the chart.

"No, I'm going home today. I don't need to move. I'll be okay." She didn't want to be disrupted. She just wanted to go home. But she also spoke from a sense of loyalty, not wanting to abandon Annette. Grennel might even be moving her out so she couldn't see any more of what went on here.

"There's a lot of commotion over there, as I think you know. That's not what I want for you right now."

Emma didn't know how to take his remark. She felt uneasy with him, with herself, her body, all those tests, and stabbed by guilt about Annette, who had her family to look out for her, while Emma was on her own. What came out of her felt like she was thinking on her feet, and slipping out a broken window but keeping clear of the sharp parts. "I really don't know for sure what happened. But they're a nice family. And she's a nice woman."

"Oh, I don't doubt that." He stood and shifted his shoulders to adjust his navy blue sport jacket, which had gotten crooked. He added a tug at the hem and used his palm to smooth his tie down his belly. "Anyhow," he said. On his way to the door, he tapped the elbow of one of the doctors attending Annette, a chunky freckled fellow, who then trailed Grennel into the hall.

Emma's throat filled up with tears, watching them go. It was like Dr. Grennel was her only hope, and she couldn't trust him. She just wanted out. She regretted having shot off her mouth to that one daughter and tried to remember all she'd said. But the fact of the matter was that the daughter hadn't seemed very interested. Like she didn't take any of it seriously. Like Emma was old and senile, and less than reliable, the way you couldn't count on a drunk. And maybe she was right. Emma had been halfway drunk in the night, drugged up the way she was on that pill.

It wasn't long before a wheelchair rolled in, some nurse she'd never seen before behind it. Where the heck were they getting them? Or was she forgetting half of the ones she met? She was just glad it wasn't that scoutmaster one walking in. It was scary to think that every time the door opened, it might be her, meaner than ever.

"Orders are to move you to where you'll get some rest," this one announced.

"Does Grennel know?"

"Of course he does. It's his orders."

"I thought he said he was letting me stay here. I'm getting discharged later on today, you know."

"Doctor's orders." She smiled and nodded, as a second nurse, this one vaguely familiar, came in. "Here comes Sally to help gather your stuff."

All of a sudden getting out of that hospital felt like the only thing that mattered. Better not to annoy these nurses the way Annette had annoyed that other one, she thought;

so she pointed out her belongings, which didn't amount to much, the clothes she'd arrived wearing, her earrings and wristwatch. These two were in one heck of a hurry, like they had to get out of there before a bomb went off, and they wheeled her past Annette, before she had her wits about her. She waved, and said, "Annette, they're moving me. So you won't be seeing me. I just wanted you to know."

"Who the hell are you?" Annette said. Her eyes looked way too big for her head and maybe getting bigger.

"I just thought—" Emma said. Well, there's no need. That was the thought that came next. She was already in the hall. No need to try. The one pushing her hadn't even paused. She felt dreary and dejected, gliding past all the other rooms on both sides of the corridor, some doors open, some shut, sick people in all of them, with who knew what happening to them.

Her new room was empty, both beds neatly made. She told them she'd like the window when they asked her preference. They explained that she would be discharged after lunch sometime, and asked her to fill out the lunch menu. She dozed a little, watching TV, until fear plucked her out of her dreams. She'd left something important behind, something irreplaceable, and though she knew it couldn't be Annette, the feeling declared that it was. She rang her call button. She kept envisioning Annette without her, all alone in that room in the night. At the thought of Marianne coming in the door, she wanted to tell Annette not to worry. She had the strangest desire to talk to Marianne. The actual thing she'd forgotten was the container to irrigate her colostomy. She was one hundred percent positive that she had told them to get it from the bathroom, but she didn't see it anywhere now.

The responding nurse said she'd run back to check, and if it was there, she'd bring it, but Emma said she wanted to go because she wanted to be sure. It was too important. She needed it. Truth be told, however, what she needed was to test the truth of the belief taking hold of her in which Annette was okay again, back to normal.

But there was no doubt that Annette, lying all crooked with her fingers curled on the bars of the guardrail, was still out of it.

"Annette, hi," Emma said, but nothing registered. She had no idea who Emma was. It was sickening to feel she might as well not even be there.

The nurse retrieved the missing container from the bathroom, and as they were leaving, Emma tried again. She couldn't help herself. "Bye, Annette."

"You can just shut up. Shut up."

One of the two daughters with her said, "Mom, you remember Emma."

"Emma? Yes, I do. I sure do."

"You like Emma."

"You bet. But why are you talking about her? It's that one there looking at me I don't like."

"Annette, I'm the same one that's been here," Emma said. "The same one I been."

"No, no. No, no." She had a look in her eye that said nobody was tricking her. She was smarter than all of them.

"Mom, c'mon. Who else would it be?"

"Emma was nice, darn it. That's not her. She's fooling you, but she can't fool me. You can't fool me, damn you," she said to Emma.

Back in her room, she felt so alone, staring at the empty bed near the door made up so neatly, like somebody had died. Like her roommate had died. There was no getting through to Annette, no matter what. Maybe she was never going to come back with her mind, and she had such a sharp little mind. Not

191

a little one. But a sharp one. Nothing little about it. Emma felt so bad. She started to cry. Couldn't keep from starting and couldn't stop. Just sobbing and shaking, another sick crazy old lady in a hospital bed, thinking over and over, What'd they do to that woman? What did they do to her? It was awful to think Annette would never be able to play with her grandkids again, or return to being a foster grandparent at that school, where all those poor kids were cast to the winds, and the parents, too, and Annette helped the little ones with their reading, or even with going to the bathroom if that's where help was needed.

Her lunch was a tasty enough slice of meatloaf in gravy, some mashed potatoes, peas, and cherry Jell-O. Already showered and packed up to go, she lay in her bed on top of the sheets and blankets, waiting for Maggie, who she had called to come get her, and who was on her way. But it was Grace, Annette's daughter, who came in when the door opened.

"Hi, Emma," she said. "I brought you some beans out of my garden. Like I promised."

"Oh, thanks." It was a nice little bundle in a baggie, all right, fresh picked for sure, bright in color.

"I wanted to get them to you before you left. Mom's settled down quite a bit now. But I have to find out what happened. The family has to find out what happened to her. And maybe you're the only one who can help, if you know what I mean."

"If I can help you, I will," Emma said. Darn, but she wished Maggie had come by sooner so she could have been out of here before this happened, as if she was a criminal in need of escape and Maggie was her getaway driver. Now she was in a pickle, caught between her wish to help Annette and her fear of the scoutmaster nurse.

"You told my sister about some nurse and scolding. So we're thinking we need a name. Is that right? She scolded Mom. See, we'd like that nurse's name."

"Oh, heck. I can't help you there. I don't know her name." Her relief felt honest and honorable, because it was true. She didn't know the name.

"We were hoping you did."

"I wish I did, too. But I don't. Nice-looking woman, if I try to describe her, maybe forty years old give or take. Kind of trim. And do you know what?" It came to her in a jolt of excitement right at that exact instant, a way out, the perfect solution. Why hadn't she thought of it before? "Here's the thing. I know for a fact that she had this other little one—like an assistant—a young nurse who was her kind of helper. She had red hair and was very pregnant, and she just kind of—she was young, see, and she kind of followed the other one's orders, and did what she said all the while everything was going on. She was right there. She heard the whole thing. So she's the one you want to talk to. She's gotta know the name of the one she was with. I don't know her name, either, but she was red-headed and pregnant, and on duty that night. She should be pretty easy to find, I would think."

FIVE

Of course, Maggie wanted to hang around and jabber after they'd landed back at the apartment. There was no way for Emma to tell her to go, after all she'd done, one favor after another, just being one heck of a good friend. So Emma boiled some water and fixed them two cups of instant coffee. It was good fortune that she'd shopped the day before she'd been hauled off to the hospital, so the milk hadn't gone bad. Maggie talked a little about Bud and the way Elroy and the others felt. Who'd said what recently. It sounded like there was a disagreement brewing about how to best go about getting what they needed from Bud, and Emma asked a couple of questions, but

Maggie couldn't seem to make the details clear. She was trying to get a meeting organized for the upcoming Wednesday evening in her apartment. Now that Emma was back home, she said she would push for it to happen. "Because times awasting." Then she went off on a golf tangent. Her putter had forsaken her, and she was about at her wit's end. She talked about the ninth hole and the seventh hole, a par three she'd messed up in a way that was unforgivable, so unforgivable she'd been about ready to just forget about golf. Give up on that one, and take up something else. And then she "sank a long putt." The sound of the ball dropping into the hole—the way she went on about it, it was like she was in love, some high school girl in love writing a poem about the ball, the hole, and the sound. Emma kept nodding, sipping coffee and making appreciative sounds when she thought she was supposed to, trying hard to be a good friend. Somewhere in the back of her mind, way back for sure, she was thinking that maybe golf was another of the wonderful things in life she'd missed out on. But all the while she ached to be alone in her little apartment, and when she finally was, she just sat in her chair with her empty cup held in both hands resting on her lap. She looked around at the photographs of her kids and grandkids, her own mom and dad, the desk her dad had made, the rug and empty chair where her dead husband had always sat when he was still with her. She was so glad to be home, her heart was beating fast. She could feel her heart inside her, thumping determinedly, just working away, glad to be home, too. She should probably call her kids to tell them what had happened. But then why call about that? They'd just worry. And the time to worry was past now. Why not just say hi. It didn't have be bad news every time. And maybe they'd call her. Wouldn't it be wonderful if one of them called her right now? Right this very next second, like they knew she was hoping to hear from them, and the ringing phone with them on the other end, her favorite voices in all the world, would bring proof of their special, lasting connection.

The next morning, crossing the parking lot on her way back from the drugstore in the little plaza across from the apartment building, she had her head down against the chill of the wind that had turned icy overnight. Late September had run out of days and October was pushing winter at them, the gray air hinting of clouds, sunless days, even snow. Bud's voice gave her a jolt, and she looked up into his round eyes deep in his round face. Headed in the opposite direction, he had paused to smile and look right at her. "Glad to see you're up and around, Emma."

"Oh, yeah," she said, wondering if he had any idea of what she and the others were plotting.

"I guess you had a rough go."

"Rough enough." He was utterly sincere as far as she could tell, and she felt treacherous, as if she was the one planning to cheat him when it was the other way around. She didn't even want to look at him. "How you been, Bud?"

"Okay. You know. Knock wood, right." He made a dopey face and then a fist, which he tapped on his skull.

"Cold enough for you?" she asked.

"Getting there. Okay, then. You take care." After a quick wave and a shrug, he went on. He had a dainty way of walking.

The front door key gave her trouble. It took her three tries before it fit. When she heard her phone ring, she still had to get into her apartment. Kind of panicky, she fumbled to get her key into the slot. Like she always did when the phone rang, she hoped it was one of her kids, and halfway believed it would be this time. "Hello."

"Hello," said the strong-voiced woman on the other end. "I'm calling from Saint Anthony's Hospital. I'd like to speak to

Emma Skayhill—the Emma Skayhill who was recently in our hospital. In Room 716. Is that possible?"

Halfway tempted to say they had the wrong number, and not answer if they called back, she said, "Yes. I am Emma Skayhill."

"Oh, good."

"How may I help you?"

"And you were in the hospital recently. I have the dates here. Let me see."

"I got out a day or so ago. Maybe yesterday."

"Wonderful. I'm wondering if you would answer some questions for me."

"Well," said Emma. "About what?"

"We're conducting an investigation into something and you might be of assistance." Now that word chilled Emma. She wanted no part of any "investigation," but didn't think she could come right out and say that, as the woman went on: "I am sure you know something happened in the room you were staying in. It's our feeling that if you answered a few questions, it would be very helpful."

"I don't know if I want to do that."

"It would be extremely helpful."

"I told one of the daughters all that I know."

"But I need you to tell me. To verify that what they say you said to them is in fact what you did say. It will go no further than my office. But we have to reprimand the nurse who's at fault, if what the family is telling us is true. And you're the only one who would know because you were the only one in that room besides the nurses."

"So that's what I'm saying. Ask them. Ask the nurses."

"We have. We have their accounts. And now we need yours."

"That little redhead. She's pregnant, that's the one I mean."

"Oh, we spoke to her all right."

"Good. Because I have to tell you, I don't ever want to be treated like that at your hospital or any other one. Because when you're sick, you're sick. You can't always control everything. Things a person has been in charge of all her life. That control just goes. It was unreasonable, the way she scolded that poor woman."

"What we understand to have happened, never should have happened, and we intend to make sure it never happens again."

"That's right. As you should. But I don't see what you need from me."

"As I hope I said, we're trying to be thorough, and according to the family, the way things unfolded is that Mrs. Olson got out of bed to go to the bathroom, even though she had been warned not to go on her own, and she had a little accident on the floor, and the nurse who cleaned it up scolded her badly. Way beyond anything that could ever be thought acceptable."

"Okay."

"Would you agree with that description of what happened?"

"Yes, I would. In a nutshell." She was losing ground, if she hoped to stay clear of this mess. Her footing was giving away. Like a fish that had taken the bait, she was getting hauled toward shore. If she didn't want to land in the dirt, she better bring this conversation to a halt. "Well, it sounds to me like you got the whole business sorted out."

"All right then. Good. That pretty much sums it up, and it's good to know you agree. We've put Marianne on suspension, but I wanted to be fair and felt it necessary to check with you and makes sure about the details."

Emma was frozen. Stopped in her tracks. "Could you tell me something? What'd you just say?"

"About what?"

Why the heck was she talking about Marianne? "Somebody is on suspension. Who's on suspension?"

"Marianne Jones. She's new here and—"

"Wait a minute now. The black lady. She's a black lady, right?"

"Yes, she is. And she's the one who the other nurses say is responsible."

Oh, boy, she thought. "Oh, boy," she said. "What was your name again? Did you tell me your name?"

"Pauline Steger."

"Okay. Because you should know, Mrs. Steger, that somebody's feeding you a line." Now she was stepping in it. Cow pie on one foot, and dog doo-doo on the other. "Because she had nothing to do with any of it."

"Who?"

"I don't know her name. I can describe her but I do not know her name." Emma had popped out of the water and come down on dry land, and there she was, squirming and flopping. So they'd all gotten together and cooked up a story to accuse the black one. "I have to tell you, it's really unfair to blame Marianne for what happened in that room. What I'm talking about. Because she did nothing wrong."

"Are you sure?"

"Yes, I am."

"I see."

"That's what I'm telling you." What the heck was this Pauline asking? As if Emma couldn't tell the difference between the white one who did it and the black one who didn't.

"Now, Mrs. Skayhill, I want you to know I am so very glad to hear you say this. Because I have to tell you—I'm the one who hired Marianne. She had good credentials. We've never had black help up here, and we should have. So I am glad to hear you say she took good care of you."

"It's just not true if the other nurses are saying she did it. Marianne did nothing. To either one of us. She was really nice."

"Well, we've got Marianne on suspension for thirty days, because this other nurse—Well, you see, we don't know who she is."

"What do you mean? Because that little—" About to say "pregnant redhead," she felt like a car screeching up to the edge of a cliff. Wait a minute. Something was fishy here. They could sure as heck find out who was on that shift, couldn't they? If they wanted to. What were they trying to pull? Was all this just because the one who did it said it was this Marianne, and the others went along with it? Annette would know—if she could know anything—that it couldn't be that big black one. That it was the other one. She was a pretty lady, so trim, and such a smart nurse, and good, too, up until she had to clean up that mess. How could she think she would get away with blaming a black lady—such a difference—my god, anybody could tell that it wasn't her. Unless the other nurses were scared. Unless the one who did it was so mean and spiteful and scary, they were all scared of her.

"You were on a lot of medication that night, weren't you?"

"I'm sorry. What?"

"According to your chart. Are you still taking it?"

"Taking what?"

"The medication you took that night."

"You mean that pill?"

"Yes. It was an opioid, you know."

"I don't." Emma looked to exit this phone call, which felt like a very small, uncomfortable room. How the heck had she gotten into it—just ran down the hall and broke in like a reckless fool.

"It's a very powerful sleeping pill."

"Well, okay. I took one. They gave it to me, and I took it. Like you're supposed to, isn't that right? Doctor's orders. You know, I have to get off the phone." She hadn't decided to blurt it out like that, but that was the way things went sometimes. She was in them before she knew what they were, like this little room where it was getting hard to breathe. "I just remembered something I have to do. I got carried away here talking."

"All right. You've been very helpful."

"Okay then."

"I may have to call you again. Would that be all right?"

"Sure. But I have to tell you I think I've told you about all there is to tell."

"I'll only call again if I absolutely have to."

"Okay. Suite yourself."

"Bye now. And thanks again."

Well, that's enough of that, she thought. She had more to do than worry about what went on over at that darn hospital. For one thing, she had her mail to bring in. Her plan to stop on her way back from the drugstore had been disrupted by the phone. That kind of bad behavior over at Saint Anthony's wasn't Emma's to straighten out, not at her age. Had everybody forgotten how old she was, for heaven's sake? That kind of mean stuff had been going on before she ever walked through the front door over there. It had been going on probably since before she was born, and it would go on long after she was in the grave. Since the beginning of time, probably. And what if there was a lawsuit of some kind? That was as likely as not these days, and there she'd be in the middle of it if she didn't watch her step. Those doctors had been swarming all over Annette. And the family would be well within their right to sue, finding out their mother was treated that way. Mad as hornets and with a good case. She wondered how Annette was doing, not that she had time to think of her. Maybe she was home and feeling better. Or at her daughter's place. Maybe a lawsuit was what that Pauline woman was getting ready for, like a spy nosing around to see what Emma knew. She worried she'd said too much. Well, she was done with it. Lawyers and testimony and what was that other thing they did to people? Dispositions. Sworn testimony. That was the last thing she needed. Some lawyer asking her mean questions and trying to trip her up. That wasn't what it was called. Not "dispositions," but something else. Well, whatever it was—no thank you. Thinking of Annette made her want to call over to somebody and see what was what. But she knew better.

A twist of her key opened her mailbox built into the wall, one for every tenant in the building just inside the front door. She had her electric bill, the cable bill, and the phone bill, too. It was that time of the month. A stack of the weekly flyers from Eagles Market with sales, specials, and coupons stood on the shelf under the mailboxes. She took the top one, and went back into her apartment, perusing the blaze of enticements that covered the front, inviting her to buy things. She stood, leafing through pages beside the kitchen table before moving on to settle at her desk under the painting her son had given her of an old man seated at a shiny table, his head bowed toward bread in a bowl, his hands clasped in prayer below his white beard. Her dad, "Grandpa Ed" as he came to be known, had made the desk from scratch. Nothing to start with but nails, glue, determination, and ingenuity. He'd cherished it all his life and passed it on to her rather than to one of her brothers, or her sister, surprising the heck out of all of them, Emma especially. Recalling that moment and the mystery of it, the way he looked up from his sickbed and told them all that he wanted Emma to have his desk, she nodded her approval for his handiwork accomplished those years gone by. He was a stickler for details, and skilled in any number of ways. The stained wood finish still shone under the glass panel she used to protect the surface from spills and whatnot. Every kind of wear and tear over the years. The glass was rectangular like the desktop, but a smidge smaller along all four edges, which was good, because if it stuck out, it could catch on something, or break easily. She retrieved her checkbook from the top-right-hand drawer, along with the letter opener with CHICAGO imprinted on the handle. Charlie had brought it back when he'd gone to a ballgame with his brother in Chicago. Though the task before her meant money going out, she was glad to do it—to be able to do it. Neatly slicing open the envelopes, peering at the official document inside, each bearing her name and address, made her feel she was part of the world. She was doing something, using things, and people knew of her activities and were holding her accountable. The dollars demanded by the electric, the phone and cable companies, all tabulated to the last penny testified to her participation in the routines of day-to-day life in a way not much else did. She wrote out the three checks, fit them into the envelopes provided, and sealed them with a sense of accomplishment.

Dusk had gathered outside, dimming the air around her. She and her desk with the friendly lamp shining down on her hands were alone in the darkening rooms. She stood carefully, her joints all but creaking. She started toward the door where she would step out into the hall to put the envelopes with her bills in her mailbox, so the postman could pick them up the next day. But then she felt like walking to the big mailbox on the corner of the plaza.

A glance out the window warned of a chill now that the sun was more or less worn out. A few bloody bands struggled through gaps between the houses and office buildings that mingled on the high ground along Tanner Boulevard. Lights burned in dozens of windows.

When she stepped out in her spring coat, she wished she'd taken the time to dig out the thicker one meant for winter. But at least there were gloves in the pockets. Nothing wrong with a brisk walk in the sharp air. With the wide mouth of the mailbox pulled open, she reached for the envelopes, but they weren't where she'd put them. She groaned and scolded herself for having forgotten them on the desk, but then they turned up in the opposite pocket.

A large figure, bundled up with their head bowed down, sped toward her on the sidewalk that ran parallel to Bergen Avenue. Whoever they were, storming on heedlessly, they alarmed her enough to move out of their way. With someone paying no attention to where they were going, you never knew what they might find offensive. But then she recognized Elroy. He had a stocking cap pulled down over his ears, big mittens on his hands, a scarf around his neck, and the collar pulled up on the padded coat that went down to his knees.

"Elroy," she said. "Hello." It seemed wrong and rude not to offer a greeting. He glanced at her out of narrow eyes, stomping past without a word. He looked furious, she thought. "It's Emma. From downstairs," she called, instantly regretting that she hadn't just let him go, as maybe ten yards on, he turned to study her. He found her threatening, even as his mouth worked oddly to form what she knew he intended as a smile. "Emma. I see you there. I didn't know that was you. But it is. How do you do. I'm getting some exercise."

With that, his big legs and big feet hauled him on down the hill. "I was a farmer," he called to her, walking backward now. "I had two hundred and nineteen acres. I worked morning to night. Sunup to sundown. Drank a lot of water. Good, fresh water morning, noon, and night. Sunup to sundown. I was active, you know. I need to stay active. I was active with tractors and harrows. Corn as far as you could see. As far as anybody could see." Still on the move and farther away, his voice had thinned as wind came up, making him sound weak and almost pitiful.

"That's a good life. You had the good life."

"Okay," he said, and went on.

SIX

Well, there'd been plenty of warning that the meeting at Maggie's might not go smoothly, Emma thought, watching Elroy stand up and sit down. She glanced at Connie in hope of an explanation, but Connie only smiled, nodding affectionately, as if her husband was a puppy given over to some animal necessity that would pass or turn into a clever trick. The fact of the matter was that weirdness and inconvenience had been all too prominent in the run-up to their get-together, with Elroy insisting that the time get changed from evening Wednesday to midmorning Thursday. It didn't make a lot of sense, but Clara Luzman, who was the only one with a conflict—a dental appointment for a cleaning—willingly canceled. Then Elroy wanted a time limit. They would start at ten thirty sharp and go no more than forty-five minutes. But they should aspire to a half an hour. That's what he was going to aspire to and they all should aspire to the same thing.

Maggie had readied a pot of coffee, and set out a plate of Oreo cookies, along with bowls of M&M's, peanuts, and Goldfish. Elroy grabbed and gobbled a handful of peanuts, before attacking the Goldfish. There was a moment when he actually clutched peanuts in one hand and Goldfish in the other, debris from each of them squeezing from between his fingers and falling to the floor. May and Clara fussed with their coffee, tittering over whether to add milk, or to use sugar or Equal, while sending quizzical looks back and forth to share their chagrin at Elroy's behavior. When Emma leaned over the coffee table to take a few M&M's, Connie, who was seated opposite her, did the same, creating an instant of clumsy proximity that prompted her to say, "You go ahead there, Emma. Age before beauty."

Emma smiled. "Don't mind if I do." She swore she smelled liquor on Connie's breath. What the heck was going on?

"All right now," Maggie said, as if the fact that they were in her apartment empowered her to move things along. "As I told Emma the other day: 'Time's awasting.'"

"That's right." Elroy stood up. He brushed at his lap so crumbs and a fine dust of yellow spilled onto Maggie's rug. "We've done nothing of value."

"I was referring to the overall issue," said Maggie in a defensive tone. "Not just the here and now."

"That's a joke," said Elroy.

"What is?"

"The here and now."

"Well, I'm enjoying my snack," May said. "Especially my Oreo."

"You think it's a laughing matter," Elroy grumbled. He looked wounded. "But it's not. At least not to me."

"I'm not laughing, either, Elroy. But I am enjoying my Oreo."

"There goes another minute," he said.

"All I know is that I ran into Bud on the street the other day," Emma said, "and I felt like a criminal." She hoped to bring practical matters to the forefront while also giving a nod to decency. "Hiding what we're up to. I don't like it. It's not my way. And so the sooner we get this out in the open, the better."

"We know what we want," Maggie said. "We know what

we need to say." Her glance around the table found nods and murmured agreement. "And so what remains is to decide on who goes to him and when they do it."

"The hell with the bunch of you," Elroy said. "Damnit, damnit. Goddamnit."

"Elroy, please." Connie's hands were up to her mouth, as if she was the one who'd misspoken.

"Don't what?" He was on his way to the door.

"What happened?" said Clara. She appeared mainly to ask May, though anyone would do.

While May answered with wide eyes and a dramatic shrug, Maggie said, "Elroy. Now, now."

"Now, now what?' I'm going over there. Yes, I am. I'm sick of this pussyfooting around. This is man business. I'll face him and tell him, the sonofabitch. I'll bang on his door and kick it in if I have to. Do you hear me, the bunch of you?" He eyed them with a dismayed frown that left no question about how small and worthless they were in his eyes. "Hens," he said. "I'm done hanging around in the henhouse waiting for the god-damn hens to tell me what to do. I'll tell him what we want. 'You son of a bitch, you give us what is rightfully ours. You're a sonofabitch, Bud Smith.' I'll tell him to his face, and if he talks back, I'll punch him square in the mush. And if he punches back, so be it. We'll fight to the death. And if he kills me, so be it. That's what you hens don't understand and you never goddamn will. Being a man means you fight. You fight to the death. You kill and die, and there's no two ways about it."

His big hand swooped into the Goldfish, jamming the tiny yellow bodies into his mouth as he plopped down on the couch, chewing grimly and surprising them all that he was still in the room. He coughed crumbs and spittle into the air. He gulped some coffee. He took up another handful of peanuts and then more Goldfish. He stood and started for the door.

"Come, Connie. We're going." He left the door open for his wife to follow. She glanced back at them and molded her right hand into the idea of a telephone that she raised to her ear, signaling that she would talk to them later.

"He's not going to do that to Bud, is he?" said Clara.

Connie shook her head "no," but her eyes were squeezed shut, like she could not bear to look at something zooming toward her.

"Is he drunk?" Emma wanted to know.

"Oh, no." She repeated both her telephone gesture and her headshake before disappearing behind the closing door.

It was May who spoke first. "One for the ages, all right. I'd love it if somebody could tell me what the heck he was doing."

"You know what I think," Clara told her.

"Well, sure. Clodhopper. But maybe off his rocker, too."

"Born in a barn. You know."

"I think he was drinking," said Emma. "I saw him on the street a couple nights ago and he was like that."

"What street?"

"Just out here by the mailbox."

"And he was acting drunk?"

"No. But odd. You know. It struck me."

"She said he wasn't drinking." Clara pondered other possibilities that seemed to lurk in her coffee.

"Well, I'll tell you one thing. She was drinking," Maggie said.

"Do you think so?"

"I don't think. I know. I smelled it on her."

"Did you?" Emma asked. "Because I did, too."

"Who could blame her?" May wanted to know. "Married to the likes of him."

"He was probably drinking, too, then. If she was."

"Maybe not."

"Poor Connie." May emphasized her sympathy for Connie with a sad clicking. "She's got a tough row to hoe with that one."

"Fifty years they've been married. Actually more than fifty."

"Is that right?"

"That's what she told me."

This fact shoved them all into reflection. In the developing silence, Emma sensed her companions depart one by one into this or that memory, while she felt the weight of time, or something, with her husband inside it.

"Let me freshen everybody's coffee," Maggie said. "I could make another pot."

"No, no," they all agreed.

"I don't know where this leaves us with the whole Bud thing," Emma wondered.

"I'm halfway ready to give up," said Clara.

"Oh, no you don't," Maggie said. "You'll do that over my dead body."

"But maybe the young people deserve a break. That's all I'm saying. And we've been paying the rent he charges for a long time. It's what we agreed to."

"Well, I'm one who could use that extra few dollars," Emma said. "And I'm not too proud to say it. Every month? You bet."

"We all could. But it's the principle of the thing, too." Maggie slipped into that tone she used sometimes, which the way Emma saw it was better suited to a soapbox. "There's nothing wrong with talking to him. We have every right."

Clara looked at May, who appeared permanently distracted. Of all of them, she'd lost her husband most recently. "You all right there, May?"

"Oh, yeah."

"Here's what I think?" Maggie told them. "The first order

of business is not to get too overwrought here because of the way Elroy acted. Just take a little time until we find out what's going on, and how to deal with him."

"And how the heck do we do that, pray tell?" Clara struck Emma as snide and dismissive, probably responding to Maggie being up on her high horse. The two of them could get that way. "The man is not exactly easy to talk to. He's a kind of mystery man and the mystery is that he's a kind of large farm animal."

"You and your sharp tongue. That's going a little far, don't you think," said Maggie.

"No."

"Remind me to stay on your good side."

"You really don't like him," said Emma.

"Well, at least you're paying attention."

Okay, so now she was going to start snipping at everyone. Emma decided that Clara's negative mood came from the fact that no one else, not even May, had agreed with her about surrendering. "I think if we want to find out, we see what Connie has to say about it. It looks like she wants to talk. I mean, she made that gesture about the telephone."

"True," said Maggie. "We can follow up on that."

"I still say we need a backup plan." Clara sounded insulted, like she'd proposed this idea a while back but no one had paid any attention. "I like alternative plans. It's always good to have one."

"Not quitting, though," Maggie said, eyeing her. "That can't be it."

"That wasn't what I was going to say. What I was going to say was that we get down to it. Move it along, so we can figure out who will be the ones talking to Bud, if Elroy's not part of it. And I have to say—I want to go on record that I don't think he should be part of it under any circumstances. No matter what. He's liable to do anything. Go off half-cocked and we'd be responsible."

"So who do you see as the ones who talk to him in this backup plan of yours?" Maggie asked, not even trying to hide her suspicion.

"Don't worry. Not me. I don't want to do it. I just want to get this over with one way or the other."

"That's what I said a bit ago," Emma reminded her. "Right at the start."

"So at least we agree on that. I think it should be Maggie, for one, because she's certain about what she wants. And you, Emma, too, because you more or less agree with Maggie on everything."

"Okay by me," said Maggie. "Emma? What do you say? I think we'd be a good team."

"Okay. Sure."

"And we need to set a timetable, too. So it just doesn't drag on. It has to be done by next Saturday." Clara certainly thought she was laying down the law.

"Okay."

"Wait. This coming Saturday? Today is Thursday, remember," Emma reminded them. "That puts it right on top of us."

"I see your point. So the next one. A week from this coming Saturday."

"Okay."

"At the very latest."

"Okay."

"Okay."

SEVEN

Emma was supposed to go with Maggie to an afternoon card game over at May's, whose building at the far end of the complex was in a really nice spot in the sense that it was the farthest from any of the heavily traveled roads nearby. Emma had always kind of envied May that location, but whenever she thought of it recently, no matter what the occasion, she was dogged by a flickering impression of the hearse parked outside waiting to take Ed, May's husband, off to the funeral home. He'd keeled over while looking for the Scotch tape less than a year ago. The dispenser wasn't in the drawer where he knew he'd last put it, and he was storming around. At least that's how May told it. Today's card game had been scheduled for her cozy little place, still kind of haunted in Emma's mind, because everybody thought it would be good for May to take on the responsibility, maybe lift her spirits to act the hostess. Bring some life inside those four walls where she sat alone too much.

But as the time grew close, and noon went by, Emma felt a strong urge to stay put. Maybe she was coming down with something, or maybe she'd been pushing too hard. She could do that. When she spoke to Maggie, she tried not to make a fuss. "I apologize and I hope I'm not hanging you up, but I am bushed. My get up and go, got up and went. So I think I'm going to just stay home and go to bed early."

"Are you sure? A little fun might do you some good."

"True enough."

"You might win a little money, too. Ever think of that?"

"Oh, sure. From all the high rollers. I've been through a lot lately, as you know better than anybody, all the ways you helped me, giving up your golf game and all. But maybe it's the smart thing to take it easy."

"Nothing all that hard about playing cards, Emma."

"You know what I mean."

"Sure. You're all right, though. Nothing more than just tired."

"That's it. Have fun without me." The relief she felt hang-

211

ing up left no doubt she'd made the right decision. Doing nothing seemed just what the doctor ordered.

The late-afternoon sky had clouded over, nondescript ruffles shifting about, unable to understand what they exactly wanted to be or to do with themselves. A bird came flying right at her, going to crash into the window for sure, this crazed robin it looked like, and she waved her arms to warn it away. The darn thing turned on a dime, like an acrobat, veering off to the left out of view, nothing but a blur. She'd missed Douglas Wenke on the radio with the obituaries at noon, she realized. Something about the bird had reminded her. She hadn't heard him yesterday, either, or the day before, a failure that she worried might become a habit, given the way her routines had been disrupted. Tomorrow she'd make certain, and she scribbled a note to make sure. The evening paper would come soon, and when it did, she could use it to catch up on who'd sailed off. She felt neglectful somehow, and the column of news print with names and descriptions would maybe lessen her guilt.

For a while she ricocheted from one disappointing TV show to the next, until she gave up thinking she could find anything she liked, and just stopped where she was, this big close-up of Maury Povich smirking at a pair of overweight black women with colored hair, purple and green on one, yellow stripes on the other. A mother and daughter, it turned out, who were trying to nail down whether or not the daughter's boyfriend, who was seated kind of crouched in a chair, was the father of her child. The boy in question was kind of a frail-looking, and Emma couldn't tell if he was right there with them or off somewhere behind the scene. The picture only showed him alone. and Emma couldn't help but think of Marianne, who had been so quiet and caring, and unlike these two, who shrieked and shouted, and wailed, too, when the DNA test said the boyfriend was not the father. He was a slim, nice-looking fellow, well dressed in a regular gray suit, and he ran down the aisle to celebrate the news, waving his arms like he'd just won a game. It must be awful for someone like Marianne to be associated with this kind of behavior the way Emma was associating her, though thinking about Marianne made her wonder about where this poor mother and daughter had gone off the track. She felt bad, especially for the little boy, who looked so worried. The women were enormous and their hair looked like somebody dumped paint on it. The daughter had been sleeping with so many men, she didn't know who was the father. Maybe this one. Maybe that one. And there she was going on television to talk about it. What went on in their heads to get them to do that? But then people did crazy things. Emma figured she'd done pretty well with her life, but there were girls she'd known when she was young, and some older, too, who fell apart. They seemed to have everything anybody could want, husbands and kids, and then they lost their way with boys and men, drinking, divorce, and that kind of stuff. Maury Povich might smirk, but it was just a crying shame. It was pitiful the way that daughter just shook when she sobbed, and she was pretty, too. The heck with Maury Povich. She felt like smirking at him and his stupid show. He could smirk all he wanted, but he'd have to do it without her, because she was turning the channel. She passed through cop shows, comedy reruns, some movie that looked familiar, feeling almost dizzy, and hungry, too, she realized, as she shut the whole mess off.

She knew she should eat better than she intended to, but she couldn't be bothered. Getting butter and jelly on toast was about all she could handle. Later on, she might try something else. Maybe soft-boil some eggs.

She went on then to get quite a bit done, cleaning out her colostomy bag and making herself comfortable in her night-gown and robe after a nice shower. But darn if she didn't end

213

up back in front of the blank TV screen, as if she might turn the fool thing back on. She put one aching foot on top of the other, and pressed down hard, rubbing the arch, thinking about something she'd heard on TALKNET the other night, this man with a soothing, strange accent speaking about "emptying the mind" as a way to relax. The idea made little or no sense though the result he described sounded worthwhile. Not the empty mind part, but the peacefulness that he claimed could come.

When she looked up and saw the time, and the gray hours coming on outside her window, she had to wonder where the day went. Same place as all the others, she thought. It was like Douglas Wenke spoke to her. His deep announcer's voice almost scolding as he told her she better remember to listen to him at noon tomorrow. To read the obituaries in the paper wasn't as respectful as the sound of him naming them in that reverent way he had, one little person after another in a kind of roll call. She peeked out the apartment door, thinking the paper should be waiting on the vestibule floor. When it wasn't, she stuck her head out the front door, hoping to see the kid who delivered them on his way, but he was nowhere in sight. Yesterday's edition lay folded on the couch, and she thought about looking it over, even though she remembered only strangers being listed. A few familiar last names, along with that famous rock and roll singer whose name she couldn't come up with just now, dead in a car crash.

The phone rang twice and stopped, done with her before she could budge let alone decide whether to answer or not. Still, she was on her feet, as if the ringing might come again and the phone in its cradle was shy and flighty like a bird or squirrel she had to pounce on before it fled. The light rapping on the door behind her confused her. What the heck? But then she picked up Maggie's voice on the other side. "Emma, are you up?" She was close to whispering.

"Maggie?"

"Oh, you're up. Good."

Emma found Maggie standing in the hall. She had a worn, secretive quality, one Emma associated more with her own unsteady moods than with those of Maggie. "What's going on? Did something happen?"

"Can you come over? Connie came down to talk as soon as Elroy fell asleep. It's not even eight and he's sleeping, and she came as soon as he was out. She slipped me a note at the card game to see if coming to talk tonight might be okay. Can you come over?"

"A note?"

"Yes."

"Why a note?"

"I don't know. She just did." Maggie backed away.

"Let me get my slippers on."

"Come as you are. No need to dress."

"I'm barefoot. I'll be right there."

"Just hurry."

"I'll be right there, Maggie. I'd like my slippers. You're acting funny, you know, like it's some kind of an emergency. My phone rang before but no one was there."

"I know. That was me. I hung up and came across to knock instead. And I have to tell you it is kind of an emergency. Connie's all shook up. So please don't dillydally. She doesn't want Elroy to wake up and find her gone. I'll leave my door open."

Connie sat on the couch, and she looked worse for wear; that was for sure. She sipped from a beer bottle, and when Emma stared at it, if only for an instant, Connie made her plea with a shrug. "It soothes me."

"Sure. I have one every now and then. Or I used to."

"Here's the thing." Connie rolled the bottle between her palms, and peered down, as if she were trying to see into the opening. "You and Maggie have to be the ones to talk to Bud. Elroy can't do it. There's no waiting to see how he's doing. He's not doing well. Good days and bad days. But it's the bad days are piling up. I hate sayin' it, but he can't handle it. All of a sudden he starts talkin' about marching over to see Bud and getting the whole thing over with. You saw him the other morning. But that's not the half of it. I have to tell you, he can get scary. If Bud wants to have it out with him, well, Elroy says he's ready. Murder if he has to. And then—and it makes me sick to say this, but I gotta before this whole thing gets out of hand—he starts to cry. Bud's going to beat the crap out of him. Can you imagine? Bud couldn't beat the crap out of you, Maggie. Or you, Emma. But something is happening to my Elroy. I wish we'd just stop the whole thing about the rent. I wish it'd never got started. I know Clara said the same thing after we'd gone the other morning. May told me, and I'm for it. But it's not the whole thing. I think it's the dementia, you know, coming on. And this is just one thing. Bud and all, but if not this, well, something else. The doctor has said that it's coming, but it looks to me like it's way past coming on. It's here. Elroy's dad had it. Took him by storm. And his older brother, Earl; he has it bad right now. Took him, too. Just wiped him away, the way a tornado knocks away a house or a whole little town. I saw that, you know. Over in Manorville, where I grew up. Half the town gone in a blink. I never forgot it. And it's here for Elroy. So he can't be involved more in any of this rent business. The other night he got out of bed and I didn't know it. But I woke up to go to the bathroom, and I found him in the living room, crouched down by the window, peeping out. Had the shade pulled down, and when I asked him what he was doing—didn't he want to sleep—wasn't he tired? Well, he said he was making sure Bud didn't sneak up on him. We got to skip it. Or forget about it. Then maybe he can forget about it. Or you two go and do it, but hurry up about it. Okay?" She put the beer to her mouth and leaned back, tilting the bottle almost straight up and down, trying for the last little drop.

Lord, Emma thought. She'd never heard the woman say more than two words at a time in all the years she knew her.

Connie placed the nozzle at a point below her mouth, and pursing her lips like she might whistle, she blew, producing a hollow sound. "So that's pretty much all I came to say."

Maggie nodded. "Okay. And it's a lot. And it's good you did it. But you better go, don't you think? I don't mean to rush you, but you said you don't want him to wake up alone."

"No, I don't." She got up and took a little step and then a big step, like walking was new to her. At the door, she said, "Sorry," without bothering to look back, like she didn't care whether they heard her or not.

"Hardly your fault now, is it, Connie."

"We don't mean to let you all down." She went, closing the door.

Emma and Maggie sat for a while, perfectly quiet except for their breathing, and a heavy sense of being burdened, almost buried under the news, at least as Emma felt it. Dementia. Poor Elroy. Then Maggie got up. It looked like she was going to walk into the wall. But she reached around the corner and dragged out this funny-looking suitcase, which Emma recognized as a golf bag because it had golf clubs sticking out. "It helps me think," Maggie said.

"Okay." She watched Maggie, who did seem thoughtful. "What helps you?"

Maggie took out one of the clubs and then, unzipping a

neat little pocket on the side, showed two white balls in the palm of her hand. "Putting." From somewhere around the same corner, she withdrew a kind of green plastic saucer. "We got to figure out what we want to do?"

"Yes, we do."

"It's all coming to a head." Maggie went all the way across the room, where she placed the saucer thing down on the rug before returning close to where Emma sat. Maggie zipped the pocket shut on the colorful bag. It was mostly plaid interrupted by bands of leather running up and down and circling above and below the pocket. It had neat little legs that kept it upright.

"You ever had dementia in your mom or dad, Maggie?" Emma asked.

"Nope. Both sharp as a tack, right up to the end. Dad especially." Maggie placed a ball on the rug, and holding the club she'd chosen in both hands, she set a square, kind of hammer part behind the ball. She kind of crouched over and twisted, and she kept looking straight down at the ball and then up and over at the saucer thing.

"Don't that hurt your back?" Emma wondered.

"I'm putting." She moved the club back a couple of inches, and then gave the ball a kind of shove. Off it went, after the tiniest click, gliding over the rug toward the saucer thing, but sliding past on the right, and bouncing off the wall. Maggie groaned and straightened up, looking glum. "This rug is fast, you know. Real greens are never this fast, so it's hard to know the speed. It's the worst part of my game. Putting. Just breaks my heart. Because it's so important."

"Was that click the one you mentioned a while back, the one you love so much?"

"What?"

"When you hit it. That click. Remember you told me?"

"Oh, no. Did I tell you about that?"

"Yes, you did. Something."

"Well, that's not it. The one I love to hear is only on the course. You have to be on a real course and then there's this sound when the ball drops into the hole. It's a really wonderful sound, but you have to be on the course." She set a second ball down pretty much where the first one had been, and she crouched all crooked again. "Would you stand behind me, Emma?"

"What? Sure. What for?" She figured that standing behind a person meant pretty much the same thing in golf that it did in the rest of life, so she moved accordingly.

"You can help me aim."

"How the heck am I going to do that? I don't know the first thing about it, Maggie."

"My alignments and all. Anyway, you can do it. Putting is more strokes than anything when you keep score. Every hole gives you two putts. So, if par is seventy-two, say, you can figure thirty-five or thirty-six are putts, and that's when you shoot a perfect round. That's how important it is."

"Sounds important all right."

"It is."

"How's this? Am I about where you want me here?" She stood pretty much with her back to the door, and something in the perspective brought back her grandkids playing miniature golf. "Wait a minute. Is it like miniature golf?"

"This part. Kind of." She raised and presented the club she was holding, pointing to the hammer-like silvery end. "See the flat part here? When I put it down behind the ball, I want you to make sure it's aimed at the hole over there."

"Why don't you do it?"

"I am. But you can do it better. I'm on the side of the line, and you can look from the back the way caddies do, and tell me. Think like if you ran a thread through the head of the club, and through the ball over to the hole, and then ask yourself—would it be straight?"

"Okay." She eyed the ball, the club, the imaginary thread, and the cup thing. Darned if she wasn't having fun. I'm playing golf, she thought.

"Anyway, the way I see it, we'd be a good team to go and do it." Maggie used a tilt of her head to peek back. "I mean Bud. Going to see Bud. I'm game if you are. I'm feeling stubborn about it. I have to tell you, I don't want to quit."

"I could say the same thing. It's not a lot of money, but there's the principle of the thing, too."

"Month by month. Year after year. Like you said the other day—it adds up."

"You know, if you went ahead and gave it a push just now, I think it would need to make a pretty sharp left-hand turn to get to the hole thing."

"Okay. See that's why this is good. It's helpful, because it looks good to me." She adjusted the hammer part carefully, and then kind of bounced on her feet, wiggling her rear end. "How about now?"

"Okay, I think. I'd say okay. But don't blame me if it don't work out."

They kept at it for another half an hour, stopping to share a Diet Coke, and then practicing a bit more with Maggie getting better and better at making the ball roll into the hole thing. Emma felt flattered to have Maggie trust her this way, and even more flattered that Maggie had remembered her remark about the money adding up. But then Maggie got it in her mind that Emma should try a couple pokes, and home started looking pretty good. "Thanks, but no thanks," Emma said.

EIGHT

With her apartment located directly across from Maggie's, she was halfway in the door before she stopped to grab up her newspaper she'd been so all-fired to have. She couldn't remember if she'd picked up her mail, so she double-checked and was rewarded with nothing worth the trouble. Mostly junk, flyers and advertisements for this and that. Waste of paper. But then the very last letter startled her with a return address of Saint Anthony's Hospital. The envelope didn't have the appearance of a bill, so she suspected it might be from that woman who'd questioned her. She hoped not and, opening it warily, found neither a bill nor anything from Pauline Steger, but a form letter and a questionnaire. To her utter amazement, the hospital wanted her to report on her recent stay. How did she feel about it all? How was she treated? Would she rate the nurses? Rate the room? The food? On and on. She was flabbergasted. Didn't they know what had happened? Didn't the left hand know what the right was doing up there? Furious at this display of gall and ignorance, she folded the pages, jammed them into the envelope, and tore the whole thing in half. She'd be darned if she was going put herself through that. Force herself to remember just to help them out with their dumb questions. She clumped the two halves of the envelope together and ripped it into quarters. She kept at it, shredding the pieces she had into darn near confetti before dropping everything into the trash can. Where it belonged. Because she hadn't been treated right, and if they didn't know that by now, she didn't think it was her job to tell them.

She couldn't believe it when the phone started ringing. Crazy as it seemed, her first thought was that the hospital knew that she'd just destroyed their property. Who would call her this time of night? She stared at the handset, both annoyed

221

and scared. The darn fools could ring all they wanted. Of course, it wasn't really all that late for most people. Nine thirty was all. It was just that she was tired. The caller was as likely a wrong number as anything. Or maybe it was Connie upstairs. Right over her head. She looked at the ceiling, listening for signs of life. Connie and Elroy were up there doing something. After what seemed an eternity, the badgering and the mystery of who was so insistent got to her and ready for the worst she answered and Bethany said. "There you are, Mom. Just wanted to say 'hi.'"

"Bethany! Oh, thank goodness. Oh, I almost didn't answer."

"It started to scare me when it took so long. Why didn't you?"

"Oh, I don't know."

"Were you in bed?"

"I was headed for it."

"Me, too, but I just thought, 'Heck, I think I'll call Mom.' No special reason."

"What a treat. That's the best. A call like that. I just love it when you or Sam call out of the blue. Everything all right?"

"Oh, yeah. How about you?"

"Good. How are you and Ronnie?"

"We're good. Weather's a bit colder out here, though. What's it like where you are?"

"Same."

"We had a little frost the other night."

"Did you now?"

"Woke up and there it was. Kind of pretty. It melted fast."

"Weather here has started to turn. But the way it goes these days, it could just as well turn back. Never quite know what to expect with the darn stuff these days."

"That's the truth. I'm glad to hear you're doing okay."

"Oh, sure. Except I was in the hospital for a couple days."

"What?"

That's how it started; just popped out of her, like somebody else had jumped on with them, the way it could happen in the old days when telephones were all party lines and you never knew who might listen in, or might speak up next. "Just for a couple days."

"What for?" Bethany sounded pained. "Are you okay?"

"I'm fine. Don't worry. I don't want to worry you. It was just those darn cramps, you know. Misery the whole night long. I had to ask Maggie to take me up to the hospital in the morning, and she did it wearing a golf outfit. Can you imagine? She was about ready to go play when I called. Dropped everything to give me a hand." Off and running, she told about meeting Annette, and the way the two of them hit it off first thing, the fun they had, how nice she was, and then she plowed on into the nurse and the night, and ran headlong into how Annette got mistreated so awful. By the time she'd finished, Bethany was fuming.

"Boy, if that had been you, I would have been out there on the first flight, Mom."

"I know you would have, honey. But it's over now. I hope it's okay that I told you."

"Of course. It's terrible, though. To treat an old lady like that. Why would they do that?"

"That's the sixty-four-thousand-dollar question, if you ask me, because it wasn't her fault it even happened with that light business and them not coming. Either they need more help up there, or they should teach them to be a little more patient when you make a mistake with that kind of stuff." She paused and might not have gone on had she not felt the heat and power of Bethany's concern radiating through the telephone all the way from Connecticut. Each and every detail she'd already told screamed out that it was linked to the rest of what happened, and so with the weight of everything wanting to be spoken pushing from behind, while the events she'd already described pulled her forward, she went on, first to Bethany, and then later on to Sam. Not wanting him to feel left out, she phoned him the instant she hung up with Bethany, and to her surprise he picked up, saving her from the ordeal of talking to his answering machine, which always made her so nervous. One after the other her kids listened, as she took them through every twist and turn, beginning, middle, and end. And while Bethany and Sam were attentive to all that went on with Annette, Emma felt their concern sharpen when Marianne entered the picture, especially as Emma spoke about how nice she'd been, how gentle, even if she had been a little scary at first.

"There, you see," said Bethany as if a long-standing question had unexpectedly received a conclusive answer. Both kids lived out East and believed in civil rights, not that Emma didn't, but she didn't know many black people. Or any, if the truth were told. More and more black people were moving into town, but she still didn't know any. So the question lacked a certain immediacy. She thought she might stop as she approached the part about Pauline Steger trying to blame Marianne, or maybe just skip it, but she didn't, everything tumbling on headlong, and thank goodness she hadn't stopped, because the kids blew a gasket. Both of them. Sam about jumped through the phone, and Bethany said, "I don't believe it. I really don't." Their shock and anger had a far greater fire in it than what they'd expressed upon hearing of Annette's abuse. The questions flew, and when she reported how she'd stood up for Marianne in spite of being intimidated by the mean nurse, they all but cheered. They were so proud of her, they said. She hadn't expected all this, or any of it, and she started getting worked up to match them with a degree of indignation she didn't know she felt. Her attitude grew harsher toward the scoutmaster nurse and that Pauline woman, too, her judgment and condemnation skyrocketing. Given this opportunity to view what she'd lived through from her kids' perspective, she wondered how she'd put up with any of it for a second. "It was just awful that they would want to blame that poor woman. First they do what they did to Annette, and then, as if they haven't done enough damage, they go ahead and put the blame on somebody they think they can get away with accusing, innocent or not. It's a heck of a thing."

"It sure is."

"I couldn't believe my ears when I first heard her say it."

"But you stood up for her, Mom. That was great of you and so brave, too."

"I had to. If I wanted to live with myself, you know." She wondered if maybe she had been heroic. She felt like someone on a TV show saying words that were perfect for the moment, but didn't quite belong to her.

"A lot of people wouldn't have done that."

"I suppose."

"You know that's true."

Within minutes of hanging up from Sam, she was at the stove, utterly famished, heating up a can of tomato soup. Her venture into the refrigerator to see what else she might find to eat put her in contact with the string beans Annette's daughter had given her. She hadn't eaten them, and wished she wanted to now, but she didn't. She crumbled crackers into the soup. Glancing at the painting of the old man bowed to his bread above her dad's desk, and feeling more and more tired, she ate in silence. She had hoped to put the whole episode with Annette and Marianne out of her mind. But it had burst out of her, like her kids needed to know.

She wandered to her recliner. She'd turned the TV on

somewhere along the line, and she sat for a while in front of it before realizing she didn't know what she was looking at and hadn't for quite some time. She was just sitting there staring at one cop talking to another about some murder and a suspect she knew nothing about. She could barely keep her eyes open.

But once in bed, the search for sleep led nowhere. If she dozed even for an instant, she jolted awake. She was in a lather, replaying the excitement in Sam's approval, the pride that Bethany had expressed, savoring the regard in their tone, and the compliments they actually said aloud. She didn't want the day to end the way it would if sleep got hold of her. That was the fear that kept waking her up. Strange as it seemed, she couldn't help but feel that her trying to help Marianne had made her kids remember that she was their mom and that they loved her. She wanted to hang on to that. Every second of it. She didn't want to let any of it go. They were right. She couldn't just step away and let Marianne fend for herself. It wasn't right. Their interest urged her to stay involved, and to check things out further. Then she could report to them what she found out. Continuing her involvement would give her the opportunity to call her kids up with more news about Marianne and what was going on, the whole mess, and what she'd done to help out.

NINE

In the morning she all but lost her nerve sitting at the table with her coffee, wanting to make sure she was good and ready, on her toes, so to speak, stirring in milk and Equal. She tried a taste, and finding it sufficiently cool, she took a gulp. Good sense was slipping into her thoughts, tampering with her decisions, warning against the calls she intended to make. It wasn't her business. She had enough to take care of. She really didn't want to risk making enemies. So much was going on. She glanced at the ceiling, as if she might see Connie and Elroy up there. There was little new in her arguments and doubts. They were like a habit she had. She wished she had some real coffee with some real kick to it, and turned the stove back on to heat the teakettle for a second cup of instant. She planned to start with Annette, saving the whole question of Marianne until after she was more up-to-date, so to speak, on the Annette front. Her time in the hospital seemed further back than it was, her time back at home more than it was.

The phone book had a ton of Kalishecks, so she dug out her magnifying glass and leaned in close to scan the tiny print until she stopped at one named "Hank," which was the first name of the husband of that one daughter, Grace, she thought. She was ninety percent positive. It was on East 23rd Street, which sounded like something she'd heard in one of the conversations. So after making another coffee, this time doubling the teaspoons, she dialed and after a couple of rings squeezed her eyes shut, like that would keep her from hanging up. The next ring was cut off by a man who answered, sharply, as if he knew she was about ready to back out. "Hello."

"Hello, there. This is Emma Skayhill. I was the one with Annette in her room up at Saint Anthony's. I think I might have met you there."

"Oh, sure. I remember you."

"You were all so nice, and I'm not just saying that. I appreciate the friendly way you all treated me. Anyway, I was with her that night when all the fuss happened. And I was sitting around this morning—and I don't want to intrude, but we liked each other—I know I liked her—and I was hoping to find out how she's doing."

"Well, she's come out of all that, Emma. I'm happy to tell you she's getting along fine now."

"Now that's a relief. Does my heart good. Is she home yet?"

"Turns out she was overmedicated."

She didn't know what to make of that. It sounded like they'd concluded they knew what had happened, and the idea of being overmedicated explained everything. "She was pretty upset, I'll tell you."

"You would know. You saw more than most."

She wondered what he meant by that, and felt uncomfortable. "Well, I'm glad to hear she's on the mend."

"We're all grateful."

"Is she home? Did you say she was home?"

"I don't know. I might have. Because she is. Came home a day or so ago in the afternoon. Off all that medication. Something got mixed up, and the doctors don't know how yet, but she got overmedicated."

His conviction annoyed her, like he was the one in the room that night, and there was no mystery to solve, because everything was aboveboard and ready to be looked at in the clear light of day. She had to bite her tongue to keep back what she felt. "Could I talk to her?"

"What's that?"

"I was hoping I might get to talk to her."

"Annette? Is that who you mean?"

She began to wonder about this guy. She couldn't say for sure that she recognized his voice, but to be fair, people sound different over the phone. "Just to say hello. I wouldn't keep her long. I'm sure she needs her rest."

"I see—that's the mix-up. She isn't here. She's at home. I'm her son-in-law, Hank. You called here."

"Of course. Sorry."

"You know."

"Could I call there, do you think? Would that be possible? Would you give me that number?"

He huffed, and a lot of crackly noise came through to her, along with muffled talk, or what she assumed was talk, figuring he had his hand over the mouthpiece. Then he said, "How about this? Let's do this. I'll see to it she knows you called, and if you give me your number, she can call you. Does that sound okay?"

"If that's what you think."

"Let's do it that way."

"Whatever's best for her. I don't want to be a nuisance to you people. You've had enough trouble."

"No trouble. Just give me your number and we'll work this out. Emma Skayhill, right?"

Well, at least he'd listened close enough to get her name right. "That's me," she said and gave him her number.

It wasn't ten minutes before the phone rang. She was still at the table. Having detected Connie and Elroy overhead, she'd gotten caught up in listening to them, halfway hypnotized by their walking around, his big feet clomping, while hers whispered after him.

"Hello?" she said.

"Mrs. Skayhill. Hi. This is Grace Kalisheck, Annette's daughter. I gave you those string beans."

"Oh, sure," she said. "Hello."

"I think you spoke to my husband a bit ago."

"I did. A matter of minutes. He tells me your mom is home and doing great."

"She is. Back to normal almost. We're so grateful, I can't tell you. The other evening, we went over to Mom and Dad's, and she was playing this card game—something silly with Paul and Brandon—and she had the two of them in stitches—laughing so hard. It gave me such a thrill to see her like that, as you can imagine. But the thing is—do you know what? When we try to find out what happened —you know, trying to get her version—she doesn't have a clue. It's a total blank."

"Is that right? Doesn't that seem a little odd?"

"I don't know. I guess that can happen."

"I guess so. Because it has. I mean shock. That's what they say. It can knock the memory right out of you."

"You mean, trauma and like that. Oh, sure. Too awful to remember. You read about that."

"It was awful, let me tell you. So maybe she's better off."

"We keep trying to get to the bottom of the name of the nurse you mentioned."

"What nurse?"

"The nurse. You said some nurse."

"I never said any name, I don't think."

"But there was a nurse. We remember you telling us—I think it might have been the morning after—and you said that Mom had an accident, and some nurse had to clean it up, and she got really mad and started scolding Mom bad."

"Balled the heck out of her. Made me almost sick to hear it."

"See—that's what I'm getting at. If all that happened, you'd think Mom would remember it. But she doesn't. Not being scolded or the accident. But then, as you say: 'shock.' You do read about it. But it sounded to me that day you and I talked that you did—that you remembered."

"Does she remember me?" Emma wondered.

"You? Oh, sure. Of course."

"Because she didn't there at one point."

She could almost see Grace on the other end changing gears, the way her voice kind of backed up before going on to say, "Well, that's tricky actually—I don't want to give the wrong impression, because she remembers you for sure, but only in the sense that she remembers the good times you had before that night. But she doesn't remember you from then on. Nothing after."

"What about now?"

"That's what I'm saying. She remembers you, but only the parts from before. So it's tricky. Anyway, we're having trouble finding out who did that to her, and we'd like to. We were all talking the other night, and we did our best to make clear to Mom everything that happened to her, and she said to tell you that if you ever remembered that nurse's name, she hoped you would tell us. We all do."

"I'm sorry. I thought I made it clear—I don't know any —I wanted to and tried to make that clear to everybody—that I'm not going to remember. Because I don't know it. I never did know it."

"But sometimes things come back to us. Time passes and they come back."

"That's true sometimes. Sure. But not in this case. I don't think what I never knew is coming back. See? I never knew it. But I can tell you one thing—it wasn't Marianne. She did nothing wrong."

"Who?"

"Marianne. Marianne did nothing wrong."

"I don't know who that is."

"She was on that night. A black nurse. She was the night nurse. That other one, though—she was a pretty lady, but tough—and smart, we thought—and good, too, we both thought. Or at least I did. But I mean, anybody could tell the difference—that the one wasn't the other. But I don't know her name."

"Mom never said anything about any black nurse."

All of a sudden it was like Emma looked into a snowstorm. All the facts, or what she thought were facts, or what might have been facts, or what she had at least hoped were facts, spun

and whirled out of whatever order she thought they possessed,
The whole thing was like a zillion white flakes packing this
wind-tossed sky that hurled them thither and yon. She had no
idea what anybody knew, or even what she knew. "I gotta go,"
she said.

"Okay. Sure. Oh, my goodness, are you okay? I didn't even
ask about you, did I?"

"No problem."

"But how are you doing? Better, I hope."

"I'm doing just fine."

"Have you tried those string beans?"

"I've been saving them. But maybe tonight. I was thinking
that earlier."

"They're simple enough to cook."

"I love string beans."

"Don't let them sit too long. The fresher they are, the better. I picked them that morning—just before I dropped by to
see you."

She didn't want to be rude, but she had to get off so badly,
she didn't know if she could keep from slamming the phone
down. "Okay then."

"You really want to go, don't you."

"I'm sorry, but I do."

"Don't apologize."

"Okay."

"Remember what I said."

"I will."

"I mean it."

"Okay. Bye."

To her dismay, Connie and Elroy were still at it, and she
heard them the second she was free of Grace Kalisheck. Like
birds, or maybe a bird and a horse, they drifted through their
kitchen situated right above where she sat. They were on their

way into their living room that grew out of their kitchen, just as hers did. They moved back then in a circular path, or maybe an oblong up on Emma's ceiling. When they stopped, Emma heard sounds she thought were tiny human words trying to escape down to her. Sometimes Elroy walked fast, and Connie's little feet scurried after him, and sometimes she sliced in a diagonal, like she was trying to cut him off before he got too far away.

Emma's neck ached from looking up sharply for so long. She felt trapped, the world crowding in on her. Not only was she sure that the phone could ring in the next instant, but she was certain that it would, with somebody else yammering at her about what they needed to tell her or she had to do. Even the impulse to turn on the TV in the hope of a little amusement carried risks, given the stories she would be asked to follow and care about, advertisements blasting, people and dogs smiling one minute and stricken the next, music and singing, and all of it wanting to make her yearn to buy something that she'd probably never thought of wanting in her entire life. And even if she did watch, it wouldn't keep the phone from jangling. Everything had a mind of its own. She needed to get out. Cabin fever, she thought, wishing there was somewhere for her to go where no one could find her. She imagined a forest and a cave, and decided to take herself down to the mall. It'd be strangers there, and even should she have the misfortune of running into a familiar face, they wouldn't have a clue about all she'd been going through with Bud and Elroy, or the hospital.

It was close by, too. She was lucky that way, a hop, skip, and a jump, she thought, looking out the window at her poor old Buick that her dead husband had babied, worried about, and left her. It looked forlorn in her parking space, where it sat day in and day out, month after month, enduring rain and snow. It was a beat-up jalopy, no two ways about that, twenty years old—twenty-two to be exact—rusted and creaky. But it still started in the cold when she needed to use it. As long as she did things the way Charlie had taught her, it got her where she needed to go. Don't flood it, she could hear him now. Goose it twice and get the choke out. Then start her up. But don't flood it. For god's sake, whatever you do, don't flood it.

She parked as close to the main entrance as possible, which was a still good city block off the way she saw it. The darn place was packed. And sure, the mall was always busy, and that was good, but it still surprised her to find the stores buzzing even on a weekday in the middle of the afternoon.

Entering through the revolving doors, she passed the infor-mation booth, where a young girl and a middle-aged woman, who really wasn't acting her age, giggled, the older one patting the younger one's arm, neither one of them giving any thought to being on the lookout for someone who might need some information. A dozen little stalls stood in a line down the mid-dle of the long concourse she strolled. They didn't sell much that interested Emma. Junk mainly, trinkets, sunglasses and coffee cups, pennants and doodads. Along the side, glass pan-els framed the garish display windows full of strange-looking mannequins in stranger-looking clothes. A perfume store let loose traces of its wares along with music as the door opened. The next shop was sports equipment, and then came vitamins followed by more windows with some other kinds of clothes aimed at teenagers, as far as she could tell. A lot of smells other than the perfume mixed into an odor that made it impossible for her to single out any one source, though meat had to be cooking somewhere, peanuts roasting, coffee brewing, choco-late baking. She felt overwhelmed, like she was someone new to the earth and the habits of bodies and appetites. A second or two of rest on one of the benches that stood at intervals along the walls would get her back on her feet. Plopped down, and gazing up at this one passing, and then that one, a cluster of teens who ought to be in school, unless it was Saturday, which maybe it was. But it wasn't, she didn't think.

She had to wonder why she felt so assaulted by everything. At home and now here. She was sick of pretending she didn't feel out of place, like a sightseer in a foreign country who didn't understand what was going on when this was her hometown. Born and raised here. Lived here all of her life. She'd been to this mall a thousand times. But today was odd, and even though she'd come here to escape everyone and have some privacy, the fact that not a single soul, not one set of eyes in all these people crossing every which way in front of her, cared to say, Hello, or even give an interested glance in her direction, made her feel alone and lonely in a large, looming way different than the privacy and lack of attention she'd thought she wanted. Back and forth they went, hell-bent on whatever it was that mattered to them. And whatever it was, she could be sure that it wasn't her. When a couple of strangers did take note of her, she knew that all they saw was the old lady on the bench. Watching them made her sad in a way she didn't much care for. She felt like a ghost. That was the sense that lay behind the feeling. Not that she knew what a ghost felt like. Unless she did, and this was it. Kind of lost and disconnected from the world, but still in it. Hanging around the everyday things, and seeing how they mattered to people and remembering how they had once mattered to her. Right there with them where they ought to see her. Involved, but unnoticed all the while.

The heck with this noise, she thought, and stood up. What she needed was a task. Something to do, and maybe she didn't know what it was just yet, but she could get started anyway, and figure it out later. Go buy something. Think of something she needed and shop for it. Find it and buy it. The problem was that she could imagine nothing in the nearby shops holding the slightest appeal. And the assessment seemed true as far as she could see. She'd be better off at Eagles, which she had to drive right by on the way home. It would be easy to find some food. Maybe even some of that sugarless ice cream. Chocolate, or fudge ripple, or strawberry, or vanilla, or that cherry something. That was a tasty one that she'd recognize the second she saw it.

Bodies shot by on either side and in both directions, one at a time, or in groups or pairs, as she tottered along. Her knees hurt from sitting. They didn't appreciate the change of getting up, like they thought she'd settled down on that bench permanently, and they were done with walking. That's what she could do, she thought. Go get some pain reliever, Tylenol or Aleve, from the drugstore at the end of the corridor. She'd turned a corner. Afterward, she could still go to Eagles for the ice cream she wanted.

TEN

Once inside the store, she tried to follow the big overhead signs identifying the categories of product, such as Pain Relief, though that one got mixed up with Cold and Flu. She hoped the smaller signs sticking out to arrange the aisles into manageable segments would help more than they did. The place was a maze, and an enormous one at that, without a single employee in sight. The heck with it, she thought. She still had to make the long walk all the way back to her car. And anyway, she had both Tylenol and Aleve at home. She didn't remember so many little things ever being so difficult, and wondered if she was slipping.

Eagles was pretty much the same deal, bigger than needed and organized by signs. But Eagles was close to home, and she went there so often, she knew the layout like the back of her hand. She made a beeline for the ice cream. But then rounding the last corner, she pulled up short, ready to stop before she had any idea why. Walls of stacked ice cream containers waited behind big glass doors, one of which was being held open by a man who shouldn't be there, who shouldn't be anywhere, actually. It was Bradley Corrigan, who was dead. Tilted forward and fishing around inside, he straightened and looked at her. After a second he smiled, closed the door, and went off carrying a pint of ice cream in his right hand. She tried to think hard. He wasn't someone she knew well. He was a little older, and a star athlete in high school, and she'd had a schoolgirl crush on him from afar. She'd known his younger sister, Doris, and she'd wanted to phone Doris when she'd heard Douglas Wenke announce Bradley's passing maybe six months ago. Or maybe a year. Could it have been more? The news had shocked her. He was dead. She knew it. But maybe it wasn't him. But how could she forget that face?

Peering around the corner that had swept him from view, she discovered that he now stood alongside the meat section. He smiled back at her, and he waved this time. She wheeled away, embarrassed to have him think she was following him. Which she was. When she tried to find him again, this time hoping to study him thoroughly, he was gone. Maybe it wasn't Bradley Corrigan. It couldn't be. But it had looked just like him. But maybe Bradley Corrigan wasn't dead, and she was misremembering. She could hardly walk up and say, Bradley, I thought you were dead. Or, Bradley, are you dead? Or, Weren't you dead? Or, I'm glad you're not dead. Or, Are you Bradley Corrigan? He was gone anyway, whoever he was.

She thought maybe she would run over to Saint Catherine's Church for a little visit on the way home. As long as she was out and about, she might as well. It wasn't far out of the way. She could ask the girl on the register for a freezer bag, and maybe even some ice to pack around the ice cream. Almost in a trance, she'd taken vanilla, a choice that had called out from a simpler past without rum raisin this, chocolate whatever, cookie dough ripple. Just plain vanilla. She would scoot over to Saint Catherine's, and she wouldn't stay long so the ice cream couldn't melt. It was good soft anyway, and should it get too soft, she could freeze it again, though she had to admit that for reasons she didn't understand ice cream lost something special when it was frozen a second time.

The church was located on a hill, and rising toward it, she blinked in the sun still high but off to the side, sending down fiery rays to splash off the slanted rooftop and the cross high on the steeple. Other than her Buick, the parking lot was empty. Once she'd hauled herself upright, she needed a moment to get her balance. She was cramming a lot into one day with all she'd been up to since morning, and probably ought to take a nap once she got home. But as she made her way to the front stairs, she felt kindness reaching out in the breeze arising just then to meet her. She'd say a little prayer for Bradley Corrigan, who could probably use it wherever he was, dead or alive.

The front door brought her into silence and startling shafts of light. There was one just a few feet in front of her, so shocking in its definition and density that she felt like she would bump into it if she kept going. The stained glass windows high above her blazed with color and fanciful figures of angels and saints. In one, Mary bent stricken over her beloved, half-naked Jesus, who was bloody and languid in her arms on the rough ground at the foot of the cross, where the two of them sprawled together. An angel in a nearby window, his trembling wings and big, intelligent eyes more alarmed than those of the youthful Mary staring up at him, announced the baby who was to come her way and who Emma was sure adorned another of the windows, though she didn't see him at the moment. It occurred to her that the angel's eyes appeared wounded because he knew all that was coming to Mary, but he'd been forbidden to tell her. Namely that the infant he announced would turn into the mangled body embraced by the older, worn down, but still beautiful Mary in the first window, which was darkening now, as the sun must have moved on or been covered in clouds, turning the brilliant images into shadows.

She went on, advancing down the side aisle through irregular light. The statue of Saint Catherine stood set into a hollow in the wall with a kneeler and a table holding rows of votive candles. Emma had her purse, and she dropped a few coins into a slot where they fell through a momentary silence until they clinked atop other coins at the bottom, reminding her of her childhood piggy bank. She'd put a lot of hope into that thing. She knelt then, filling with a blast of need she had to let out, a desperate, mindless, nameless begging that made her shut her eyes and nod. This was her appeal. She was appealing. She waited, not exactly expecting a response. She didn't know much about Saint Catherine. But the idea that came delivered that soothing funny accented voice she'd heard on TALKNET speaking about the comfort of having an empty mind. But her mind wasn't empty. She was appealing. Nothing about this was empty. Not the light, the church, the shadows, nor Emma on her knees.

Was that a prayer? she wondered. What did she have to do, or better yet, what did she have to feel in her heart to make a good prayer? Her heart that in the hospital that girl, smart as a whip and trained to run her fancy machine in the echo chamber way down in the basement of Saint Anthony's, couldn't find. The one she and Emma had worried she didn't have. Like it was a game about whether or not Emma had a heart. Or where it was. Or if it was hiding. She drew her rosary out of her purse and started at the beginning. The Apostles' Creed, the

Our Father, and then the Hail Marys, fingering the beads, and trying to have her mind become empty of everything but the words dedicated to Mary. But she wanted things, was scared of things, needed things, and she could not escape them for a second. What did real prayer feel like, she wondered, the prayer the saints knew and spoke of?

She stood up suddenly, imagining her ice cream melting all over the front seat of her car. Hastily she lit a votive candle, which she should have done sooner. She anticipated the world outside becoming as vague around her poor old Buick as the dimness dissolving the inside of the church.

But then she emerged to find the sun still had a distance to go before it was down, and the ice cream in its freezer bag wasn't in bad shape at all.

Emma was almost home when she worried that her Buick being gone from its regular spot was such a rare event that it might have caused a stir in the apartment complex, rumors and guesswork afoot, but particularly with Maggie. And so, to pull in, as she did, and find that Maggie's cute little Honda absent from its parking space was a relief. It meant Maggie was out somewhere doing something, saving Emma from having to contend with even one question about where she'd been, why she'd gone, and who she might have seen. The only answers she could have given—the mall, drugstore, Eagles, and Saint Catherine's, while leaving out the ghost she saw selecting his ice cream—would have seemed so limited as to feel like lying.

She pushed her way in the front door and then on into her apartment, where she met welcome and refuge. At the sound of a papery crunch, something moved under her foot. She stood on an envelope that she didn't remember. Someone must have slid it under her door. It was sealed, adding mystery to the surprise, as she went to her desk for her letter opener. It looked like Maggie's handwriting, which she was pretty sure

she knew, and she discovered she was right, her eyes falling to
the signature before she read the message.

Dear Partner,
I took it upon myself to go see Bud today. Not to do
more than set a time for the three of us to meet.
I wanted to get the news to you since I won't be back
until late tonight, and you'd already left. Where the heck
did you go? I was flabbergasted to see your spot empty. So
anyway, I resorted to this note. I told Bud we needed to
speak to him as representatives of other tenants. Boy, did
that open his eyes wide. As you can imagine, he wanted to
know what we wanted to talk about. But I said I couldn't
tell him without you there. So we set a time for next
Friday. Ten in the morning. I told Connie, and May
and Clara, and they're glad. Hope you are, too. It
just struck me the time had come for us to get things moving. I think you'll be glad to know that I did
get a little nervous without you at my side.
Talk soon.
Maggie

Okay, Emma thought, making her way from the desk chair
to the recliner, rereading as she went. If that don't beat all. She
had half a notion to be irritated at Maggie for acting in such a
high-handed way, but the truth was she didn't have the where-
withal for much of anything. And that was Maggie's way, after all. And what the heck, she was right. Somebody had to
do something to get the ball rolling. This rent thing had been
hanging over her head—over all their heads—for too long.
Next Friday seemed about right. Not so far off she would feel it
might never happen, but not so immediate that it felt right on
top of her. She'd have time to think about what she wanted to

say. She and Maggie could meet to talk the whole thing over. Consult, so to speak.

She figured she better come up with a note of her own, even though she didn't have the energy to write much. She was making too much of it, she knew. It ought to be simple. But nothing ever was. She wanted to make sure Maggie had some kind of an answer when she got home, so she didn't worry that Emma hadn't gotten the information, or that she was annoyed about Maggie going ahead without her. She knew darn well she had better get those questions settled if she didn't want Maggie phoning her when she got home, or knocking on her door, which she didn't want to deal with tonight. Or maybe ever. Now that was a heck of a mean thing to think. But that was just how tired she was. She looked forward to dealing with it tomorrow. Just not tonight. She'd call Maggie bright and early. But first things first, which meant getting her note written. Back at her desk, she dug out her best stationery with the matching envelopes. The ideas came out pretty easy, and she worked to make her writing clear, thinking back to the nuns who'd taught her, the ruled paper they used to give capitals their proper height over the lowercase letters.

> Maggie,
> Great that you did what you did. Got us going. I'm proud of you. And grateful. Thanks for doing it. And thanks for letting me know. I bet Bud's eyes did almost pop out of his head. I'll call you in the morning. Had my car out as you noticed and I didn't do much to speak of, but I'm bushed.
> Thanks Partner
> Emma

ELEVEN

Once she had eased the note under Maggie's door, she realized she had a bit of a dilemma. It was too early for bed, and worn out as she was, she had the nagging feeling she wouldn't fall asleep without a struggle. Anyway, she needed to eat something, and not exactly because she was hungry, but almost more because she had the urge to chew and chew hard, to taste and enjoy and swallow. The dilemma was that if she kept her lights on, or even watched television in the dark, Maggie, getting back, parking where she did, and walking in the front door, couldn't help but see that Emma was still up. It'd be perfectly natural for her to want to step in to say hello, especially tonight. Maggie was one to do that kind of thing, with or without anything out of the ordinary, like the note business as an excuse.

She heard the toast she'd put in the toaster pop behind her as she opened the meat keeper in the fridge, looking for the ham and cheese she knew were in there. That's when she saw the ice cream. Not in the freezer, but on this refrigerator shelf. She didn't remember putting it there. She didn't remember putting it anywhere, but there it was in the refrigerator rather than the freezer. All flummoxed by the envelope, she must have misplaced it. Absentminded for sure. But on the other hand, she had a lot on her plate today, and none of it food. That was a joke, Emma. You should laugh. You're the only one here.

The ice cream wasn't a puddle, more like vanilla pudding that tasted dreamy when she took a big spoonful. Still she closed the container and stuck it into the freezer where it belonged. She put her sandwich together with some mustard and sat chewing at the table. The thing to do, she decided, was turn out all the lights except for the lamp on her bedside table in the bedroom. She could watch the little TV she had in there on top of the dresser, if she wanted. Of course, she had to deal with her colostomy bag and take a shower first, and not rush things so she took a spill and knocked herself silly the way she did in the hospital that time right after the surgery. It was a wonder she'd lived. What she needed was to hurry but stay careful, and if her luck held, she might have it all done before Maggie pulled in. If the living room lights were out, not even Maggie would get it into her head that it was okay to come banging on Emma's door.

It was the same darn dirty tasks night after night, and she was never going to get used to it, and never going to like it, emptying the poop out of her bag. Oh, she had a load tonight, she thought, putting wads of toilet paper into the bowl to keep the water from splashing, and then getting the bag loose from the stoma. And always alone. Every night alone. She dumped the poop and went on washing and hooking the new bag up, making sure it fit, making sure it sealed on the stoma, the warmth of her hand pressing the bag close to get the adhesive to stick. Nobody to help her or for her to complain to, even as a joke. She got to feeling so blue all of a sudden, lonely and wanting to call her kids. She wanted to call Bethany. Or maybe Sam. Or maybe both. It was less scary to call Bethany. She didn't know exactly why that was true, but had no doubt that it was. She could call Sam, though, and she did it if she needed to. She wished she had something new to tell him about Marianne and all that business. That would be a good reason to call. And Bethany, too. They'd both been so interested. But she really didn't know anything new. In fact, she felt that after trying to look into things the way she had with Annette's family, she knew less than she had before. Particularly with that Grace telling her she didn't even know who Marianne was. "What black nurse?" she'd said. That was a shocker. For goodness' sake. The whole thing was starting to look like Emma might be the only one who cared; the only one trying to get to the bottom of it all and make sure the right one got blamed. What would happen, she wondered, if she tried to talk to Annette again? It had almost seemed like the family was guarding her. Protective custody, sort of. And who could blame them? She had to think that maybe the only way to find out more, if that was what she really wanted, and if she was willing to take the risk, would be for her to call that Pauline woman, and ask a couple questions. Maybe pretend she thought she was supposed to get back to her. Of course, that could be dangerous, making her seem nosy, and putting her in jeopardy with that scoutmaster nurse should she get wind of what Emma was doing.

But she really wanted to speak to Bethany. Or Sam. That was the thing. It was funny how she could get this pang out of the blue every now and then, this hunger for her kids, and it was a hunger, too, a real deep gnawing that wanted a lot more than talk could satisfy. It was a fierce animal loneliness inside her craving them in a way that went beyond the realm of anything that could ever really happen. Getting ahold of them on the telephone, hearing their voices, chattering about something, nothing, or anything was a poor substitute for what she really wanted, which was probably something like a time machine, or maybe a flying carpet. Still, a substitute, even a poor one, was better than nothing.

She was in bed now with a bowl of ice cream and the small TV atop the dresser lit up like a cook fire in a cave. That's how she felt. Holed up like an animal in its den. She didn't even have the bedside lamp on, and she had no earthly idea what was going on between the man and woman on the TV, except that their marriage was on the rocks. They yelled and ran around in maybe the plushest bedroom she'd ever seen, and the woman shot in and out of a closet big enough for a whole family to move in and live just fine. The woman started grabbing clothes, beautiful dresses and underwear and shoes, too, off the longest row of shoes anybody could imagine. She was just throwing it all into a suitcase. She looked drunk, or on drugs. Probably drugs. She was pretty in a trashy kind of way, and then the man started ripping the clothes out of the suitcase and throwing them, and he hurled the suitcase, and Emma turned them off.

If figuring things out, if coming up with a way to help Marianne, was what she wanted, these two were not the ones to do it. They had no sense whatsoever.

Maybe what she ought to do was to listen to TALKNET. There were always all kinds of problems there and solutions being offered. There might even be one about how to help black people who were being unfairly treated at work.

She came in midway on a woman who sobbed every other word, making her story hard to follow. But then Emma started to catch on, understanding first of all that the woman's name was Dana. The host kept saying, "That's okay, Dana; that's okay." But how could it be okay that Dana had come in on her best friend, Carol, "doing stuff" with her little boy. Eddie? "Eddie," she wailed. "He's only seven and there she was—I can't say it."

"It's okay, Dana. It's okay."

Well, maybe. Maybe not, thought Emma, and she wished the host would stop saying it was okay. She did like the advice he gave, though. He had a voice a lot like that of Douglas Wenke, only wiser and more watchful. "Go to the police. Maybe what happened in the past wasn't your fault. Forgive yourself. Even if you suspected, you didn't know. But now you know. Any more of it is your fault." Eddie had burst into tears at school and they'd called Dana. The principal wanted to see her and Eddie.

They went on awhile with Emma trying to imagine what Carol had been up to with little Eddie. She thought she had a pretty good idea, and she wanted to take that dirty Carol and slap her hard.

All of a sudden, she worried she'd been maybe half asleep, or daydreaming, stuck on Eddie and Dana, because Jacqueline—that's what the host called her—was bawling that her mother was "a terrible nasty bitch." Her father had run off when Jacqueline was seven, and she knew why. Her mother was "a monster who had no soul. Not now and never would."

Trish and her husband were fighting morning, noon, and night. At least that was how it looked to Trish. Their sex life was gone and it had been the glue that kept them together for almost nine years. She didn't know why it was gone, but it was. Everything was hopeless. Sex was the way they'd gotten over their fights in the past, but it didn't work now. They couldn't even do it. They'd start and one of them would get annoyed at something the other one said, or didn't say, or did. Or used to do different. Sometimes it was her. She couldn't help it. She would feel cold. So cold.

Poor Dan had the saddest, most broken way of speaking that went from a whisper to a squeal. He had to be encouraged to speak up and keep trying as he told how his daughter had killed herself. Jumped off a bridge. At night. He'd seen it. He sounded strangled at that point, and Emma was sure he was done. But he came back, panting like he'd run to get away, and then had run all the way back. His daughter was sixteen and in the back seat of his car. They were stuck on a bridge in slow-moving traffic. He'd been upset and cursing the traffic because he had to get her somewhere, drop her off, and then get somewhere else for work, and he was cursing, and she got out and ran. Before he knew what to do, he saw her go over the side of the bridge, her pale legs uncovered by the skirt rushing up around her from the updraft as she jumped feetfirst. He used that word—"updraft." For an instant he couldn't move. How could he get out and leave his car in all that traffic? He looked in the back seat like she might still be where she'd been trying to catch up on her homework. And then he bolted to the railing, shouting her name, "Kimmy, Kimmy," into the dark so heavy, he couldn't even see the water.

No black people, Emma thought. They didn't call in. Or maybe they called but they couldn't get through. Or they were put on hold until they gave up. She couldn't see the callers, but nobody sounded like a black person, not like Marianne, or like those ones she saw fighting on Maury Povich.

She was dozing, and had been off and on, the radio voices a hazy background, like a church choir practicing clumsily to learn some new song, or like her singing to her kids way back when they were little and needed help getting to sleep. They begged her to lie with them, and she did, offering a lullaby.

All those problems, and people calling to talk about them. She had to admit that it amazed her—the different ways people came up with to get themselves into trouble. She'd seen plenty in her lifetime, the troubles of this one or that one, her own mistakes, too, though what she did, or even the worst of what the people she knew did, couldn't hold a candle to the crackpot stuff people got fouled up in today. But back when she was young, people were ashamed and secretive, so maybe it all went on. Now they just blabbed away—taking the trouble to phone in to do it. All these strangers out in the dark somewhere, different states all over America, some in the Midwest, others far and wide, places she'd never been, all baring their souls because they thought it would help, their secrets sailing about on the airwaves. She could halfway see them hung out in the night sky, apologies, sad faces, mistakes. Dan watching his daughter drop out of sight in her skirt all puffed up, falling past Dana and her little boy waiting for the principal, and past Trish and her husband, too, walking around, hunting for their lost sex life maybe near the moon, calling for what was gone. Like it was a dog they'd lost, or they were birds who couldn't find their nest. Eddie and his mom, too.

It was late. The wee hours, and with the trials and tribulations of so many souls on her mind, she realized something else. She had not heard Maggie come home. At least she didn't think she had. She might have dozed and then not realized that a sound she heard was Maggie pulling in. Or she could have missed it. Because she had gone in and out. She hoped Maggie was home safe and sound. She had to shake her head and smile, even chuckle at the fact that in spite of the way she'd hidden in the dark, hoping not to be found, she felt a touch hurt and neglected that Maggie had come home without trying to check in on her. Unless she hadn't come home at all.

It was a real struggle between her sense of responsibility to Maggie, pushing her to check out the window, and the cozy comfort of the bed on her poor old bones, urging her to stay right where she was. But she moved, finding her way to her feet, remembering and kind of reenacting the way she'd been called on to wait up and worry any time Bethany or Sam were out too late, back in their teenage years.

Light from the parking lot framed the shade, which she didn't raise, but plucked at the edge to open a crack out into the courtyard, where snow fell on Maggie's empty spot. An array of flakes, faint and sparse, melted as they touched down on the pavement, or the hoods of the other cars snuggled in their slots. Darn, she thought. Snow. Goodness. She gazed up into a halo of dancing white specks sharply visible as they passed through the spell of the streetlight. Where the heck was Maggie? Emma sure hoped she was all right. Slick roads now to worry about on top of everything else. This type of wet snow made for tricky driving. She was pretty sure she was right to remember that Maggie's note said she would be out late. But according to her bedside clock, it was two in the morning, for crying out loud. She hoped Maggie hadn't gone someplace where she had too much to drink. She had it in her to like a little more wine than might be good for her. She was a bit younger than Emma, too, and had some even younger friends, who could get a little wild. She'd heard stories. Mainly ones Maggie told her, almost bragging, as she tried to make what had been reckless, if you asked Emma, sound like a good time.

She slumped down in bed feeling more tired than ever. Everyone wanted something from her, and it didn't seem to matter if they were alive or dead. They just showed up at her door. Or they looked at her funny, the way Bradley Corrigan had done at Eagles. And now the people on TALKNET seemed to think they had the right to her attention. She had to laugh at that one. Maggie and all of them—they were barking up the wrong tree.

When she heard footsteps on the ceiling, her surprise and puzzlement turned into disbelief. She gaped up, as if intensity could pierce through the plaster, the lumber, the Sheetrock or whatever, to take hold of Connie and Elroy, give them a good shake and tell them to get back to bed. They were on the prowl. Did this happen every night? she wondered, only she missed it being sound asleep, as she usually was. His big feet padded around, followed by her little ones. And then Elroy started to talk. It sounded like he said, "Gimp." Or "Gimp me," and nothing the least bit hushed about him, either. What the heck? Then he growled and it fell to her, clear and scary, like she'd actually parted the floorboards, or he knew she was down there and wanted her to hear. "You pimp me," he groaned to someone he hated, who could only be Connie, his voice bitter and forlorn. "You pimp me. All my life. It's all you ever did. You pimped me, damn you. You pimped me."

Nothing more happened. Not a word more from him. Not a sound from Connie, either. Not another step more from either one of them. It was like he'd never spoken. Like they hadn't prowled. Like they weren't even up there. Emma waited, holding her breath, truly afraid to breathe for seconds that went on long enough that they had to turn into a minute, and then more than one. But it was over. It was like they'd vanished. Like she hadn't heard what she'd heard. Like it hadn't even happened.

Lord, she thought, as the scarlet glow of the vigil candles below Saint Catherine's feet emerged in her head. There had been only a few burning in the church full of shadows, a scattering of ten at most among the unkindled majority waiting in neglected rows. What a terrible thing for Elroy to say to poor Connie. How awful to hear your husband of all those years say that to you. Emma regretted lighting only one vigil candle, and that one only for her troubles. At least she'd included Bradley Corrigan, or had intended to anyway. She hoped she had. But she should do it every day—light one every day. And for everybody. If she really believed, why didn't she light them all every day? She had her problems. That was for sure. She could use a little help. And maybe some TUMS. Her stomach burned. She could darn well phone into TALKNET, as well as all the ones who did. Call in and bend their ear about plenty, and maybe she darn well ought to do just that. See if he had some answers. If only she had the nerve. Or could find the nerve. Which she couldn't. Or wouldn't. If she was certain about anything in this life, it was that she was never calling into a nighttime talk show to air her dirty laundry. But she had reasons enough. Offenses and disappointments galore. She'd done her share of bad things. Thoughtless, hurtful things. Regretful things. Dumb things. Like eating that cheese and ham that might have been in the refrigerator too long and gone bad. Her stomach was in a tumble. She couldn't remember exactly when she'd shopped for that cheese and ham. And ice cream on top of it. She should have had better sense.

She turned onto her side. Like that time with the birds. Anybody could have done it, but she was the one, and it stuck in her now like a bone in her throat ready to make her gag, a sharp, physical dig, bringing such remorse that she tried not to think of it. She'd been sitting one day, and when she got up, she passed by the sliding glass doors, and she saw all these strings and sticks and everything all over the patio. What the heck, she thought. And then these birds were headed in her direction, two of them. They were bringing in little bitty twigs and strings; they had pieces of tissue, regular Kleenex, and they just came flying up with all this stuff hanging in their mouths. It was so cute. At first Emma thought she was seeing things, that they weren't doing what she saw them doing, just dropping this mess all over her patio. If they were making a nest, she didn't see it. But then her air conditioner came into her mind, the way the flat part on the top stuck out. It wasn't running yet in the spring. She got a little step stool and looked, and there it was, the nest they were building, all braided and partly put together. It was their supplies they were bringing in piece by piece. She recalled seeing cardboard boxes on patios and air conditioners around the neighborhood. She didn't think much about them at the time, other than finding them odd. But with these birds coming to her apartment the way they were, she decided the boxes were how other people had dealt with the same problem. It had never happened before on her patio and air conditioner. Her place was close to the roads with their traffic noise, so maybe the birds had stayed away as long as they could. Maybe their coming now was some kind of last resort. And she thought, I really should let them do it. And once she did, she started to really enjoy watching them. They'd fly up with one little twig and one little piece of string and then a little piece of ribbon they'd found from here and there. Oh, she remembered it now, how darling and sweet they were, and the nice way she felt watching them put it together.

But then one day something got into her and turned her to thinking about it in another way. It was on top of her air conditioner, and so she realized, Well, I can't have that. When I turn on that air conditioner, those poor little baby birds will all die. So she went and got the broom and got up on the step stool to take another look at how they made their nest, and it was just this twig thing all interlaced so cute. But she had to knock it down, she thought, so she did, using the broom. She put all of the twigs and pieces outside the patio railing in the grass. It wasn't long before both birds, the one the mother and the other the father, showed up, swooping. They knew Emma was doing something that they didn't want her to do. It was like they'd watched her and waited for her to go back inside, and then they came right down into the yard to pick up all those same pieces and put them back together on top of the air conditioner.

Well, that made her kind of mad. She wasn't going to stand for it. The babies would get born and they'd be slopping all over and shitting all over. She knocked it all off again, even if it was maybe the cutest thing ever, the way they cared. She went and found a cardboard box about two feet high and sat it on top of the air conditioner like her neighbors had done. When the mother bird came along after a while, she didn't understand what the box was. She flew up with this string hanging in her mouth and then she squawked and went away. But she came back again, really wanting to build her nest there for whatever reason. No reason Emma would ever know. It was maybe early evening, if Emma remembered right, the next time the bird came back. She fluttered around, looking at that box; she scolded it a little bit and then she went away again. At least three more times she returned, and once Emma watched from behind the sliding glass doors that opened onto the patio, and the bird saw her. She flapped her wings and zoomed, like she knew what had happened and whom to blame for it. Outraged and indignant, you'd have to say. Because Emma had fixed it so she couldn't get to that spot anymore. And Emma thought—

Well, she didn't remember what she thought. She no longer had any idea. But she knew what she'd done.

And then the really crazy thing that happened next was that those same two birds went over to Maggie's patio, and they went to work on her air conditioner. One day Maggie said, "Emma, I don't know what's going on. My patio is full of junk all the time. String and twigs and junk." Emma told her, "Well, why don't you put a box there like I did. It's some bird trying to build a nest to lay her eggs." Well, Maggie got angry. "Why the heck didn't you tell me?" She got very angry, because when they went and looked, it was too late. "It's there, already. The nest," Maggie said. "And I can't touch it now, because there are babies in it."

Emma's stomach did a flip, or half a flip, then shot this burning glop up into her throat and back down into her chest. She had to sit up. "Ouch," she said, shaking her head in annoyance. What the heck was she thinking about those birds for? Of all things? What got her started on that? Somebody had done something. It might even have been her. But whatever it was, it had sent her off the beaten track. Because she had a lot of more pressing stuff that was actually real to take care of than worrying about those birds. Mainly, she had to get to sleep. Getting tied up in knots about things that were long past, and that hadn't even mattered when they happened, let alone now, wasn't going to get her anywhere.

Darn, she thought. Because if the way she felt indicated what was coming, she would never get to sleep. Her stomach swirled and a whole bunch more of that really scalding gunky mess jumped up into her throat. Why hadn't she had the good sense to check the "use by" date on that ham? It had to have had one. She hoped she didn't throw up. It was only a hope and a thin one, but throwing up would be the last straw. It had to be the ham. It tasted of ham, all that bile.

Anyway, since it didn't look like sleep was a possibility, the least she could do was put the time to good use, and make some decisions. First off, she would be kinder to Connie from now on. She'd make a real effort to say, "Hi," and ask how Connie was when they ran into each other. That wouldn't be asking too much. Should she tell Maggie what she'd heard going on upstairs? She had to call Maggie first thing in the morning to assure her she wouldn't have to face Bud alone—that she could count on Emma. But Connie and Elroy, and Emma overhearing what she did, that was a different matter. She should be kinder to Elroy, too. Not think so mean about him, every chance she got, his big feet and all. And she was going to call that Pauline woman. That was the most important thing. She would take the risk. Somebody had to worry about Marianne and her rights and all that, and if it was up to Emma, well, then so be it. She'd figure out what to say, and maybe practice it out loud to get the feel of it. Maybe even sit with the phone up to her ear to practice. Those birds should have known better. If they'd understood the simplest thing, well, they would have known that nurse was a bad one, mean and nasty, and the boxes, well, well, they made everything different. But they were birds, and so—What was happening? Oh, look. She saw it coming. A wave of dark and velvet rising up.

Sleep.

TWELVE

She had to get ready. Dad was trying to help, but he had the wrong shoes on. *No*, she said. But he kept at it, wanting to fix everything. But after she left the room and he was there at the table, and she came back, he was bowed over, sitting with his head down. She didn't like seeing him like that, and she said, *Get your head out of the food, Dad.* Oh, she could see him so plain but he wouldn't talk to her. And she couldn't hang on to the meat. She couldn't stop dropping the meat in the kitchen. She couldn't get it in the oven, even though it was sliced up for her. Sam's wife had cooked delicious steaks with little ropes on them. So Emma had her nice piece of beef on this string. If she connected this string to that one, the meat would cook quicker, so she was working to get the two hunks apart first, and she was dropping the meat and then this man came in and said he was a doctor.

You'll have to listen to Melissa, he said. Emma hated Melissa. She used to work in the office at the store and she was real bossy.

Well, you have to get everyone out of here by two thirty, Melissa said to Emma.

Emma said, *WHY?*

And she said, *Because my group's coming in.*

Emma said, *IN MY HOUSE?*

YES, she said back. *In your house, and if you're not out, they'll just come in and eat with you.*

HAAAAH, Emma said. *They will not.* She was ready to punch her square in the nose.

Oh, that was so dumb.

She was really upset, her hands clenched in fists, but she

was glad to recognize the ceiling of her bedroom—the one in her apartment—that she knew so well, and the silent, blank TV on the dresser, and the blinds open on the windows, where the snow fell outside.

Whew, she thought. But there had been another part to the dream in which more had happened and which she needed to remember. Or maybe the dream was still going on. Maybe that was it. Because there was this big hole in the floor, and it went right on into the basement. The carpet and everything was burned and scorched, and she said, *Dad, have you seen this?*

He came out and he said, *Yes, your friends did that when they were here.*

She said, *None of them smoke.*

He said, *Well, somebody burned that and it was burned bad, and it was burned right through to the basement.*

I know, she said, and she tested it, tapping with her foot to see if it might hold her, because somebody had put something over it, a carpet or something, so she couldn't see where the hole was and where it wasn't. Not wanting to fall in, but needing to see how deep it was, she managed to look down into it, trying hard to think of somebody. Who was it she was trying to think of? Somebody she knew and had seen at Eagles. What was his name? She really wanted to remember if he was dead or alive. Teddy was down in the hole. Her little brother was down there lying in the sand under the desert winds blowing over him, knots of sand, whirling, twirling dust making him hard to see. But it was him, her little brother, and her big brother was there, too. And her sister and mother and father. And Grandpa and Grandma Weber. Uncles and aunts, too, Glenna and Clyde, she thought. Or maybe it was Matt. Not all in the desert, but all in the hole.

What was it she believed had happened to whoever it was she couldn't remember, no matter how fierce her desire, and no matter how strong her determination, no matter how she tried? Who was he to her even? Grade school or maybe high school. Some kind of school. She knew other tidbits about him, but she couldn't quite gather them in. It was frustrating, because somewhere inside her she had all the information she needed, but she couldn't summon it up, try as she might. She had a sense of what she knew, an impression. Or rather, if she was more careful about how she looked at it all, she had the feeling of something elusive which might not even be connected to what she was trying to figure out. It might even be some other notion entirely trying to barge into her head. It was a funny deal, all right, this living business. No two ways about it. When you got down to brass tacks, it was a mystery show like those detectives programs on TV with clues ducking in and out, and she was supposed to make sense of it all, when half of it came and went without her even knowing it was there. Busy with one thing and in comes another. And yet she was expected to know what to do. Know right from wrong. Supposed to know who she was starting way back when, and who she was now, and if that wasn't enough, she had to know who the heck everybody else was, too.

Upright on the side of the bed, she rocked from side to side, and lurched back and forth. Boy, did she have a stomachache. This clot of fire, like she'd swallowed a red-hot coal that she had better cough up. Gathering all the breath she could, the sputter she managed hurt enough that she yelped. It hurt just to breathe. Oh, boy, I'm getting pneumonia. Oh, boy. I hope not. Everything hurt, so she twisted and turned and fell back and admitted as much as remembered that this had gone on all night, and it was not getting better. If she was honest, it might even be worse than ever. But it was no picnic either way she looked at it. She should probably get up and see how much snow had fallen and whether or not Maggie's little Honda was back where it belonged; and she should probably get some Vicks to rub on her chest. Oh, she hoped it wasn't pneumonia. She flopped down, coughing with such pain that she squealed and hit her fist down on the bed.

In the bathroom, she realized the time—almost eight in the morning, and she hadn't taken care of anything. Not a single one of her regular, morning things. I gotta get going around here. The idea of engaging in the tasks that made up her daily routine consoled her. The colostomy bag didn't have much in it, so she thought it could wait. It would have to anyway, given how she felt. Her skin was a little irritated from the adhesive. She needed to put something on it. But she'd do that later, too. She should irrigate tomorrow. Didn't want those cramps coming back. She let the water run to heat up, and then she cleaned up a little, dabbing away with a washcloth soaked in warm soapy water. Normally she'd want a bite to eat before too long, toast and jam, or maybe an egg, but that wasn't in the cards today. Not with the miserable heartburn she had, the worst indigestion of her life.

Her big jar of Vicks sat right where it should, right where she remembered it in the medicine cabinet. She lugged it with her back to the bedside table. Trying and failing to get her socks on wore her out, like it was this bizarre athletic event at which she had no hope of succeeding. She did wiggle into some clean underwear, and a pair of slacks, but that was the end of all she could handle. Collapsed in bed, she stayed quiet a moment before wrestling the Vicks jar open and slathering handfuls of greasy glop onto her chest with the pungent stench squirming up her nose. Too weak to finish what she'd started, she closed her eyes, knowing that the ointment she'd failed to rub in sat on her in lumps and waves. She had this misery coming to her, staying up so late instead of getting a good night's sleep. She coughed and everything hurt. Absolutely everything. She took a penetrating, Vicks-flavored breath that made her feel sicker. This is what she deserved, fretting about foolishness instead of paying attention to what was important, like the rotten ham she was too dumb not to eat.

She dozed and woke up in tears; little tears slipping from her eyes down her cheeks. She was sick. It was definitely getting worse. She should do something. But she continued to lie there and to hope and to think that rest could fix what was wrong. Or that she could outlast it. She vowed to gut it out a bit longer, hoping for the best, praying for it, too. Her rosary lay on the bedside table, where she grabbed it, her fingers squeezing their way along the beads to the crucifix at the end. Maybe another hour. One more hour, and if things didn't improve by then, she'd call somebody. Amacare. They were the ones. They were close by. Right over in the little plaza. She could call them and see if she could get that nice little PT to stop by today—that Anne—she was nice—and she'd done a really good job with the therapy on Emma's shoulder not so long ago. Maybe that's what it was. Her darn shoulder acting up. It hadn't been bad for a while. Anne had pretty much fixed it up.

She found the Amacare number on the piece of paper she kept taped to the wall by the kitchen phone. Her glance darted between the paper and the dial, as she punched in the numbers. A woman cut the second ring in half, she answered so fast.

"Hi. This is Emma Skayhill and I'm wondering about Anne. If she's around. Or free. I hurt so in my chest, and Anne's been really helping me. Do you think she could come over?"

"Oh, Emma," the receptionist said. "That sounds hard. You're suffering. I can hear it in your voice."

"Yes, I am. That's right."

"I can really hear it. I'll try to locate Anne for you and call you right back. When did it start?"

"Today. Last night. All night. It was one heck of a night I put in, I have to tell you."

"I'll call you right back."

Ten minutes, five minutes, an hour. Two hours. How was Emma to say? Time underwent something funny, the pain, and the haze it produced in her head stretching everything out, leaving her suspicious of the measurements she normally trusted. Who knew how long it was before the phone rang with the Amacare receptionist calling back. "Emma, this is Joanie." She had a wide-awake sounding voice. "I can't locate Anne."

"Oh, darn. Why not? Where is she?"

"I don't know. But I just can't. What's your problem?"

Right then and there Emma decided that Joanie was an imbecile. Asking such a question. Or maybe she'd been hit on the head by a rock since they'd last spoken, because Emma was sure she'd already explained everything to whatever ability she had, and so she said, "That's okay. I'll call back."

"Emma, wait now."

"Don't get pushy."

"I know you told me, but I want to be sure, so tell me again. What's going on? Your symptoms, I mean. I want to help you."

"You're not a doctor, are you?"

"Just tell me."

"Okay. Sure. But remember it this time, will you? It's burning and miserable in my chest. Under that bone thing. In between. I told you. How many times do I have to say it?"

"Okay. That sounds awful."

"It is awful. It hurts awful. And my cough goes right through me—this shock right through my body from top to bottom. Stem to stern. Do you know? Do you hear me? Please try to find Anne."

"Have you spoken to your doctor?"

"No. I'm sure that little Anne can—"

"Emma. I think you really need to call him. I'll try to find Anne, but you call your doctor's office."

"I'd rather not."

"Right now. I'm telling you."

"Okay."

"You don't sound like you mean it. You have to do it. Promise me you'll do it. Don't just say 'okay.' As soon as you're off the phone."

"Will you do it for me? Call for me? I'm laying down. I've got to lay down. I've got to stay laying down. I can't really breathe very well. And dialing, you know. And talking."

"I think you better do it. You're the one who knows what's going on."

"The heck I do."

"They'll want to talk to you."

"Why?"

"They'll need to ask you things, Emma. Questions. Now I'm hanging up. Do you think I need to call back in a few minutes to make sure you did it?"

"No."

"Because I will."

She was panting as she hung up. And tired beyond anything she'd ever known in her life. Going way back. Even when her kids were born. She needed a second, a chance to collect her thoughts. She sagged slowly onto her bed until she was flat on her back. And sick as a dog. She'd told Joanie that she was already lying down, when she hadn't been. She'd lied, because she desperately wanted to get into bed and now she'd done it at last. But she couldn't get comfortable. Her whole body was jumpy, like it wanted to run off. Some far-off deep part of her body was watchful, like a scared animal that knew it was way off in the middle of nowhere with danger all around. She was in for something. Trouble was coming, though she didn't know what.

The HMO number was carefully printed right under the Amacare number on the piece of paper Scotch-taped to the wall by the kitchen phone. What a dumb place to put it, she thought, making her way out of the bedroom into the little hall by the bathroom. She had no idea what notion had convinced her the kitchen was a good place to put such important phone numbers. But she needed to do what Joanie had told her and telephone Grennel because if she didn't Joanie would call back and scold her.

Emma was barefoot with nothing on top except globs of Vicks. No blouse, no bra. Bras and blouses struck her as unreasonable, uncomfortable, and utterly beside the point. Now she had to go around the bathroom corner. Ahead, the dining room area waited with the table and the four chairs she had to get past, and everything seemed so much farther than ever before. She had to think about breathing, both the need and the method, warning herself to be gentle, trying to smuggle her breath in without her body knowing what she was doing, because she dreaded coughing ever again. It hurt so. For a second she couldn't remember her doctor's name, though she knew his nurse was that what's-her-face—Irene—the one who gave the flu shots. Emma jabbed in the number, and didn't even let the receptionist get halfway through her spiel before she said, "I need to speak to Irene—Dr. Grennel's nurse."

Irene was a narrow rod of a woman with a pleasant enough voice, who Emma had come to believe over time concealed the heart of a shrew, or a witch even, some figure of unspoken threat that made a person like Emma know to be on her best behavior, or Irene might turn around and bite her head off. "Hello, Irene. This is Emma Skayhill and I have to tell you, I'm not feeling well."

"I'm sorry to hear that, Emma. Would you like an appointment?"

"I think so."

"What seems to be the problem?"

"I'm having such chest pains. Terrible ones. What should I do?"

"I'll say this once, and only once!" Irene shouted, turning into a crazy kind of army person and leaving no doubt that all hell was about to break loose. "And you better listen. Do you hear me, Emma?"

"Yes, I do."

"I'm calling 911. You stay right where you are. Don't you move from that spot until they get there. Where are you?"

"What?"

"Where are you, Emma? Are you at home?"

"I'm—in the kitchen."

"Are you sitting?"

"No, I'm—I just—"

"Is there a chair near you? Sit if there is."

"Well, the dining room table and chairs are—"

"Sit down on one of them. Right now."

"Okay, but there's a recliner just across the—"

"No. Sit in the nearest chair. I told you to listen."

"Okay. But I don't want to go to the hospital."

"The ambulance will come once I reach them, and you just let them in when they get there. That's all you have to do."

"I don't want to go up to the hospital."

"Well, you're going! Now are you sitting like I said?"

The tyranny of Irene's orders could only mean that she thought Emma was in the middle of a full-blown emergency, and the realization just about scared the heart right out of her. "Yes. I am."

"Good. Stay there."

Irene disappeared behind a scratchy sound and a click. Emma felt so alone, so very alone in all the world, just this stupid old woman plopped down on a dining room chair in front of an empty table. "Irene?" she said, like Irene might still hear her, because Emma had the phone pressed to her ear. But Irene was gone, hung up and shouting orders at somebody.

Across the room, the recliner looked much more sensible and inviting and she thought she might go there. She had to hang up the phone in the kitchen, which meant a few short steps back from the dining room chair, and she made it, but barely before the energy expended by even this little act triggered a punishing cough that froze her where she stood.

It was faint and so far off, she squinted as if narrowing her eyes would help her hear better, the ambulance siren rising and falling. Oh my god, they're coming for me. It was like something aimed at her, an arrow or bullet already fired and flying straight at her. She staggered to the recliner, and sat, grateful for the afghan she'd crocheted and kept folded over the back, where she sometimes rested her head. It was her heart. The problem was her heart. Not pneumonia. Not heartburn. But her heart trying to choke and kill her. She dragged the afghan down onto her lap, worried that she might never get up from this chair. That this was it, her last stand. Now her lack of a blouse and her lack of bra appeared to be as big and stupid of a mistake as any she'd ever made. Why had she done it? She'd been tired, but there was more to it. She tried to get the afghan to cover her shoulders and across her front, and the hard work made her gasp. She was glad they were coming. She couldn't do more than she'd done. They'd have to take her as they found her, nothing on top but Vicks and her colostomy bag. What a sight.

For a second, trying to sort out the sounds screaming toward her, she heard more than one siren, maybe five or six. For

goodness' sake, who had Irene called? She sat huddled, awaiting the din of rescue coming like a whirlwind to find her. And
then the throbbing engine and the dying sirens were right outside in the street in front of her window, and she put her hands
over her ears. Still she heard the voices of men along with the
curious cries of her neighbors. The hubbub moved toward her,
and someone she was sure was Connie called out to someone
else that someone needed help. The firemen were here. Emma
knew that Irene had ordered her to open the door to the building to let them in, and then the door to her apartment so they
could help her, but everybody and all their commotion had
scared her into a kind of paralyzed helplessness. She didn't
think she could move.

Loud manly voices said loud manly things. It was the firemen, she knew, coming for her. They tromped over the lawn
in their big black rubber boots and heavy black raincoats and
their big fireman hats, those helmets with those high, bright
skull parts rimmed and red and the brims sticking far out the
front and the back. Their big hands waved and made fists and
carried axes, ladders, and hoses.

"Emma's right in here," Connie said. "Her apartment's
right to the left as you go in. You can't miss it."

The front door opened and their booming footsteps
filled the hall. They knocked on her door and called her
name, banging and saying, "Emma Skayhill, let us in." She
stood, lugging the afghan, fearful that they would give up
on their effort to summon her, knocking and calling her
name, and start hacking away with their axes to break her
door down.

"They're looking for Emma," Connie shouted at an angle
that indicated she was talking to someone up the stairs that
started right past Emma's door.

"What do they want?" Elroy demanded.

"I don't know."

"Ask them."

The pounding fists of the firemen, and their urgent voices expressed desperate need by the time she pulled the door open. One took her by the arm and moved her back. "Sit down, ma'am."

Another one said, "Thank you."

By the time she hit the recliner, the afghan was gone, though she had no idea where it had ended up. She could hear Connie yammering to someone who wasn't Elroy. Emma knew by the tone. The one who'd moved her had a pill he fit under her tongue, while Connie blabbed about waiting for the minibus, because she was going to the mall, and so dumb luck had put her there in the right spot at the right split second to let them in. The one who had given her the pill said it was nitro, and she nodded, halfway expecting to feel better in that exact instant or the next one. He worked to hook her up to oxygen, he explained, slipping this mask over her head and down to cover her nose. Connie excitedly told whoever was with her how the truck pulled up and the firemen jumped out and they asked her to let them in the front door and she did.

If Emma had the count right, there were four big firemen. One had come and gone, and two were carrying on like madmen with her furniture, shoving it everywhere, picking up the footstool and the little table, and then knocking the other recliner onto its back they pushed it so hard. The floor lamp jumped and went sprawling when one got tangled in the cord. She felt flimsy as tissue paper. The nitro hadn't done a thing. Not as far as she could tell. The one who'd given it to her was fiddling with the mask he'd slid onto her. And they weren't firemen. None of them were, no matter what Connie said. They were those other ones. Paramedics in those outfits. No big boots and raincoats, or fireman hats.

Catching sight of her eyes on him, he said, "We're going to get you out of here now, Mrs. Skayhill."

"Okay, but I need my robe. Can you get my robe or something, please?"

He had eager serious eyes and he looked straight at her. "Yes, I will. Where is it?"

"In my bedroom. In the closet."

He looked around. "Where's that?"

"It's there," she said, pointing, and he startled her the way he took off, almost running.

Somebody yelled, "Ed, what are you doing? We gotta go." This was one of the pair of other ones wheeling in a stretcher contraption. "Ed!"

"She wants her robe. I'm getting her robe."

"Hurry it up!"

Partway in the bedroom door, Ed wheeled around, ran back, and bent close. "What color is it? The robe. Ma'am, what color is it?"

"Blue."

"We don't have time for this, Ed!"

"I know," he shouted, but off he went anyway, angry, or maybe just edgy from all the pressure he felt to find her robe and save her life, too.

The one who'd scolded Ed crouched down. He had very blue eyes behind thick glasses. "We have to get you out of here, Mrs. Skayhill. Timothy and me are going to lift you onto the gurney, while Ed gets your robe."

"Okay."

Ed scurried up with a blue nightie in his big hands.

"Oh, no, that's not it. That's a—"

"Never mind," said the one with the glasses. "We're just going to wrap you in a blanket, and go."

Ed tossed the nightie, and maybe he aimed for the couch, but it fell in a sad swirl onto the floor.

"I don't have a blouse on." She was stupid to say it, because surely they could see.

"We don't care."

They picked her up and moved her toward the gurney, where one of their big thick blankets waited already spread. "You've seen worse, I guess," she said.

"Yes, ma'am."

She gathered what breath she could, and said, "Be careful of this bag. You know what's in it." She wanted to make them laugh, betting a good chuckle would make them like her. "You don't want it coming loose. Take my word for it."

One laughed, and the other didn't. But they moved her gently, all their muscles working to take care of her and not hurt her, like she was something that mattered and that might even be worthwhile. They set her down, rolling the blanket around her, one of them pulling it up to her chin while another buckled these straps around her.

"Wait," said the one who wasn't Ed. "She needs a key to get back in. Do you have a key?"

"To what?"

"To here."

"To my place? Yes, I do. I sure do. It's right over there." She indicated the table they'd moved. It made her giddy to be helpful. "On the table."

The one who went looking said, "I don't see it."

"Maybe it got knocked on the floor."

"You have to be able to get back in here when you come home."

"Yes, I do. But where is it if it's not there? I don't know. I want to be able to get back in when I come back."

"I think I saw some keys in the bedroom," said Ed, darting off, like he was starting to know his way around.

The one who was down on his hands and knees by the table said, "I don't see them."

"You have to have your keys," Ed shouted, coming back. He held them high so they jingled, the three of them against one another, the front door key, the one that opened her apartment door, and the one to her mailbox.

So that was it then, they were going. They wheeled her out of her apartment and out the front door into the bright air where the snow fell. Not much had collected on the ground overnight, so it may have just started up again. The air was brisk and sharp on her skin. They lifted her down the stairs to the sidewalk but then they angled off onto the grass, the wheels bumping up the slope toward the waiting ambulance. She saw Connie standing beside Elroy and May, too, who'd come from somewhere. Oh, she felt so bad. Too bad to even wave. She was so disappointed in herself. She was supposed to go talk to Bud. Who would do it if she couldn't? She was letting them down. She was letting everyone down. What a failure she was. Poor Maggie would have to go it alone against Bud. And that would be hard. May couldn't do it. Connie couldn't do it.

Snowflakes tumbled toward her, touching her face, dissolving against her skin. But there were more above her, gathering multitudes as far as she could see into the gray where clouds were massed. Something was wrong with the ambulance door, it seemed. They couldn't get it open and they were yelling and getting really mad at each other. Nobody seemed to know who had closed it.

Ed appeared over her, looking down. "How are you doin', Mrs. Skayhill?"

She smiled up at him, but didn't know if she wanted to speak, her chest was so heavy.

The other one with his intense blue eyes behind his glasses showed up. "We got it," he said. "Don't worry."

They lifted the whole stretcher thing with her on it, and the snow on her face was cool and almost refreshing, though the moisture of its melting felt like tears.

And what about Marianne? She had to help her. She'd decided she wanted to and was going to. Somebody had to. It didn't seem anybody else could be bothered and so that left only her. Only Emma. She didn't want Marianne to be on suspension. It wasn't right that Marianne was on suspension because of what that other one did. But what could Emma do? She could barely breathe.

The doors to the back of the ambulance swung shut with thumps that shook the stretcher under her, wiping out her last glimpse of her neighbors bunched in a tight little group, craning their necks and adjusting where they stood to keep an eye on her, as long as possible, Connie, May, and Elroy, and Bud. Bud was there, too, arriving at the last second. But no Maggie. Where was Maggie? And where were Emma's kids? Why weren't they here? Or at least living close enough that she could call and they'd be waiting at the hospital, or rushing to see her the way Annette's family did, all those kids and grandkids. Emma must have done something wrong, though she couldn't say what it was. But she'd been hurt and angry for a long time about the way Sam and Bethany were off so far from home, knowing, too, that they had their lives, and there was no changing any of it. Oh, well, she thought, that was the way things were for her. That's all.

Now the ambulance was on the move. That was what all the rattling and rocking was about. The siren started up, scaring her all over again, warning everybody about something, only this time it was like she was inside the shrill cry; like she was part of this huge noise rising and falling; like she was making it happen. Her neighborhood, the street where she lived, had been shut away by the closing doors, and now she was leaving it behind. Good old MacDougal Road. How many streets had she lived on in her life? There'd been Crispin Street and then Jefferson and Johns and Milwaukee Avenue and Garfield. There were more, too, she bet. She'd think of them in a second. The snow had been beautiful as they shoved her over the grass and she lay looking up, the whole of everything above filled with the white flakes falling on her.

Ed and the one with the glasses were in the back with her. The other two must be up front. She saw now that they'd put a blood pressure cuff on her arm. Ed had a stethoscope to her chest. When he realized she was looking at him, he nodded and smiled, like the news was good, but she wasn't sure she could trust him.

Oh, and who would help Maggie do her putting of the golf balls on her carpet so they rolled all the way across the living room into the little saucer thing? Maggie had to get good at it so she got to hear the sound she loved so much on the real course. Who would help her aim? If Emma didn't come home, who would live across from Maggie? Who would look for her to drive up and park where she belonged?

And what about Dan—that poor Dan on the bridge watching his daughter disappear? She wanted to help him, and Marianne, too. What about everything that had ever happened to her? Not just the streets where she'd lived, but everything that had happened? Who would care if she was gone? Who would remember Emma Skayhill's life? And what about all the lives she remembered? What about them? Her brothers, and her sister. And her neighbors, going all the way back to when she was a child, the Santacruzes and Dwyers and Schemmels. What about them? Oh, boy, she thought, feeling the size of all she would take with her. Oh, boy.

Ed was looking out the back window, while the other one, who had removed his glasses, put them back on and reached down to pat her wrist. They were racing now. She could feel the speed in the body of the ambulance and in her body, too. She'd seen this kind of thing. Stopped whatever she was doing and looked up. Been a bystander watching an ambulance flying by. An onlooker wondering what had happened. Wondering who was inside.

ACKNOWLEDGEMENTS

As these stories began and came to fruition they benefited from the patient, thoughtful consideration of certain trusted readers, who plowed through multiple versions of these stories: my soul brother, Pat Toomay; Marsha Rabe; and Rachel Berg, who more than once occupied the room with me where an idea came or walked with me when an adjustment popped into my head, giving her keen mind and support. Another to whom this book and I are indebted is Tony Giardina, if not for these particular stories, then for his friendship and thoughtful reading of my work over time, which has contributed to my overall ability to keep at it.

It is worthwhile, I think, to recall one's earliest hopes, and there I find the sharp eye and blue pencil of Raymond Roseliep, with whom I studied creative writing at Loras College. He was the first to let me feel I might have a chance. A few others from the past whose attention and passion stays with me are Jim Childs, John Cashman, Tom Reiter, and Tom Hummel. My mom and dad, William L. Rabe and Ruth McCormick Rabe, and my deceased wife, Jill, have their influence, still.

It goes without saying that I owe a debt of thanks to my agent, Deborah Schneider, but I'll say it anyway. She read the content of this book with care and enthusiasm, some of the stories in several versions, and one in particular that morphed radically, ballooned, shrank, and then found shape.

A very particular thanks is due to Joseph Olshan and Lori Milken of Delphinium Books, who welcomed this collection for publication. Jennifer Ankner-Edelstein, an editor there, helped me through some self-induced confusion in biographical matters. And then Joe and Lori with a few questions prompted me to do a large amount of work on those sections of the stories and novella that had not been through an editing process at either the *New Yorker* or *Narrative* magazine.

Which brings me to Deborah Treisman, Fiction Editor, at the *New Yorker*, who accepted three of these stories, "Things We Worried About When I Was Ten," "Uncle Jim Called," and "Suffocation Theory," and then with an attentive, wise editorial touch shepherded them onto the *New Yorker* pages. I am also indebted to Tom Jenks, Carol Edgarian, Jack Shiff, and Mimi Kusch, the dedicated, caring editors at *Narrative* magazine, where a portion of "I Have to Tell You" was published under the title "Roommates," and a portion of "The Longer Grief" was published as "Grief."

My muse through much, if not all the work on *Listening for Ghosts*, was Phoebe, a sleek Labrador retriever who, if busy with dog matters when I went to work, would wait, poised to come in with her nose almost touching the office door. When I checked and let her in, she would join me, adding her trust, patience, and companionship to my hope that what I was up to might be worthwhile.

ABOUT THE AUTHOR

David Rabe was born in Dubuque, Iowa. Drafted into the army in 1965, he was stationed in Vietnam in a medical headquarters unit. Discharged in 1967, he returned to Villanova University to study theater under Richard Duprey, Robert Hedley and Jim Christy. Many of his early plays were written during this period. *The Basic Training of Pavlo Hummel* was his first play performed in New York in 1971. It was followed by *Sticks and Bones*, *The Orphan*, *In the Boom Boom Room*, and *Streamers*. Other plays include *Goose and Tom Tom*, *Hurlyburly*, *Those the River Keeps*, *A Question of Mercy*, *The Dog Problem*, *The Black Monk* (based on Chekhov), *An Early History of Fire*, *Good For Otto*, *Visiting Edna*, and *Cosmologies*. Four of Rabe's plays have been given Tony nominations as Best Play on Broadway. Other prizes and recognition include: an American Academy of Arts and Letters Award, the Drama Desk Award, the John Gassner Outer Critics Award, a New York Drama Critics' Circle Award, and the Elizabeth Hull-Warriner Award. Over time he has increasingly devoted himself to writing fiction with three novels: *Recital of the Dog*, *Dinosaurs on the Roof*, and *Girl by the Road at Night*, as well as a book of stories, *A Primitive Heart*. In recent years, he has had stories published in the *New Yorker* magazine and at *Narrative* online. His three children are Jason, Lily and Michael. He lives in Northwest Connecticut.